Nandini Bajpai grew up in New Delhi, one of four sisters and many cousins, in a family that liked to read. Although she has dabbled in corporate finance, business analysis, and fostering shelter animals, her first love is writing. Her novel *Red Turban, White Horse: My Sister's Hurricane Wedding* was published in 2013 by Scholastic, India. She lives in the Boston area with her husband, kids, their dog Yogi and cat Rakhan.

Starcursed

NANDINI BAJPAI

RED TURTLE

RUPA

Published in Red Turtle by
Rupa Publications India Pvt. Ltd. 2013
7/16, Ansari Road, Daryaganj
New Delhi 110002

Sales Centres:

Allahabad Bengaluru Chennai
Hyderabad Jaipur Kathmandu
Kolkata Mumbai

ISBN: 978-81-291-2931-4

10 9 8 7 6 5 4 3 2 1

Printed at Parksons Graphics Pvt. Ltd, Mumbai.

Author's Note

The twelfth century in India was a turbulent time. The fragmented kingdoms of North India waged war on each other and also faced the threat of invasion from Muhammad of Ghor. In the middle of this upheaval, an Indian mathematician of the period, Bhaskara Acharya, wrote a path-breaking book on astronomy—*Siddhanta Shiromani* or, *The Crest Jewel of Astronomy*. It contained four parts—*Leelavati, Bijaganita, Grahaganita* and *Goladhyaya*—which deal with arithmetic, algebra, the mathematics of the planets and the mathematics of the sphere. Interestingly, he chose to name the section on arithmetic 'Leelavati'—a woman's name that means 'beautiful' or 'playful' in Sanskrit.

Not only did Bhaskara Acharya name it so, he also addressed some of the problems in that section directly to someone of that name. Other verses in the book were addressed to 'auspicious woman', 'intelligent girl', 'pretty girl with tremulous eyes' and so on. But there is no indication anywhere in the text about her identity.

Leelavati became a standard textbook on mathematics and was widely studied, commented on and translated. In a sixteenth century Persian translation of the text, commissioned by the Mughal emperor Akbar and carried out by his poet laureate, Faizi, there is a story about who Leelavati may have been.

Quoting other sources, the book tells this story:

Leelavati was the daughter of Bhaskara the teacher. She was born under an unlucky star and could not marry. But Bhaskara calculated a rare, auspicious moment when she could wed. Everything was made ready and a water clock set up to tell the exact time when the wedding should take place. But Leelavati, being curious, leant over the clock to see how it functioned. As she did so, a jewel fell from her hair into the clock, blocking it. The clock did not tell the time correctly, the auspicious time passed without anyone knowing and Leelavati could never wed.

It is impossible to tell if this legend is true. According to some people, Leelavati was Bhaskara Acharya's wife, not his daughter, or even a fanciful invention to make the verses of *Leelavati* more poetic. But the character—who shares her name with my grandmother—has always fascinated me. As I read the verses of *Leelavati*, I could just picture a young girl—clever and beautiful, encouraged to study by her father, one of the best minds of his age. But a girl cursed by fate, who decides to follow her heart and try and make her own luck. This is her story.

Part One

Dear intelligent Leelavati, if you are skilled
in addition and subtraction, tell me the sum
of two, five, thirty-two, a hundred and ninety-
three, eighteen, ten and a hundred, added
together; and the remainder, when their sum is
subtracted from ten thousand.

—VERSE 13, *LEELAVATI*,
BHASKARA THE TEACHER

1

I WAS BORN UNDER AN EVIL STAR.

Baba knew that dark forces shadowed the moment, for no one read the stars as well as he did. He kept it from me for many years, but I sensed it. A secret sorrow clouded my mother's eyes when they rested on me—a secret never mentioned, yet ever-present. One that won me the freedoms denied to other girls, as if in compensation for the misery that lay in my future.

Why else did Baba let me study with him at the observatory, even though it set tongues wagging, even though it made the scholars grumble and sulk? No, when I learned that Mangal ruled my star chart, I wasn't surprised.

I've studied the portent in Baba's books. Anyone I marry is doomed to an early death—reason enough for my single state at the advanced age of fifteen. Only a doddering old man at death's door would now consider taking my hand.

Baba, being Baba, is certain he can calculate an auspicious time when Mangal is weak, and still give me a chance at happiness. No one knows the stars better than him it's true, but I have no faith it can be done. Still, I pretend to believe it for his sake.

There are some advantages of being unmarriageable. If you have a liking for mathematics, you needn't suppress it. If you loathe cooking, you needn't cultivate it. And, above all, you needn't worry about leaving your mother's house for a stranger's.

So, it wasn't the news of my fate that astonished me.

It was the face that flashed before my eyes the moment I was told of my prospects, or lack thereof.

I hadn't seen Rahul Nagarseth in two years, ever since he sailed away with his father's trading fleet, yet I remembered him well.

The first time we met I was ten, he a year older, and new to Baba's class in Ujjayani. I had always taken pride in being the first to finish the tasks Baba set us, but right away, Rahul had been quicker than I. And he had stared at me wide-eyed as if he had never seen a girl before. There was only one way to deal with it.

'What are you looking at?' I had demanded, staring back. I was almost his height and so could look him level in the eyes.

Reaching over he had tugged a ringlet that had escaped my braid to dangle over my brow. Then he had smiled and dimples had deepened in his cheeks, catching me by surprise.

'Your hair is pretty,' he had said, in his funny accent, and run off.

After that I had always braided my hair tight before going to class. Little by little he stopped being the strange son of a wealthy merchant from far across the seas and became one of us.

Then, two years ago, he vanished without any word of when he would return.

It had felt like the most unjust cruelty for the Nagarseth to have taken him away then, but I had forgotten my childish attachment since, or so I thought. Knowing the barriers between us—of caste, faith, wealth, and now, of astrology—it seemed fitting that he left.

We were bound for the port of Bharuch in Anhilwara, to my grandmother's house, for Baba was sorely short of funds for the observatory, and there were none to be had in Malwa. The

Sethani—Rahul's stepmother and the power behind the purse strings in the Nagarseth's absence—lived there now, and ignored Baba's reminders of her husband's pledge of support. Meanwhile, the observatory was in dire need of repair, and the books in its library were falling to dust for want of scribes to copy them. Baba hoped that seeing the Sethani in person would perhaps change matters—a vain hope, in my estimation.

But on the long, dusty journey from Ujjayani in Malwa to the port of Bharuch we heard rumours. More than the rains were expected in the seaports this monsoon—the Nagarseths' trading fleet was sailing back.

2

'A PIGEON LANDED IN THE NAGARSETHS LOFT TODAY,' AMMA said, combing back the heavy weight of my hair. 'It was injured, poor creature, so they sent for me.'

I sat cross-legged on the straw mat before her, my face turned away. A good thing, for her news drained the colour from my cheeks. An injured messenger pigeon from the trading fleet could only mean one thing—pirates.

'Were you able to save it?' I asked. The fleet would be loaded with spices, silk and porcelain, not to mention gold, ready to be traded for the cotton and indigo of Anhilwara. Rich pickings for coastal pirates, but from what I remembered the Nagarseth had never lost a ship yet.

'I was able to set the wing,' Amma said, deftly dividing my hair into sections, and plaiting them tightly, over and across, over and across. Her touch was firm but gentle—that of a healer. 'They were safe as far as Surat, according to the Sethani. They've made it across the ocean, she said, and called in every port from Calicut to Surat—they're not about to fall to pirates now, she's sure.'

'Sounds like something the Sethani would say,' I said. The mention of the Sethani was enough to put me in an ill humour, although her confident claim did calm my fears a little. 'At least Baba won't have to deal with her anymore, I'm sure the Nagarseth will fund the repairs at the observatory, unlike the Sethani.'

'She isn't as bad as you think,' Amma said, flipping my braid

6

over my shoulder. 'There, you're done.'

I raised a sceptical eyebrow and followed her to the verandah that circled the courtyard—the heart of my grandmother, Ajji's, house. The sounds of children playing spilled from it. The voice of my brother, Loky, was the loudest.

The lamps had been lit, and set in their niches. Overhead, a crowd of sparrows in Ajji's fig tree chirruped busily. A faint aroma of woodsmoke—and of rice, ghee and spices from our dinner—still lingered in the air. The deep voices of Baba and grandfather saying the evening prayers swept over the hum of the birds. I chanted silently along with them, for I knew the verses as well as they did.

To my usual devotions to Saraswati, I added a fervent appeal to bring the fleet safely home:

Fair as a jasmine, the moon, or a flake of snow; dressed in white; your hands graced by the staff of a veena; help them Saraswati, vanquisher of ignorance.

Perhaps it made no sense to entreat Saraswati, for how could she protect anyone with her rosary, her holy books and her gentle swans? Yet I could not bring myself to turn to the more warlike gods in place of my favourite.

'Loksamudra,' Amma called. 'Time for bed.'

Loky grappled gamely for a hold on one of our larger cousins, though he was clearly outmatched. But reinforcements from the smaller boys piled into the fray.

'Five minutes more,' Loky begged from deep within the scrum.

Amma crossed her arms, unrelenting.

Loky knew that look, and disentangled himself reluctantly. 'I'll get even with you tomorrow,' he said. 'I've learnt moves from the wrestlers of Ujjayani. Wait till you see the Flying Tiger!'

'Flying pussycat, more like,' snorted Dhruv, the large one,

still under attack by his own younger brothers. 'Don't worry, I'll be waiting.'

It had only been a few days since we arrived at Ajji's house in Bharuch, and already the cousins were bonding, as if the months apart had never been. Loky loved the company of our uncles' children, though they were all too young to be my companions. But Bharuch had other advantages I appreciated, its busy seaport that was home to Anhilwara's merchant fleet, and the tower that watched over it—a tower from which one could always sight the first glimpse of any approaching ship.

'Loky,' I said in a low voice. 'Want to go to the lamp tower tonight?'

Baba planned to station himself at the viewing platform atop the tower tonight. At home, he had an army of students to take astronomical readings for him, so it was a rare treat to be able to help him, like old times, before he became head of the observatory. But Amma had refused to let us join them—it wasn't proper for me, she said, and Loky needed his sleep. I'd been tempted to sneak off nevertheless, and now, with the trading fleet within sight, how could I not?

Loky nodded quickly, his dark eyes sparkling back at me, and I quickly tousled his hair.

Small as he was, I needed him to come with me. If we were caught, he would serve as my chaperone, and so save my prospects of marriage from further ruin. Lucky for me, he was always up for adventure.

When I woke up, the seven stars of the Saptarishi had marched around the polestar to the eastern horizon in the still-dark sky. Baba and Aajoba, my grandfather, were probably at the tower already—we had to hurry if we had to beat the sunrise.

I reached over to shake Loky awake.

'Wake up,' I whispered.

Loky yawned, showing his tiny, perfect teeth in his round brown face. He opened his eyes a crack, rolled over, and fell back, snoring. His sacred thread hung over his shoulder and across his small, sturdy body, glowing white in the dim light.

I shook him again. 'Don't you want to dodge the watchmen?' I whispered. 'Come on!'

He sat up and gazed at me drowsily. 'What about the watchmen's dog?' That vigilant creature, bless its dutiful soul, had landed us into trouble more than once.

'I have a plan,' I said, unlatching the window to lure him out of bed—he could never resist a climb, the steeper the better. I stepped out on to the ledge that ran along the side of the house. The drop into the lane was too steep, we'd have to climb down to the cowshed, then into the back garden, and let ourselves out through the back door.

'Wait!' he said, climbing hurriedly out of the window and inching after me on the ledge. We edged along until we reached the cowshed. It was a six foot drop, but the thatched roof muffled our landing. I slid to the edge of the roof and landed in the hay. Loky followed, nearly landing in a cow patty. The musky, damp smell of cow and hay surrounded us. The cow lowed from her corner, and her bell clanged alarmingly loud.

'Shh,' I whispered and offered her a lump of sweet cane sugar. She chewed thoughtfully, watching us with her large, placid eyes. I strained my ears to see if the noise had roused anyone. No, the only sounds I could hear were the buzz of mosquitoes, the swish of the cow's tail and the chirp of a few invisible crickets.

We crept to the back door, which was always kept only latched, not locked. I opened it cautiously, and we were out into the dark alleyway.

'Stay alert, brother,' the watchmen called out to one another. 'Jaagte raho!'

The thudding of their wooden staffs echoed from one neighbourhood to the next. We waited till the watchman reached the corner of our lane, then, keeping to the shadows, ran through the twisting alleys of the Brahmin neighbourhood. Our nemesis, the watchman's dog, ran off, tail waving, to examine the treat I had dropped for him.

The tower loomed in the distance, alight with lamps. We ran to the giant banyan tree that bordered the temple compound. With any luck, the monkeys there wouldn't awaken and give us away.

As Loky raced ahead of me—up the steep stone steps, past the lotus tank, around the carved pillars of the dance hall—I guiltily joined my hands into hurried namaskars in the direction of the shrines we passed. There was no time to make proper salutations to Vishnu, Shiva and Surya. We had to reach Baba before the rising sun blotted out the night sky and the stars.

Our footsteps echoed in the winding stairwell as we ran up seven levels and arrived, breathless, at the windswept viewing platform on top. It must have taken Aajoba an age to climb to the top with his stiff knees. The cool sea breeze whipped strands of hair free from my braids; it was a welcome relief from the stifling heat this time of year.

'Baba!' Loky launched himself on to our father, sitting cross-legged next to Aajoba on the low cotton mattress. I studied Baba anxiously. The moonlight shining on his intelligent, high-browed face showed only surprise, not anger.

'Ah, here are my eyes at last!' Baba said. Typical Baba! Amma may worry that I stole away to help Baba, but he was always glad to see us. His eyesight wasn't what it used to be, and Aajoba could barely see the moon, a terrible fate for a scholar once known as the best astronomer in the West.

I looked up at the sky, as familiar to me as the palm of my hand. The always-changing moon, the wide starry sweep of the sky Ganges, the constellations, fixed in their places, and turning slowly on the axis of the two poles and the wandering planets moving between them, controlling the fates of countries, empires and kings—crushing the dreams of ordinary mortals like me.

Doubtless, a good clear night for taking observations, but today I was far more interested in scanning the horizon. Below us, the dockyard and the harbour were dotted with lights, as was the estuary of the river Narmada winding out to the sea, but the bay itself was uniformly dark. I bit back my disappointment; perhaps dawn would reveal more.

'Leela,' Baba said. 'Do you see a star, just there?'

He was right; a point of light had just appeared in the west.

'I see it,' I focused fiercely on the strange yellow star twinkling low on the horizon, willing it to be more than a star. 'Is it a ship?'

Now, more than just a light was visible. From the darkness emerged a mast, then sails, the dark shape of a hull, and then, other lights behind the first one; other ships. My pulse quickened as each new one came into sight.

'So many of them!' Baba said, his eyes crinkling into a smile. 'It can only be the Nagarseths' fleet.' He touched a torch to his flickering oil lamp, and waved the blazing flame over his head to signal the Watch.

'About time! I have been waiting for that heretic to return ever since I received his letter from Java.' His affection for the heretic was clear from his tone. 'He promised me three translations of astronomical texts from China.'

'Is it really them, Bhaskara?' Aajoba came over, leaning on his cane, but had to take our word for it, since it was too far away for him to see. Loky couldn't see over the railing at all, and had to be raised on to Baba's shoulders for a better view. Below, a few dockhands emerged from the surrounding warehouses and raised a cheer—the Watch had seen Baba waving the torch and roused them, for the fleet's return was an event worthy of celebration.

Their excitement was nothing compared to the wild hammering of my heart.

3

'THERE SHE IS!'

Amma's voice greeted us as soon as we entered the courtyard. Relief dulled the anger in her voice, but not by much. Amma and I looked quite alike, though I was taller than her by over a head, but that didn't mean I could stand up to her when she was in a temper—and she was fuming now. She didn't offer well-water to the men to wash their feet, an oversight that didn't bode well for anyone. Lucky for me, she directed her wrath at Baba.

'Leela isn't a child any more,' she said. 'She can't run around in the middle of the night helping with observations. What will people say?'

Baba was in no mood to argue. 'Nothing they don't already,' he said, rinsing the dust off his feet himself. 'Stop your scolding, for we have excellent news! The Nagarseths' trading fleet has returned safely. They'll be in port today.'

'Everyone knows that,' Amma replied, unsurprised, 'because of the pigeon.'

Baba looked bewildered, but Amma turned away without volunteering an explanation. She didn't often quarrel with Baba, but today she was laying the blame for my behaviour at his door.

I followed her in. Better grovel as abjectly as possible now, before she took away any other privileges, or escalated the disagreement with poor Baba. 'Loky begged me, Amma,' I said, lying remorselessly. 'He wanted to spend time with Baba; he's always so busy with work in Ujjayani. And, of course, I couldn't let him go alone.'

'You will get yourself a bad name,' Amma said, shaking her head. I cringed—not that lecture again.

'Will you check on the bird today?' I asked, trying to distract her. 'Can I come along?' In hindsight, it was a useful plan. If anyone would know for certain if the fleet brought in the Nagarseth son, it would be the staff at his haveli.

Amma said nothing, but continued serving breakfast, waving off Ajji's maid. I helped her, hoping she'd change her mind, for her anger never lasted long. I rushed through my morning bath and dressed hurriedly, just in case she did.

'Leela, bring me the small grinding bowl and my pouch of medicinal herbs,' she called when I was done. I smiled at her tone. It meant I could go with her.

'You are not a child any more,' Amma chided once again, as we made our way along the narrow winding alley, no longer empty as it had been last night, but thronging with children playing, vendors selling, cows munching, servants gossiping.

'Word gets around. The other day Trivedi's wife was saying, "Why does Bhaskara teach her all the Shastras, Siddhantas and Vedas? It is not fitting for a girl. What next? The sacred thread of the twice-born, too, like a boy?"'

This was just the sort of talk that angered me most. Loky received his sacred thread and the status of a scholar-in-training, a symbolic rebirth, earlier this year. Heaven knew I was a better scholar than him. I had mastered advanced texts and commentaries that conferred titles, honours and offers of employment on Baba's graduating students. Yet, I couldn't even be a twice-born like Loky and other boys.

'Women *did* study the texts in ancient times,' I countered. 'Some even took the sacred thread.' I counted off my heroines on my fingers. 'Gargi, Maitreyi, Ghosha, Lopamudra...'

'Those days are gone,' Amma said firmly. Her tone held no promises of indulgence anymore. 'In the Kali Yuga, such things are not possible.'

The Kali Yuga, our dark times. Why was I was born now, instead of the Golden Age, when women were scholars and poets and teachers?

'Leela, there are already so many obstacles to finding you a good match,' Amma said. 'Do you have to complicate things further with your conduct?'

Several rude things about good matches sprang to my lips, but the worry on her face made me hold my tongue.

We had walked through the modest homes of the Brahmin quarter, with their close-set houses and winding alleys, to the opulent waterfront mansions of the merchants. A Jain temple of white marble, dedicated to the twentieth Tirthankara, watched over them from a nearby hill. White-clad monks and nuns thronged around it today—probably there for the monsoon retreats, when they gave up their wandering to preach to the laity.

The most handsome of these mansions belonged to the Nagarseth—the wealthiest of the Jain merchants. It stood in its own lush grounds, a vision of sculpted sandstone rising above the riverfront. This wasn't their primary residence, however. They had homes in six cities spread along the coast, and inland, in Malwa and Rajputana. And who knows how many overseas in Java and Srivijaya.

Amma lifted the heavy brass knocker and rapped it smartly against the sturdy wooden door. A smaller door, set into the large front gate, opened up.

'Ah, here you are, mistress!' the old manservant said. 'We have been expecting you.'

We followed the man into the massive courtyard behind the gate. Intricate balconies, delicately carved from red sandstone, overlooked the central garden. It was flooded with sunshine, except where a tall neem tree shaded the well. Sounds of pigeons cooing spilled over from the chabutros, the carved bird lofts set on tall pedestals. They were everywhere in Anhilwara, from simple wooden ones in village squares to marble beauties such as these. Deep verandahs surrounded the courtyard on three sides.

He led us through the main verandah, up three long flights of stairs, to the open stone terrace at the very top of the house, the view from which rivalled that of the lamp tower. Many more chabutros covered this section of the terrace. These housed carrier pigeons, so they were set lower to the ground for ease of handling.

Amma clucked softly as she gently lifted an injured bird from one of the lofts and examined it. 'He's doing well. The wing will set, I think.'

The pigeon stared at us with his ruby-red eyes. He shivered a little as Amma lifted him, but then grew still, trusting Amma's sure touch.

'Hold him while I ready the bandages.'

I took the bird carefully and stroked his soft grey feathers with my fingertips. 'What is he called?' I asked, as Amma briskly ripped strips of bandages.

'Shan,' the manservant replied. 'He was named by the young master; he took an interest in the pigeons' training the last time he was here. I think it means lightning in his mother's tongue.'

'Sh-an,' I repeated softly, warming up to the injured creature, liking the way the sound of his name rolled off my tongue. Rahul had named this bird.

'Leela!' the accented voice was familiar, but deeper than I recalled.

I turned around, the injured pigeon still cradled to my chest, the blood singing in my ears.

A young man stood in the bright light of the morning. It couldn't be, and yet it was! My hair damp and messy, hastily braided, my sari chosen without thought and tied in a rush, there were probably dark circles under my eyes too, from waking up early. And here was Rahul, smiling at me like he had never left.

'Leela,' he repeated, hurrying towards us, the dimples deepening in his cheeks, just as I remembered them.

'Rahul,' I smiled back, too surprised for moderation, so happy to see him I could have floated right off the terrace. So much for the witty greetings I'd crafted for this very moment. Every last one of them vanished from my mind.

His straight black hair—a mark of his mixed ancestry—was clipped short. He wore a dark tunic, cut in the Chinese fashion, so unfamiliar, yet well suited to him. With his skin sun-bronzed from weeks on the sea, he looked more like a boy from Malwa than a foreigner. And he seemed delighted to see me.

'I had not dared hope to see you,' his gaze fell on Amma, '... all of you, so soon. What a marvellous homecoming!'

'It's good to see you safely back,' I said.

'You've grown tall,' he noted.

I was suddenly conscious of my awkward height. I had been sprouting up like a wild vine, as Ajji had said, all stem and no buds.

'You haven't,' I replied.

He had grown, no doubt, but I was still at least two finger widths taller than him. He flushed faintly, and I wished I had not said it.

'Welcome home,' Amma said, smiling. 'We thought the ships had not yet anchored.'

Rahul bent to touch his hands to her feet. 'My father sent me ahead to complete the trade formalities.'

Amma laid her hand on his dark head in blessing. 'He must trust you greatly,' she said with approval. 'You went away a schoolboy, and have come home a man.' That last sentence was probably intended to take the bite out of my unthinking comment. Rahul had lost his Chinese mother at an early age in the far-off colonies; he had always appealed to Amma's maternal instincts.

'I was anxious about Shan too,' Rahul said as he watched Amma wrap the tiny splint around one feathery wing, while I held the bird still. 'Will he heal?' he asked.

'Yes, he just needs rest,' Amma said, splitting the end of the fabric bandage in two and tying a neat knot.

'Was it pirates that hurt him?' I asked.

'A pirate's hawk, yes,' Rahul said. 'They snatch carrier pigeons, hoping to gain information about merchant ships and then plan their raids. We evaded them this time, thanks to Shan.' He smiled ruefully, 'We were not so lucky in the straits of Malacca.'

Pirates, danger, far-off lands, what hadn't he seen? And here I could not even leave the house with my brother without admonitions from Amma.

'Well, you're here now,' Amma said, 'and in need of home-cooked food. Will you take lunch with us?'

I stroked Shan's tiny bobbing head, and tried hard not to care about Rahul's reply.

'I have business to take care of at the port,' Rahul said. 'But wait a moment before you leave. I have something for your Baba.'

'He'll grow, mark my words,' Amma remarked, sizing up Rahul with a physician's eye as he walked away. 'Boys shoot up overnight like green bamboos in the monsoon season.'

I placed Shan gently back in the loft. He settled in on the fresh hay and fluffed his feathers, making me smile.

Then Rahul was back, bearing a large package. 'Baba did not think the Acharya would be here. But I had hoped that all of you might be here for the rains, so I brought this with me. Here are the scrolls that my father promised the Acharya,' he said.

'What scrolls are they?' I was eager to know more.

'Chinese scrolls on astronomy, mostly,' he said. 'You will find them interesting as well. But I have something special for you and Loky.' As I took the package, he clasped my hands into his, and smiled straight into my eyes. 'I hope I chose well.'

I blinked in confusion. 'Thank you,' I said. 'It was kind of you to think of us.'

He dropped his hands and stepped back. 'My pleasure,' he replied.

The package was heavy and the fragrance of spices and paper scrolls rose from it. I hugged it close to me as we walked home. Did he say there was something in it for me?

4

'*I* CAN'T MAKE HEAD OR TAIL OF THIS INFERNAL LANGUAGE,' Baba mumbled distractedly. 'Who can understand what this says!'

A lectern had been set up in the courtyard and a group of wide-eyed boys sat cross-legged in front of it, cradling their best slate boards and chalk. Baba ignored them.

To teach was what Baba liked most. He had personally arranged for this class for the boys from the local school. But when I gave him the package from Rahul, he had abandoned the class without a word of explanation.

'I think I can guess what this diagram means...' he muttered, and vanished into his room. It was useless to follow him. He was gone from us as surely as if he had left the city. I debated following him to glimpse the treasures he held in his hands, but instead settled on waiting.

One of the boys stood up. 'Will the Acharya still take the class?' he asked. 'Or is it cancelled? The Acharya was just about to teach us when you came along with that package...'

I studied the diagram Baba had started to draw—Meru prastara, a sequence of numbers progressing down the steps of Mount Meru—very advanced material. These must be the brightest children in the town. It would be a pity to send them home without their class. I reached for Baba's staff and turned to face the class.

'*You* will teach us?' The boy's eyes widened.

I smiled at his surprise, pulling the free end of my sari tightly around me and tucking it in at the waist in a businesslike way.

'Yes, take your place,' I wrote the next number in the sand as they crowded around me. 'Now, who can tell me what comes next?'

Hands were eagerly raised. I looked at them and noted there was no trace of discomfort in their young faces. At what age did boys stop believing that women could teach as well as men?

Amma watched the scene unfold from the verandah without comment. I had not asked for her permission, but she didn't try to stop me, so I went on. I liked working with the young ones, especially such a clever group as this. The morning flew by quickly and soon it was time for lunch and for dismissing my charges.

I sent them off, pleased with their performance, and returned to the courtyard. A delicious aroma of simmering spices wafted in from the direction of the kitchen. I suddenly realized I was very hungry.

I flipped my braid over my shoulder and shook the sand from my knees. Maybe there was time to examine my gift before lunch and pick out something clean to wear in case I saw...

'So you teach now?' Rahul must have come in through the side entrance. I stared at him in dismay. Here I was, just as he saw me this morning, dusty and dishevelled, with a layer of sand and chalk over my clothes adding to my charms.

'Why am I surprised?' he continued, smiling. 'You were always the best in our class.'

That was true enough, and made me smile in spite of my crumpled clothes. 'Only since you left,' I said, furtively wiping my hands behind my back. 'I was only standing in for Baba. He's mesmerized by the texts you brought, you know.'

'I'm glad he finds them of interest,' he said.

I gave up trying to dust off the chalk and stared at him

somewhat accusingly. 'I understood you had business to attend to?'

'Am I intruding?' he said, looking dismayed. 'The business didn't take as long as I expected. And I know that the Acharya will need my help to understand the texts.'

I was already sorry for my jibe. 'It's no intrusion,' I assured him. 'Baba will be happy to see you.' I did not add that I was happy to see him too.

He didn't look messy. He had traded his strange Chinese-style clothes for more familiar garb—a fine white cotton dhoti, a jewelled belt clasped around his narrow waist and a wide shawl arranged over his left shoulder and swept under the right arm, leaving his right shoulder bare.

And he had changed after all; he looked leaner, deeper in the chest, more muscled than I remembered. I flushed as I realized I was staring, but then, so was he.

Suddenly Loky erupted from one of the rooms and launched himself at Rahul, who grabbed him in a headlock under one arm.

'When did you come?' Loky squealed in delight. 'What did you get me? Let go of me!'

'Nice to see you too, Lokasamudra!' Rahul said laughing. 'I'll release you if you let me speak to your sister.'

'What are the texts you brought Baba?' I asked. 'I didn't get a chance to look at them.'

'The Kaiyuan Star Observations and the star catalogues of Shi Shen and Gan De,' Rahul said, letting Loky go.

'And how do they compare to the records at Ujjayani?'

'I have not seen those records in years,' Rahul said, smiling at my interrogation. 'I must wait to hear how they compare from you.'

'Rahul! Come here, son, let me look at you!' Baba had finally emerged from his room.

Rahul bent down to touch Baba's feet as Baba placed both

hands on his head in blessing.

'Live long, live long, my son. I am thankful that you have come back to us safe and sound. How is your father?' Baba said.

'He is well, sir,' Rahul replied.

'He must know that war is looming again,' Baba said. 'Multan has fallen to Muhammad of Ghor. Who knows where he may strike next.'

'We heard the news,' Rahul replied. 'That is, in part, why we returned earlier than planned.'

'War makes it hard for anyone to care about the sciences,' my father's sighed. 'Translations, teaching staff, accurate copies, everything takes money. Leela is learning the language, but she has not yet mastered it.' He fixed his eyes on Rahul, struck by a thought. 'You must know Chinese?'

'I do,' Rahul said. ' As do others we employ. If you would like translations made, my father's scribe may be spared for the task.'

'I'd like that,' Baba said. 'But meanwhile, tell me, did they observe the large guest star that appeared a hundred years ago and shone for two years before disappearing?'

'Yes, I believe it is noted,' Rahul said.

'And what is this circular diagram, divided into four?' Baba said.

'Those represent the directions,' Rahul explained. 'The Azure Dragon of the East, the Vermillion Bird of the South, the White Tiger of the West and the Black Tortoise of the North. Each is divided into seven mansions that constitute the twenty-eight celestial mansions.'

The descriptions were fascinating. I leaned in so I wouldn't miss anything.

'Just like our Nakshatras!' Baba exclaimed, nearly walking into the closed door to Aajoba's study. Rahul held the door open for

Baba. He threw me an apologetic glance over his shoulder before vanishing over the threshold. Baba shut the door after them.

Uff! I seethed at the injustice of it as I walked to the kitchen. I would have liked to hear about the guest star and the twenty-eight mansions. Even Baba, who knew how much I loved such things, had casually excluded me from the discussion.

'Leela!'

It was Amma. 'Go get changed and then help me and Ajji with lunch. We have guests.' Something about the way she said this made me look at her sharply, but she avoided my gaze.

'But it's just Rahul!' I said.

Amma sighed. 'There are…others. Wear the new sari that Ajji bought for you, and your gold chain too.'

I went off without comment to do her bidding, which made her cast a worried glance after me. Meek acceptance was not my usual response when asked to dress up.

I scrubbed my face and hands by the garden well. I had washed my hair this morning with soapy, sweet-smelling reetha pods. A few silky wisps now escaped from the braid I'd twisted my hair into. I attached a garland of jasmine and harsingar flowers to the braid, at the nape of my neck.

In my room, I pulled off the crumpled cotton sari I had been wearing, took the bright pink sari that Ajji had bought me out of my trunk and shook out its starched length. It smelt of the sandalwood shavings Amma kept in the trunk.

I tied my sari quickly, pleating the fabric into fan folds between my fingers, tucking them in at my stomach so they fell level to my ankles. I tucked the other end of the pleats into the waistband at my back, glancing over my shoulder to make sure they were centred. The fabric fell in crisp, graceful folds, enveloping me in a warm glow of colour. The little jewellery I owned would have to do; the old-fashioned but pretty drop earrings that Ajji had passed down to me, and a thin gold chain around my neck.

I looked in the polished silver mirror on the wall, carefully applied a thin line of kohl to the rim of my eyes, and then drew a tiny black flower between my eyes.

My face looked flushed and excited. I practised a calm smile. It was a little weak, but it was all I could manage.

'Leela, look at you, so beautiful!' Ajji said delightedly as she saw me. 'Let me dot a black spot on your chin to ward off the evil eye.'

I smiled ruefully. Didn't she know? I had a permanent evil eye cast on me since birth, and no amount of Ajji's love could remove that.

5

'WHY DID YOU INVITE THESE PEOPLE?' BABA ASKED, annoyed. 'I am much too busy with Rahul to have time for them.'

'They're from your village, and far from home. It would be rude to not show some hospitality. Besides, they have a son,' Amma said with quiet emphasis.

'Oh? Oh, right!' Baba said, catching on. '*That* boy. Half of his planets align with Leela's, is it not? Except for Mangal, of course, but maybe that could be managed by a tree wedding, perhaps? And did you say they were from Bijjadi Beda?' The mention of his home village gave him pause, but then he grumbled regardless. 'I have heard of the family... More into ritual than learning, I always thought. Still, no harm in being hospitable.'

I bit my lip and dropped the straw screen, behind which I stood, back into place, so they wouldn't know I'd heard their conversation. A tree wedding to confuse the planets indeed! They were always on the lookout for an astrological match for me, even though a partial one was all that could be expected in my case. Normally, I would be civil to a suitor for Baba's sake, but it was hard to submit to a bridal showing with Rahul present. I should have known Amma was up to something. I thought of my closest friend, Brinda, too far away in Ujjayani to offer advice. What would Brinda do?

'Cross you eyes when you greet him,' Brinda would have urged. 'Spill hot lentils in his lap when you serve lunch.'

I might yet do it.

'Leela, come here!' Ajji called from the kitchen. I had never seen the kitchen so busy; Ajji didn't entertain much except for at feasts and festivals.

Amma and my aunts stirred pots of lentils, vegetables, rice. It was hot and smoky in the dark kitchen, but the food smelled delicious—all vegetarian dishes, appropriate for Brahmins and Jains alike. Funny that while they disagreed on every doctrine, they could still share the same kitchen; although Jains were, in fact, stricter than us. Some grains, fruits and vegetables that were allowed in Brahmin diets were restricted in Jain kitchens, or so I had heard.

'Leela,' Ajji said, interrupting my thoughts. 'Go set up the thalis for lunch.'

'Thalis?' I asked. 'Why not banana leaves?'

'Those are all right for family, but we have guests,' Ajji insisted. 'Mind you don't crumple your sari.'

There would be a mountain of dishes to do after this meal; unlike banana leaves the used plates could not be discarded. Apparently it was worth the extra work to impress my suitor. Ajji's mehri, who came after every meal to wash up, would need a hefty bonus today.

I laid out the wide copper dinner plates with their matching bowls, in which all the individual dishes would be served— Basmati rice, puris, lentils, pumpkin, okra, yogurt and mango pickle—and returned to the kitchen. I could hear Baba and Rahul deep in conversation in Aajoba's study.

New voices rang out from the direction of the courtyard I had just left. The guests had arrived. Amma and Ajji hurried to greet them. Soon Amma appeared with two women in tow—a matronly woman, around Amma's age, and a young girl around mine.

'Leela, pay your respects,' Amma said.

I folded my hands in a formal namaskar. The woman grabbed my hands and drew me to her.

'She looks just like you!' she exclaimed. 'Such clear golden skin, such dark lustrous hair, and what eyes! I'm surprised she hasn't been betrothed yet!'

I dropped my head, willing pimples to pop up on my nose to stop her from going on so. 'And here is my Asha. It is *her* birth chart that we wanted Leela's father to draw for us.'

Asha smiled a shy greeting and handed me a bunch of beautiful lotuses.

'We bought these at the temple,' she said. She came with me as I found a shallow pot to float them in so that they would stay fresh. We set them by the sunny spot in the verandah where Baba liked to write, and hurried back to the kitchen where our mothers were still talking about her birth chart.

'What? It was not done when she was younger?' Amma asked.

'Her exact date and time of birth is unknown,' Asha's mother said. 'She came in the middle of the monsoon, the year our village flooded, and no one had the time to note it down.'

Amma nodded sympathetically. The monsoon could be a life-giving boon and a catastrophe all at once.

'We think it was two watches after sunrise on the full-moon day in the month of Kartik, thirteen years ago. That's my mother's best estimate,' the woman continued.

The star chart was drawn by the solar calendar, but most people reckoned their days by the lunar calendar. If you counted the total number of days from the start of the current age, you could calculate one from the other. Baba had taught me that long ago.

As the others chatted, I idly calculated the lagan chart for Asha in my head. I had the panchang almanac memorized for that year.

The full-moon day in Kartik thirteen years ago would make it a solar rashee, or zodiac sign of the maiden, which would put the sun in her second house, Jupiter in her fourth, and Mars in her...

My heart stopped cold.

'Aunt?' I whispered to the woman from Bijjadi Beda. 'Are you *sure* it was the full-moon day? You said before that you were not certain.'

'Almost positive,' she answered. 'Why, child? Is that your birthday too?'

'No,' I said. 'But...but perhaps you are mistaken; people always default to a full-moon day if anything happens close to it, because it's easy to remember. Maybe it was the day *after* the full moon?'

She fell silent as she absorbed my intent gaze. After a minute she said, 'Why, yes, it was the day after the full moon after all.'

'But, Amma...' her daughter began, but was quickly shushed with one wave of her mother's hand.

Amma had been too busy to hear our exchange.

'The men are being served right now. Would you like to eat with them?' she called from the kitchen.

'We will wait and eat with you,' the woman replied. 'Can Asha help you serve the food?'

'Yes, girls, can you take the puris and pumpkin curry out?'

Asha and I picked up the platters Amma had prepared and headed for the courtyard.

The men of the household—Baba, Aajoba, my uncles, my cousins and Loky, of course—were all seated on low wooden patras, along with Rahul, and two other people I did not recognize. Asha nudged me.

'Who is the handsome one?' she asked.

'Which one?' I asked, feigning ignorance. She was staring at Rahul, of course.

'Oh, *him*,' I said nonchalantly, following her gaze, 'that's Rahul, the Nagarseth's son.'

'Wealthy *and* personable,' she said ruefully, 'but a Jain, I hear. Why couldn't he be Brahmin too?' Then she added with a giggle, 'and that's my brother, Mahendra, right next to him.'

So that was the suitor. I considered him carefully. He was rather odd looking—all arms and legs, with a long nose and a wide, wolf-like grin. He had clever eyes, that looked around in a challenging sort of way. Loky was making faces at me behind his back, while Baba was more restrained. But I could tell, since I knew his every mood, that he was carefully watching Mahendra.

The suitor was engaged in a spirited argument with Rahul. 'I'm sure none of their methods or inventions are as good as ours,' Mahendra was saying.

'Some are better,' Rahul said matter-of-factly.

'I cannot believe that,' Mahendra scoffed.

'They have a way of arranging characters on a printing plate so that a text may be duplicated repeatedly,' Rahul countered. 'That's useful, isn't it?'

'A roomful of scribes is more useful,' Mahendra argued.

I was so taken with the thought of such a device that I forgot to be quiet. 'So anyone can stamp a copy of a complicated text?' I asked. 'Over and over, without a single mistake?' Heavens! How much work, expense and heartache could that save the observatory!

Rahul's face lit up. 'Ingenious, isn't it?' he said.

Ajji flashed me a warning look, so I said no more, but I remembered to serve Rahul an extra scoop of pumpkin curry. Was it still his favourite? His warm smile said yes. Flustered, I turned to Mahendra to find him staring at me more boldly than I liked, disconcerting me. I slopped the pumpkin clumsily over the side of his plate. Rahul's eyes flicked from Mahendra to me and his smile vanished.

Just as well. Another smile and I might have followed Brinda's imagined advice and dumped the steaming curry in the wolf-boy's lap.

'What did your mother say your birth time was, Asha?' her father asked.

'The day after the full moon of Kartik, thirteen years ago,' Asha recited, 'two watches after sunrise.'

I held my breath. Had I calculated correctly? What if I made a mistake and made matters worse? I should not have interfered; it was none of my business.

I watched Baba out of the corner of my eye as I continued serving. His face had the intense look it always wore when he was calculating mentally.

'Good,' he said finally. 'Do you know if she had been born the day before it would have been disastrous? She is very lucky to have missed a terrible fate so narrowly.'

Asha gave a quiet gasp. She linked her arm with mine and gave it a tight squeeze as we made our way back to the kitchen with our empty platters.

Intentionally or not, I had made a friend.

6

'FIREWORKS!'

Loky came dancing through the courtyard, brandishing something like a war trophy. 'Rahul got me fireworks!'

'Let's see,' I snatched the parcel out of his hands. The scrolls for Baba were gone, but there were other items in the box. A few small pots of fireworks with twisted cotton wicks lay on top. My heart warmed to Rahul. He knew what would make Loky happiest.

'These are for you,' Loky pushed a narrow roll into my hands. I turned the roll over—paper. All my anticipation leaked away as I studied it. A practical gift, fit for a tall, studious bookworm. Not silks or jade or fine china, but paper.

I shook off my disappointment. It was a thoughtful gift from a former classmate, and I did like paper, after all. Chinese paper was just as hard to come by here as fireworks, especially such fine paper as this, thinner and stronger than any I had seen before.

I unrolled it carefully, smoothing it down with my fingers, and was rewarded with a surprise. A letter for me in the centre of the roll! There was a carefully drawn diagram and a few lines in Rahul's familiar hand:

Leela,
This is special kite paper. Use the instructions to make your
own. When I missed my friends from Ujjayani these past

years I flew kites as high as the monsoon clouds and imagined
that they took my greetings to them across the many miles
between us.
Rahul

My heart skipped several beats. This would need careful analysis. He had missed me, or rather, all of us from my father's class in Ujjayani. But messages by cloud hinted at 'Meghaduta', the classical cloud messenger love poem by Ujjayani's own master poet, Kalidas, which could mean—

I shook the thought off. There was no point indulging in sentimental speculation. Better to concentrate on the instructions. What in the world was a kite? I had never heard of such a thing. I didn't want to be critical of Rahul's statement, but 'as high as the monsoon clouds' seemed like a gross exaggeration. How could something as fragile as a piece of paper fly that high?

Still, it would be an interesting challenge to build the contraption. I would need thin slivers of bamboo, glue made from flour, scissors and a long string of cotton. All of which we had in the house.

'Loky, come help me with this, and I'll make sure Amma lets you light some of the firecrackers tonight,' I promised. I knew how his mind worked.

Sure enough, I instantly had a helpful, attentive assistant.

We collected our materials and ran up the steps to the flat terrace roof. In a shady corner, where the crown of the fig tree that grew in Ajji's courtyard loomed over us, we got to work. The house sparrows chirped around us, trying to eat the flour glue. Some girls on the neighbour's terrace stopped hanging up laundry to watch what we were doing. A couple of them even leapt over the narrow space between the houses to take a look. In the distance, a peacock called its catlike *pmeaw*, making me long for the rains to wash away the sticky heat of summer.

An hour later we were done.

'You have bits of paper stuck to your hair!' Loky said. I laughed because I didn't care. I had eyes only for our masterpiece; a bright colourful diamond of paper that fluttered from my hands, pulling against the slight sea breeze that blew across the terrace.

We ran down for our evening meal, carrying our handiwork carefully.

'Leela, you have paper stuck all over your brand new sari!' Amma said.

I danced around her. 'I don't care, Amma,' I said. 'Look what we made.'

'What is that?' Amma asked, taking it from me. 'It is beautiful. What lovely colours! What does it do?'

'Rahul said it can fly as high as the monsoon clouds!' Loky announced.

'Oh, I doubt that,' Amma said. 'But butter and sugar in your mouth for speaking of the rains, my child. They are well past their due time. Another week like this one and the crops will surely fail.'

The delay in the monsoon was serious. The farmers in Anhilwara, Malwa and the rest of India depended on it. If it did not come on time the crops could not grow, since there wasn't enough water even in the Narmada to irrigate every field.

But even the thought of failed crops and famine couldn't keep me down today.

'Amma, Loky and I can't get this to fly more than a few feet. Can we go to the Nagarseths' tomorrow and ask Rahul to show us how it is done?'

'Yes, of course,' she said. 'Rahul would like to see what Loky made of his gift, I'm sure.'

I didn't correct her when she assumed that the kite was also meant for Loky. 'And can we light a few fireworks tonight?' I asked pleadingly. 'Please, Amma?'

'Fine,' Amma said. The possibility of my match with Asha's brother had put her in a good mood, I suspected. I banished the thought. Just for today I resolved to enjoy Amma's light spirits and ignore the cause behind it.

That night we lit the firecrackers on the rooftop terrace as the fireflies sparkled round us. The cool breeze hinted of approaching monsoon clouds and Loky whooped with delight as a golden rocket shot up in the sky and exploded in showers of sparks.

I woke before dawn. For a while I lay still, taking in the noises of early morning—birds chirping, dogs barking in the distance and Ajji bargaining with the vegetable vendor at the back entrance, by the kitchen verandah.

Loky had crawled into bed with me sometime in the middle of the night, and was breathing heavily in my ear. I moved him aside and rose. If I hurried, maybe Baba would tell me about the manuscripts before breakfast.

It was quiet downstairs. The smallest children were still asleep.

'Leela,' Ajji called. 'Help me with these vegetables, girl.'

Vegetables didn't rank as high in importance as manuscripts for me, but I couldn't refuse Ajji. 'For a hug,' I said, wrapping my arms around her middle and snuggling against her frail old frame, wrapped in a cotton sari soft from many washes.

I took the basket filled with okra, squash, pumpkins and herbs and followed her to the kitchen. I had to stand on tiptoe to hang the basket to the hook on the low smoke-stained ceiling.

'Where's Baba?' I asked.

'At the bathing ghat by the river, saying his morning prayers,' Ajji said. No chance of studying the manuscripts then. 'Why do you want him?' she asked. 'Come sit by me on the swing instead, and help me clean the rice.'

A wide plank swing was suspended by brass chains on the back verandah, the favourite place of the women of the house. I sat down with a platter of rice, sorting through it carefully, removing tiny pebbles and debris, while Ajji chatted. She told me the miserable tales of refugees from Multan fleeing the devastation in the wake of the latest attack by Muhammad of Ghor. Soon Amma joined us and the conversation turned towards our youngest aunt, who was expected back from her mother's house any day with her newborn twins.

'Leela?'

I looked up, startled, from my platter of rice. It was Amma. 'Didn't you and Loky want to go to the Nagarseths' today? Will you take some ointment and dress the pigeon's wing?'

'Yes, of course,' I said. I held in the smile that tugged at my lips and hurried upstairs to fetch Loky.

On the way to the Nagarseths', Loky wanted to stop and play a stick and spindle game with a crowd of kids, buy a clay pot of sticky sweets, and bring home a puppy tottering on wobbly legs beside its mother in the marketplace.

'You know Amma won't let you keep a dog,' I said, taking the puppy gently away from him. It licked my fingers trustingly with a warm pink tongue.

'But I want to keep it,' Loky said, tears streaming down his small face, which had somehow become dirty again, although he had bathed before we left. 'Amma won't mind.'

I grabbed him by the arm and marched him to the Nagarseths' haveli. Smoothing my clothes down, I rapped smartly on the door.

'Ah, young miss, you've come for the pigeon,' the old manservant said. 'He's doing much better now.'

Better take care of it first, before thanking Rahul. I followed him to the roof and the pigeon lofts. The beautiful birds—silver grey and purple or milky white—cooed softly in their pretty chabutros.

Loky cheered up a bit when he saw them and even helped me with my task, spreading Shan's wing carefully while I unrolled the bandage and splint and massaged Amma's ointment on to the wound. He was doing much better.

The dressing nearly done, Loky skipped off across the wide terrace, dragging the kite behind him by the string. 'Careful with that!' I shouted after him, still working on the wound. 'Oh no! It's getting away! Loky!'

The colourful diamond was twenty feet in the air. 'Pull it in, you little monkey!' I yelled.

'Right away, mistress,' a mock serious voice that did not belong to Loky replied. I looked over my shoulder and met Rahul's amused gaze.

I picked Shan up, his feathered body squirming in my hands, and placed him carefully in his coop before turning to Rahul. 'What do you think of the kite? Did we build it right?'

'You built it very well, sound and symmetrical,' Rahul said. 'But I knew you would.'

'You did?' I said, pleased. He knotted a new reel of string at the base of the kite with quick competence. 'How could you not, with my excellent instructions?'

'Your *excellent* instructions?' I spluttered. 'I had to guess half the steps, without any idea of what I was building!'

He laughed and beckoned me to come closer.

'Go to the other end of the roof, Loky, and hold the kite like this.' He held the kite between both hands with its nose pointing up, 'And when I say "go", throw the kite up into the air.'

Loky nodded and ran off, the newly attached string trailing after him.

'Like this?' he asked, turning around at the end of the terrace. Rahul nodded and pulled the line taut.

'Here,' he said to me. 'You hold the line; I'll tell you what to do.'

I took the line and hoped I wouldn't make a fool of myself.

'Now, when Loky launches the kite, pull the line up. When you feel the wind tug the kite, release more line so it can go higher. If you feel it drop, pull the slack in. Got it?'

'If it tugs, release line, if it drops, pull in the slack,' I repeated. Could it really be that easy?

'Good. Loky, go!' he said, and Loky threw the kite up. I tried to pull the line up, but the kite simply dropped, clattering to the terrace.

'It's not broken, is it?' I asked, disappointed. Was it even possible for that scrap of paper to take flight? Maybe the bamboo made it too heavy.

'It takes practice, and the wind isn't very strong,' Rahul said. 'Here, let me show you.'

He reached over from behind me, both his hands over mine. I froze. I could feel his breath on my cheek and the warmth of his body against my back. Sneaking a sidelong glance at him I noticed that his eyelashes were dead straight, not curled up like mine. He glanced down and caught me staring.

I could hold his gaze for only a heartbeat before dropping mine. Blushing, I pushed his arm aside and moved away. 'You fly it,' I said, twisting my gold bangle around my bare arm, willing the goosebumps there to vanish. 'I'll watch for now.'

As Loky launched the kite, Rahul pulled up sharply and fed

the line out with both hands, the spindle spinning wildly on the floor beside us.

The kite rose higher and higher until it was just a dot in the sky.

'How does it do that?' I asked, amazed.

'The wind pulls it up and the tension in the line pulls it down. So when I let the line out there is no way but up,' Rahul said. 'Make sense?'

'Yes,' I said. 'How high can it go?'

'How much line do we have?' Rahul said by way of reply, laughing at my surprise. 'Here, you take the line. It's easier to fly it now that it's up.'

The line felt alive in my hands. Far above us, the kite danced and dove. I could feel its every movement passing down the line to me.

'Pull in, pull in,' Rahul said, as the kite dropped with a lull in the wind. 'You'll get it stuck in a tree, Leela.' He grabbed the line.

We pulled the line in, hand over hand, till the kite was safely back on the terrace.

'My turn,' Loky cried.

Rahul launched the kite and I helped Loky fly it. We were both getting better at it. Down below, some people in the lane alongside the haveli were pointing and looking up at the kite.

'You can tie it to a post now and it will keep flying,' Rahul said. 'Loky, will you run down and ask the steward to bring up some cold sherbet for us?'

Loky disappeared down the stairs, and Rahul turned to me.

I looked away to where the generous sweep of the Narmada widened into an estuary before pouring into the sea of Khambhat. The Nagarseth fleet lay anchored in the inland harbour of the river, safe from the monsoon clouds that could arrive any time.

'My grandfather taught me how to fly kites,' he said. 'You'd like him.' The warmth in his voice suggested he was close to his grandfather.

'I'm sure I would,' I said, turning back to him. It was rude to look away when he was talking to me, but I was afraid of what he might see in my eyes. So I focused instead on his shoulder.

'Is there something the matter with my drape?' he inquired politely, a laugh hidden in his voice.

'No,' I said, taking a deep breath. I couldn't keep talking to his shoulder. And he was not the sun, after all, that I could be blinded from looking at him.

Bracing myself, I looked into his eyes, and it was as if I was the kite, climbing giddily to the clouds or falling free through air, I don't know which. Maybe both...

'Sherbet,' Loky's voice suddenly piped up behind us.

We sipped the sweet, rose-scented drink that the attendant poured into polished silver cups, and went back to flying, slowly improving our technique, until I could fly the kite nearly as well as Rahul.

We never noticed when the western horizon started to turn dark with clouds. Only when a flash of lightning, followed by thunder, announced their arrival did I see them; towering clouds rolling inland from the sea, and the hawks gliding the updrafts beneath them as if in praise and welcome.

'It's the rains!' Loky yelled.

Rahul opened his arms wide to the sky as if greeting an old friend. 'Hail, friend of Indra, counsellor divine,' he murmured, 'illustrious offspring of a glorious line.'

The first lines of 'Meghaduta'—he *had* read Kalidasa after all.

7

*T*HUNDER SHOOK THE TERRACE, MAKING ME JUMP. RAHUL snatched the line from me and started pulling the kite in, hand over fist. He hauled it in just as the first exhilarating downpour drenched us to the skin. 'Here,' he said, handing it to me. The soggy kite looked in danger of ripping anyway, but I took it from him, glad that he had managed to save it.

'Run!' I grabbed Loky by the arm and the three of us ran through the stinging downpour. Just like the day the rains arrived in Ujjayani two years ago, signalling the end of school. The last time I saw Rahul before he left for Java. We'd run through the street, lessons abandoned, splashing in puddles, not realizing that the next day he would be gone.

I looked to Rahul to see if he remembered, but he had called for the steward and was busy giving orders.

'Bring fresh towels,' Rahul said, 'and move the wooden pigeon chabutras to the roofed terrace. Are the bales of silk covered at the docks? How about the saffron that is shipping out? Has all the merchandise been moved into the storehouses?'

He had transformed in an instant from a carefree boy to a leader giving directions. I bit my lip. It was admirable that he took his responsibilities seriously, but the rains were here! The whole city had been waiting for it for weeks. Who could possibly think of merchandise at a moment as magical as this?

'We should go,' I said. 'Amma will be worried.'

'Wait a while,' Rahul said, 'the rain may stop. Or take someone with you to carry a chhatri.'

Stop? It wasn't a spring shower that would stop, it was the life-giving, famine-stopping, crop-saving boon we'd been praying for.

'Thank you,' I said, with dignity, 'but no one carries a chhatri in the first rains of monsoon.'

He tilted his head at my withering tone. 'Is that so?' he asked, as he walked us to the door.

'Yes, it is,' I said firmly. 'Good luck with your saffron. I hope it doesn't suffer any harm from the rains.'

I stepped outside, fuming, and shut the door firmly in his face.

Outside, the world had gone mad!

The streets and narrow alleys were full of children splashing and soaking in the first showers of the monsoon. The distinctions of the marketplace were gone. Potters, farmers, soldiers, scholars all milled about, enjoying the rains, caste forgotten. Foreigners from China, Arabia, Egypt and Africa rubbed shoulders with the Anhilwarans, Kuchiis and Gujjars. Strangers laughed together, for with the sheltering shadow of monsoon clouds came a feeling of camaraderie. Today, no one was a stranger.

The musky smell of parched earth turning moist rose up from the ground. Somewhere at the end of the street, a drummer was beating a joyful rhythm on a dhol, keeping time with the torrent. I wanted to lift my soaking sari high and dance.

A girl caught my hand. 'Keekli with me,' she said. Keekli is but a child's game: you hold a partner's hands crosswise—both partners leaning back, letting one's weight hold the other—and then twirl in a circle until you're giddy. I hadn't done it since I was ten. But the excitement of monsoon was infectious. 'Stay right here,' I told Loky, and clasped hands with the girl, our hands slippery with rain, and spun, laughing, until the world was a blur around me.

Somewhere in the blur, I knew I was being watched. I stopped, dizzy from the spinning, and there was Rahul, soaked to the skin, grinning recklessly.

'But you are getting drenched, sir,' I observed, hiding a smile. 'Where is your chhatri?'

'I have it on good authority,' he said humbly, 'that *no one* carries a chhatri in the first rains of the monsoon.' There was a mischievous glint in his eye as he added, 'And if I were fool enough to bring one for your benefit, I suspect you might hit me with it.'

'What about your saffron?' I asked. 'I hear five palas of it is worth nearly a nishka now.'

'But the first rains are priceless,' he said.

I laughed with him, not caring that my wet sari was plastered to my skin, and his robes, it must be said, were less than modest.

A single-stringed tumbi picked out a merry counterpoint to the rhythm of the drums. A few men, Punjabi farmers by the look of them, started a slow dance to it.

'Dance, my boy!' The tumbi player nudged Rahul. Rahul stepped in, following the lead of the men. It was a heel-kicking, thigh-slapping, arms-flying dance usually reserved for harvest celebrations. He kept pace effortlessly as the tempo built, rising to frenzy, following the pulsating music with his whole body. He might have been a farmer himself, the way he danced. A crowd formed, blocking my view, but I stayed, clapping along with them, catching an occasional glimpse of Rahul past elbows and heads, my feet tapping to the music.

And then the crowd parted and the men, led by Rahul, circled around Loky and me. I covered my face with my hands, laughing, embarrassed by all this attention. My fault, I suppose, for encouraging him to celebrate the rains. Loky grabbed Rahul around the waist and was hoisted on to his shoulders as Rahul kept dancing.

Then the tumbi stopped. With a few backslaps and winks to Rahul the men dispersed into the crowd. Rahul lowered a shrieking Loky to the ground.

'We're nearly home,' I said, my teeth chattering as my wet clothes clung to my skin. 'We should go before Loky catches a cold.'

Rahul took my rain-wrinkled hands in his large ones, still warm from the dancing, and rubbed them together.

'You forgot the kite,' he said gently. 'I'll bring it next time.'

Next time. The promise of it was as warm as his hands.

I pulled my hands away, shivering from more than the rain. Grabbing Loky by the shoulder I headed homeward, but turned around, searching for one last glimpse of Rahul. His gaze caught mine through the crowd and he bowed slightly in my direction—a quick graceful gesture that made his wet black hair fall in his eyes.

The teekedar came to visit a few days later. The rains bring water for the crops and rivers, but also bring disease, so getting a teeka was essential. Amma insisted on us getting it every year and Baba agreed. There was no treatment as painful, it was almost better to risk the pox! No, I didn't mean that. It was thought that those who printed their skin with teeka needles and applied the pox patches harvested from last year's patients did not get the dreaded disease.

Amma believed it, so I did too, and besides, I really had no choice. It was certainly true that no one in our family had been afflicted.

I rubbed the round scar on my arm where the previous year's teeka had been given. Just the sound of the rains made it ache again.

The teekedar had set up his equipment in the main courtyard

and the whole household had assembled there.

Dhruv and our other cousins had already had their teekas and were sobbing in my aunt's arms, their little boy bravado gone. The maids were hunting under beds and in trees for Loky, who always hid himself the day the teekedar came, in a vain attempt to escape. I wished I could hide with him.

My turn, gods help me. I held my arm out, eyes squeezed together. The large hands of the teekedar held my arm firmly. The needle made its first prick. It was even worse than last year, but at least it was soon over.

I joined the hunt for Loky. I knew how his mind worked, so I found him in no time, crouched behind the bags of flour in the granary, and carried him down to the courtyard of doom.

Downstairs, there was a commotion. The entire Nagarseth clan had chosen this moment to descend upon us. Rahul's father, stepmother, uncles and cousins were gathered in Ajji's small courtyard, dripping with lavish displays of silk, gold and jewels.

Baba was deep in conversation with Rahul's father. Among other things, they talked of war. It was no secret that Ghori was restless, and sought to emulate Mahmud of Ghazni—who had raided the country seventeen times, a hundred years ago. The last of Ghazni's raids had been against Anhilwara, when he ransacked the temple town of Somnath, slaughtered its defenders and carried off its wealth. Would Ghori march against Anhilwara too, tempted by the weak target of its young boy-king Mulraj? Or would the reputation of the hot-headed Bhimdev Solanki, his uncle and the regent, be enough to deter him?

Baba confirmed that the reconstruction of the Somnath temple, a joint endeavour started by Raja Bhoja of Malwa and Bhimdev I of Anhilwara, was complete. The Nagarseth was thrilled that the fabled Somnathi sculptors would be free to work on the Jain temple the he wanted to commission in Ujjayani.

Two cavalry divisions of the Malwa army were expected in Bharuch, on their way back from the rededication of the Somnath temple. They had pledged support to Anhilwara in case of an attack from Ghori.

Amid the conversation, Loky, the only one left without the teeka, had started to inch towards the door to escape, but Amma hadn't forgotten him. She motioned for me to deliver Loky to the teekedar. I gripped his arm and marched him forward while he glared at me. 'It will be fine,' I lied. I was so busy with Loky that I hadn't even looked around for Rahul, but there he was, right beside me as I firmly held the struggling Loky, struggling like a cobra caught in a noose.

'Loky,' Rahul said. 'You can't count up to koti, can you?'

'Yes I can!'

Loky blinked rapidly and started counting, reluctant to appear less than brave before his idol. 'Ekum, duee, teen, char, panch, chai...'

Gods be praised, the teekedar was done before Loky had got to a hundred.

'That was well done,' I said, smiling gratefully at Rahul.

He did not return my smile but silently held out my kite. It had dried off well and looked none the worse for wear.

'It wasn't damaged,' he said quietly, nothing like the bracing tone he used with Loky only a moment before.

'Thank you,' I said, puzzled at his tone. Was the talk of war getting to him too?

'Leela!' said a nasal voice.

Rahul's stepmother was talking to me. I didn't think she knew my name. I looked up to find her sizing me up like one would a vegetable vendor's wares.

'How pretty you've turned out,' she said after a while, somewhat grudgingly. 'A bit scrawny, though. You take after your mother.' Her words were complimentary, her tone was not.

I flushed at the attention. I had always been intimidated by her. While Rahul's father, the Nagarseth was away, she controlled all his finances, including the endowment for Baba's observatory. Baba hated dealing with her, and I resented her for his sake. I supposed I could be civil to her for Rahul's.

'I don't see why you're not married yet,' she continued. 'Why doesn't your mother put you in silk? It would suit you much better.'

As if we could afford silk! I fumed inwardly. She was handsome, though not beautiful like Amma, and decked out in fine silk, which was embroidered with gold and silver in the latest fashion. You could barely see the fabric of her sari because she was covered in jewellery. Chains, no, ropes of gold hung around her neck. Truth be told, it was good that the shade of the dark clouds hung overhead, for it would have hurt my eyes to look at her gaudy display in the bright sunshine.

We were not rich, but we had our pride. I would not be made to feel embarrassed about my simple attire.

'Cotton is better suited to the weather,' I said, 'is it not?'

It was true that my sari was cotton, but it was fine muslin, dyed a light blue, with a thin gold border. It was more suited to the humidity of the season than the heavy silks she was wearing. The single gold armband I wore on my, admittedly thin, upper arm wasn't new, but it had been fashioned by the finest goldsmiths in Ujjayani, even if it was three generations old.

Her eyes held an amused respect this time. 'Perhaps,' she condescended.

A hearty voice chimed in, 'A diamond is a diamond, set it

in brass or in gold.' The Nagarseth turned to Rahul. 'Isn't that right, son?'

'Yes,' Rahul agreed quietly.

'It is nice to see you,' I smiled at the tall, kind man with his full head of grey hair. He had the same sincere charm that radiated from Rahul. I had always liked him.

Rahul's face stayed dark. What could possibly have happened since yesterday, I wondered.

I was about to find out.

His stepmother was still speaking. This time about the pitfalls of teekas and teekedars. 'An unhygienic practice, if you ask me. I would never allow them to allow such an assault on my person. Doesn't it actually give you the disease?'

'Only a mild form of it,' Amma said quietly. 'In my experience, it does provide protection from the smallpox. A little fever and a few eruptions but worth the peace of mind it affords.'

'It is very common in China and the kingdoms of Champa and Singhpura. Rahul and I have had them every year,' said the Nagarseth, stepping in.

'Well, you will never convince me that such a thing is safe or beneficial,' she said. 'But let us not talk of such things on an auspicious day like this.'

What auspicious day, I wondered. There were no festivals I could think of. Janmashthami, the birthday of Krishna, was still weeks away. Not that the Jains celebrated it anyway. Did she mean the Jain retreats during the monsoon rains?

'We have some good news,' the Sethani was saying. 'We're here to invite you to Rahul's betrothal next week. He is to be engaged to Roopmati, the daughter of Seth Oswal.'

My eyes went to Rahul, but he was staring at the ground.

No, I thought, stricken beyond words. *No!*

8

*W*HY WAS I SURPRISED? I MAY BE UNMARRIAGEABLE, BUT HE, clearly, was not. I looked away. Dimly I could hear murmurs of congratulations. Where was the door? I had to leave, to escape. I concentrated on moving my feet. Walk, just walk, I urged them. I made it as far as the kitchen verandah. Then I closed the door to the courtyard behind me and ran.

Up to the terrace, two steps at a time, up where bright wisps of paper still lay in the corner from yesterday, when we had made the kites in the shadow of the fig tree.

Lightning cracked above me and fresh showers poured down. Thankfully, the rain hid the tears that were streaming down my face. I held a scrap of wet paper to my face and wept.

'Leela!'

It was Amma, calling from the bottom of the stairs. 'Don't you get wet in the rain again! You'll fall sick.'

'C-coming, Amma,' I choked on my words a little. 'I…left my earrings here yesterday. I didn't want to lose them.'

'Ajji's earrings? I thought you had them on,' she said. 'Careless child! You're lucky the monkeys didn't take them.'

She was waiting with a warm, dry towel when I came down the stairs. She wrapped me in it and looked at me enquiringly. 'What's wrong?' she asked. 'There's something else, isn't it?'

'I don't feel so well,' I said. It was not entirely untrue.

'Ah,' Amma said, 'you might be falling sick already. And the teeka doesn't help.' In the past I'd had a fever after getting the teeka. Not an uncommon outcome, but a worrying one.

'The last thing you need is to get cold and wet again!' She marched me down the stairs and towelled me dry with rough cotton sheets. 'And Leela?'

'Yes?' I said.

'You're not fretting about your birth chart, are you? It is just the teeka, right?'

I nodded but didn't look at her.

'Just making sure.'

She hugged me tight. 'I know it's hard every time your friends get married. But you know Baba will set it right for you, don't you?'

I nodded. If only she knew.

She let go. 'Let's get you changed.'

I climbed into bed after changing into dry clothes. My face was burning. Hot tears threatened to leak out from behind my tightly closed eyelids. It was hard to lie still. The strings of the cot creaked under the thick cotton mattress beneath me as I tossed and turned till at last, I slept.

I had bad dreams. Rahul was in a ship in the middle of an angry sea. The prow of the ship was a woman's face. His stepmother's. She was talking and talking in her nasal voice. Someone was playing a dhol drumbeat. Thick dark clouds rained down on the ship as it tossed. Rahul was flying my kite. I wanted to warn him that the lightning would strike him. There was a flash...

I woke up. I was drenched in sweat. A cool hand stroked my forehead. Ajji.

'You have a fever,' she said. Her voice had a note of worry in it. I didn't want her to worry.

'I'm fine,' I said, trying to sit up. 'It's the teek...ouch!' My arm throbbed.

'No, stay still. Your Amma is preparing a special lunch for you. She will bring it up.'

'But you have guests...' I said. Was Rahul still here?

'They left. They have a lot to do. The Sethani, she doesn't like teekedars. Thinks they bring pestilence instead of protecting us against it.'

Her nasal voice rang in my head—*Rahul is to be betrothed to Roopmati, the daughter of Oswal Seth.* Her doing, I was sure.

'Good,' I muttered. 'If the pox takes her, Baba will have his grant money without the hassle she puts him through.' Bitter words, and I was only half joking.

'Her words are sharper than her deeds,' Ajji clucked reprovingly. 'I know you hear no good of Jains from your teachers. They may not be believers, but they have been generous to your father.' She tucked the sheets around me. 'Wish ill on people sparingly, child, a Brahmin's curse is potent.'

I hung my head, ashamed of my pettiness.

'You're looking better!' Amma carried in something that smelled delicious in a large copper bowl. It was a hearty stew of lentils, rice and clarified butter, simmered with spices, cooked by Amma herself, not by one of my aunts or the serving maids. Even Amma's food had healing powers.

I spooned it into my mouth and felt better with each steamy morsel that went down my throat.

'Stay in bed,' Amma said. 'I've told Loky not to bother you today.'

That wouldn't keep him away, I knew. But Amma made sure he promised to only play quiet games while I was sick. He brought a bag with the cloth mat for pachisi, our favourite game, and spread it out, jingling the cowrie shells we used for dice. I didn't have the heart to refuse him, for this was a big sacrifice. He would rather be out splashing in the puddles, playing with Arya and our other cousins, but he was staying in to keep me company.

He had me laughing in no time. They should bottle Loky and sell him as medicine, I thought indulgently. But after two rounds, I began to feel dizzy.

'Loky, run along now,' Amma ordered as she came in to check my pulse and feel my forehead.

'I have something that'll cheer you up,' she said, opening the window to let some light in. 'A letter from Brinda.'

Dear Leela,

Why have you not written? Aren't you going to give me your news? Yes, I know Rahul has arrived in Bharuch, so write me every last thing.

Ujjayani is tedious beyond bearing without you. Only imagine enduring music classes all alone with Nishikantji. I swear he is in a permanent rage because he misses your perfect pitch, and he takes it all out on me. The only diversion we've had is our new maid, who is trained in Turki beauty treatments. She has a novel way of shaping eyebrows with just a twist of thread. Amma wouldn't let her touch us without trying it on someone else first, so old Dhanniya volunteered. Now guess who has the most perfectly arched eyebrows in Ujjayani? Toothless Dhanniya! We're waiting to see how long it takes for the hair to grow back before Amma lets us try it.

Speaking of new fashions, I'm sending you a dress in the latest style. The skirt and choli are stitched to fit you and no one else, imagine that! The way it twirls makes me feel like dancing. Amma thinks saris are more practical since they drape to fit anyone, but I love the new style. I had a few made for myself, so I had to get one for you. If it doesn't fit, have it altered and send me the tailor's bill.

Kanwar Ranveer Singh is in Anhilwara with Prince Subhrata. I feel like I'll be engaged forever and never married. I wish the rains would come soon and then pass away so at least I can have you back.

And Leela, if you see Rahul, speak your heart, for he'll not care a cowrie for your wretched horoscope. I've heard of a plan to align the merchant houses of Nagarseth and Oswal through marriage. Promise me you won't wait until it is too late.
Your friend,
Brinda.

I read the letter over and over. How right Brinda was about the business alliance the Sethani had planned and executed. How good of her to try and warn me, but it was already too late.

I pulled out a fresh palm leaf page and my sharpest pen and wrote a long letter back to Brinda. The lies I told her! Rahul was betrothed and I was happy for him. I had an exciting plan to convince Baba to let me teach at the observatory, and to start using Chinese printing to copy books at the library. Well, that part was true enough. By the time I finished I almost had *myself* convinced, if not her. A fragile conviction, since one wayward thought of Rahul was enough to upset it all.

But I wouldn't let him back into my thoughts. Two days passed. I started to feel a little better.

'Tomorrow,' Amma said as she sat by my bed and smiled, 'you must get up and go downstairs for a while. It will do you good.'

9

HERE WAS NO AVOIDING THE DETAILS ABOUT RAHUL'S betrothal, for it was all everyone could talk about. It was a good thing I had an excuse for looking ill.

The first part of the ceremony—the pradan, when the bride-to-be had been gifted ornaments by the Sethani—had occurred even before Rahul had reached Bharuch. The second half had taken place the week I was ill, when the men of the Oswal family had, in turn, visited Bharuch to present gifts to Rahul. The bride hadn't been there, as per tradition. It was not uncommon for a couple to meet only at the wedding altar.

Roopmati—the name suggested that she was fair and beautiful, and by all accounts she was that and more. She was the oldest grandchild of the business house of Oswal, a merchant family nearly as old and powerful as the Nagarseth's, though they were more feared than beloved. They traded in jewels and moneylending and were known to extract their debts by all means, fair or foul. But to their associates and their family they were generous, so the bridal gifts had been lavish.

The Nagarseth had hosted a feast for Jain monks and nuns, to which Baba had been invited, one of the few Brahmins included in the ceremony.

'Atheists,' sniffed Ajji. 'They don't respect Brahmins as they should.'

Normally I would have sprung to the defence of the Jains,

but I was too dispirited. Baba, of course, did so.

'The Nagarseth makes no distinction between us,' Baba said. 'And he's intelligent enough to agree with most of *my* theories instead of theirs. Was I not invited?'

'He seated you with the Jain monks,' my middle uncle said. 'Who knows what caste they were? They allow anyone to join their order. Sweepers, farmers, weavers; eating and reading with Brahmins, like they are our equals.'

'They reject more than caste, they reject the gods too,' Ajji pointed out. 'They're no better than the Buddhists,' she added. A silence fell on everyone at the mention of the Buddhists.

'Our own son rejected caste and traditionalism,' Aajoba reminded her, an old pain throbbing in his voice. 'So how can you blame others for doing so?' He withdrew to his room, leaning a little more than usual on his cane.

My eldest uncle, Amma's oldest brother, had surprised everyone years ago by declaring *Buddham sharanam gacchchami* and going off to take refuge in a Buddhist order. Last anyone knew, he was meditating in a mountain cave.

The Jains are naastika too, preferring good work and compassion as a route to salvation rather that belief in rituals, gods and avatars.

'The real problem with the Jains,' my middle uncle said to Baba, 'is that they emasculate the kingdom with their talk of non-violence. Who will fight off the Turkis if all our warriors drop their weapons and become monks?'

White-robed Jain monks, with their wool fibre whisks and their white breathing masks—used to ensure that no harm was caused even to the tiniest of creatures—were a common sight in Bharuch, and in every town and village of Anhilwara. This land held their most sacred shrines, after all. And the staunch support of the Solanki rulers of Anhilwara also encouraged them to settle here. Young Mulraj's father had been an exception, with a bitter hatred of Jains, but every king before and since had patronized the faith.

'Who will speak for morality if everyone plays at arms?' Baba replied. 'The warrior clans squabble while that Turki bides his time, waiting for Ajmer, Anhilwara and Malwa to destroy each other so he doesn't have to.'

Amma had had enough of the discussion.

'Did you hear about the jewel necklace they sent the Sethani?' she asked, trying to strike a lighter note. 'It had eight rubies, ten sapphires, a hundred pearls and five diamonds. It must have cost a fortune.'

'Well, they are jewel merchants, after all,' Ajji said. 'The Sethani is the one who arranged the match, so they had to show their appreciation. Even before the boy left Java, it was all done.'

Rahul had never met her. The Sethani fixed it all with the girl's family before he had even landed in Bharuch. It was possible that he had not known about it until the day the teekedar came.

'It certainly makes sense as a business alliance,' Baba said. 'They are the two richest merchant houses in Anhilwara and Malwa, maybe even in all the kingdoms of the north. Together they will rival the Five Hundred Lords guild of the south.'

It was just the sort of match that would make sense to the Sethani. But what about compatibility? How well did Roopmati match Rahul's interests and values? Did the Sethani know him well enough to pick someone whom he could be happy with?

Unkind thoughts about the Sethani crowded my mind. Perhaps his happiness did not concern her at all. Yes, I thought, warming to my tragic theme. She did not like him anyway, because he reminded her of his Chinese mother—the Nagarseth's true love—a mysterious woman whom no one here had ever seen. Everyone knew that Rahul's father had fallen in love with his mother far away in Java. She had succumbed to tropical fever when Rahul was six, and the Nagarseth had mourned for five years before agreeing to marry again. His marriage with the Sethani was not a conventional one. He was often away, travelling on business, and there had been no more children.

I shook myself out of my speculations. I had to think about myself. Where would *I* end up with my evil planets?

Just when I couldn't bear any more talk of Rahul's betrothal, there was a welcome diversion. A crowd of people at the door had brought exciting news: my youngest uncle and his wife had arrived from her parents' home with their three-month-old twin boys!

The household erupted in a joyful uproar. There had been great anticipation for their return—these were the first ever twins on our side of the family. All my cousins helped bring in their baggage from the bullock cart a block away—the alley was too narrow to allow the cart to pull up to the house.

The babies were so new and small. My youngest aunt, the wife of Amma's youngest brother, was just a girl herself. She had travelled to her parents' home for the birth. My youngest uncle had left to bring her home a month ago and looked equal parts proud and exhausted.

The news spread in the neighbourhood and soon Ajji's house was flooded with well-wishers, come to see the new mother and the babies.

Soon there would be a naming ceremony. Arrangements had to be made. The women brought out the small dholak used for singing at weddings and festivals, and began to sing auspicious songs wishing healthy lives for the babies. I was known to have a fine voice, so they insisted I sing, and I did so, gladly at first.

Baba, who could only stand a brief exposure to crowds, shut himself in Aajoba's room. I soon tired of it as well and escaped into the study after him.

The calmness of the study, with its dusty, silent books, was just what I needed.

'See what I have here, Leela,' Baba greeted me, happy to have me share his sanctuary. 'The first translations of the Chinese star charts. I got them this morning. You know the language a little. Tell me if it's true to the text.'

I didn't need to be asked twice. We spent all afternoon poring over the text, but were disappointed, it was poorly translated. The first part that Rahul had translated for Baba was well done, the meaning clear and precise, but the sections translated by the scribe loaned by the Nagarseth were crude and confusing. We grew frustrated puzzling over it.

'I think the only thing they are good at translating are bills of sales and goods lists,' Baba sighed.

'They are accountants, not scholars. They have no idea what the author is trying to say,' I said.

His eyes brightened. 'Do you think we could talk Rahul into translating the whole text for us?'

'He won't have time, Baba,' I said. 'It'll take years. And now, what with his...' I stopped, unable to go on.

'His betrothal and marriage, of course, I keep forgetting about that,' Baba said. Then his eyes sparkled.

'Leela, I have it!' he said.

'Have what?' I asked warily. Baba's ideas could sometimes be a little impractical. It was strange how little common sense he had for a man as wise as he was.

'The solution to my translation problem!' Baba said. 'You've already begun to understand the hanzi script, is it not? And you've only been learning for a year.'

'I'm really not very proficient,' I said. I had only been interested in the language because it reminded me of Rahul. And when a visiting monk had offered to teach it to me it was too good an opportunity to pass up.

'If Rahul stays here for the rest of the monsoon, he can teach you better than your tutor in Ujjayani,' Baba finished.

Bad idea, I thought. Very bad idea. I never wanted to see Rahul ever again.

'No,' Amma said firmly when Baba told her about it.

'But it is the perfect solution,' Baba argued. 'Leela reads and speaks five languages fluently. She's the only one who can pick it up fast enough to be of any use. What is your objection?'

'How do you think it will look—a young boy and an unmarried girl spending so much time together? Rahul is betrothed and we should be thinking of a match for Leela sooner rather than later.'

This was a big speech for Amma, who rarely spoke much. Baba blinked and opened his mouth. Then he shut it, and a rueful smile spread across his face.

'You raise a good point, Leela's mother,' he said at last. 'I keep forgetting that our Leela's all grown up now.'

Amma folded her arms and looked at him. But her eyes had softened too.

'Perhaps if we have a chaperone?' Baba suggested.

Amma considered it while I fumed. Neither of them had thought of asking me what I wanted. Neither of them seemed to think it necessary. Could I treat Rahul as a teacher and nothing more? Brinda's words echoed in my head. *Promise me you won't wait until it is too late.*

'It will have to be someone respectable and responsible, an adult female from our family,' Amma said. 'Not a child like Loky.'

'Well, if you can find someone suitable, let me know. Meanwhile, I will talk to Rahul,' Baba said.

And that was that.

I put it out of my mind. My aunts were all busy with housework and children. There was little chance that Amma would find a chaperone before it was time for us to leave. We only had a few weeks here, until the end of the rains made it safe to travel again.

I had been studying the qualities that my birth chart had forecast for me. They were a terrible list of vices—pride, arrogance, quarrelsomeness. *I* wouldn't want to marry me.

'Baba, if the birth chart says that I am quarrelsome, do I have to grow up like that?' I asked Baba. 'Can I not choose to change my nature? I do not want to be quarrelsome.'

'Of course you can!' Baba said. 'It is but a guide. And you are not that way to begin with. It makes me wonder sometimes if...'

'If what?' I asked.

He passed an agitated hand over his face.

'Nothing,' he said hastily. 'But I don't want you looking at the chart again. You must be who you choose to be.'

It pained me to see Baba uncertain. He always had the answer. But there was conflict in his advice to me today—you must choose who you want to be, one moment, you must not look at the chart again, the next. I knew he didn't think very highly of astrologers. He thought true astronomy was a higher science than horoscopy. But did he doubt the stars?

That evening, I went to the shrine in the backyard that was

dedicated to the nine planets. Nine stone icons on a pedestal as high as my elbow, meant for circumambulation. There they were— Surya, the sun; Chandra, the moon; the five planets: Mangala, Budh, Brahaspat, Shukra and Shani; and the two lunar nodes: Rahu, the head of the dragon; and Ketu, the tail of the dragon, that caused eclipses.

The most dreaded one of them was Mangal—Mars, the angry one, the god of war. If he is situated inauspiciously in a person's birth chart, that person is called Manglik. The one cursed by Mangal. Like me.

I lit an incense stick and walked silently around the shrine seven times in the dark. Help me fight the vices I've been fated, I prayed silently. Please help me, gods.

'Leela, listen,' Amma said, a few days later.

'Yes?'

I had one of the chubby twin baby boys in my arms. The barber's wife had the other one on her lap while she massaged him with mustard oil in preparation for his bath. He wriggled and wailed lustily, unhappy with this treatment.

'I think your aunt needs some time away from those babies,' Amma said quietly.

'I'll help the barber's wife with them, Amma,' I said.

'It isn't enough. She can't let go. She's watching them from the verandah even now,' Amma said. 'To carry twins to term takes a lot out of a girl as young as that,' Amma shook her head. 'I've seen it happen with new mothers, especially with firstborns.'

She was right, my youngest aunt was watching the barber's wife and the baby with worry writ on her face.

'She is not much older than you,' Amma continued. 'Two

babies together are a lot for anyone. She has been crying too, when she thinks no one is watching. I think she misses her maternal home.'

Oh? I had been so wrapped up in my own miserable thoughts that I had noticed nothing.

'Do you remember that Baba wanted you to learn the language of the manuscripts from Rahul?' Amma asked.

I was suddenly all attention. I nodded quickly.

'I think it would do her good to get away from the house and the babies for a little while every day. She could chaperone you. That would work for everyone.'

'Yes, Amma,' I said automatically.

'Good, then you start tomorrow.'

10

ℐT WAS A DAY OF SUN AND SHADOW. THAT RAREST OF monsoon days when sunshine could suddenly streak through the mass of dark clouds to dance on the hills and rivers below. A day for surprises. I told myself I was ready for them.

But as we walked down to the Nagarseths' haveli, I knew my composure was as thin as kite paper. My youngest aunt seemed quiet and subdued too.

'How is everyone at your mother's house?' I asked, hoping that conversation might soothe my nerves.

Her lips started to quiver. I changed the subject hastily.

'What a nice sari this is!' I tried.

'It is from my brother...' she said. Her voice changed. 'Don't ever marry too far away from your parents, Leela. Make sure they find a match for you in Ujjayani.'

'Don't worry,' I said, linking arms with her. 'I'm not going anywhere.' A wise move—holding on to her meant I couldn't bolt before we got to the haveli.

As we reached the gate, my youngest aunt raised her hand to rap at the massive door, but it swung open, revealing not the doorman but Rahul himself.

My heart stopped. We stared at each other over a chasm of two feet.

He joined his hands in a namaskar to my aunt, but his eyes were on me. 'Are you well, Leela?' he asked, abruptly. 'I heard you were taken ill.' He looked taller than before. Amma was right about boys shooting up like green bamboo in the rains.

'Yes, I've recovered,' I said. 'And I wish you well on your betrothal,' I didn't stumble over the words, and felt oddly satisfied to see his face tighten. 'Thank you for agreeing to instruct me.'

He didn't acknowledge my felicitation. 'I'm always glad to help the Acharya,' he said instead. 'I've set up some paper and ink brushes for us. Follow me.'

We walked with him past the courtyard. The door to the gaddi, the room where business was conducted, stood open, showing low desks covered in ledgers and a crowd of busy clerks and accountants. I was surprised to see not just the Nagarseth, but the Sethani seated within, consulting with the accountants. So the Sethani was an active partner in the business as well.

Rahul led us to a spacious room—a study from the look of it. One wall of the room was made entirely of an intricately carved screen of sandstone, letting in plenty of light. Another wall had wide windows whose shutters had been flung open to invite in the cool monsoon air. On the ground were long floor cushions covered in crisp white cotton. The other two walls were lined with wooden shelves filled with pothi after pothi of birch bark and palm leaf documents, and many paper books of a style I knew to be from China.

'This is quite a collection,' I said, genuinely impressed.

'You think only Brahmins value learning?' he said lightly, pleased. 'Baba and I trade in more than spices and cotton. Anything worthwhile we've found, we've acquired. And we have more at the library in Srivijaya,' he added, with quiet pride.

'So modest,' I observed wryly. 'No, no, I'm just jealous,' I added, seeing the look on Rahul's face. 'I've never seen a better selection.'

I reached out to touch a wooden counting frame strung with sliding beads in different colours. 'Is that a suanpan? I've heard of them.'

'From me!' Rahul corrected.

'True,' I smiled. I had forgotten that he was the first to tell me of them.

'What language is this?' I asked picking up a beautifully painted book.

'Careful, it's very old,' Rahul said, 'and you may regret touching it.'

'Why?' I asked.

'Because it's made of calfskin,' Rahul said, deftly catching the book as it fell from my hands.

'How can they write on the hide of animals?' I asked, horrified at the thought.

'Because, with care, that book will last for hundreds of years,' Rahul explained. A great advantage, I had to admit. We had to copy palm leaf manuscripts every two decades at most, or they were lost to mold and mildew. It took constant effort to keep the library current.

'Would you like to share what your tutor in Ujjayani has taught you so far?' Rahul asked. 'That way we won't repeat lessons.'

'Laoshi taught me most of the characters,' I said. 'But there are so many of them, and I'm out of practice.'

'You must never stop practising,' he said, quoting one of Baba's favourite sayings.

'Yes, Laoshi,' I said, mock respectful. How would he like being called 'teacher'?

He almost smiled. 'You don't have to call me that,' he said. 'I'm not very much older than you. But let us make a start.'

He may not have been a teacher, but his instructions were

sound. He set me an exercise and watched as I traced characters, correcting me when I made an error. There were many. His brush strokes, in contrast to mine, were fluent and quick, and made me wonder if I'd ever master them nearly as well.

My youngest aunt sat nearby, fanning herself with a palm leaf fan. She looked relaxed for once, and soon I heard a gentle snore. We may as well have been alone.

Rahul leaned over to correct a clumsy brushstroke. Too close! I caught my breath and turned away from him, frowning fiercely at the letters before me, willing myself calm. There was nothing here but the warm bright room filled with rare books. Nothing but the sound of Rahul's voice, with its slight accent. Nothing but...

'Rahul turn schoolmaster?' The voice at the door snapped me back to reality. 'That's absurd!'

The intruder, a young Arab in traditional tunic, stopped short at the sight of us.

I grabbed the edge of my sari and pulled it forward to shield my face. *Never let a Turki see your face*, Ajji had always told me.

'This is my student,' said Rahul, smiling widely. 'Rashid, meet Leelavati, the daughter of my teacher, Bhaskara Acharya. Leela, this is Rashid Al-Hamdani, an old friend.'

I let my sari slip from my face. Rahul trusted this man, that was enough to make me feel safe in his company.

'Adaab!' Rashid raised a hand to his temple in a showy gesture of greeting. Then he turned to Rahul with a knowing smile and said, 'I'm reminded of the words of my favorite poet: A book of verses underneath the bough, a jug of wine, a loaf of bread—and thou...'

'Your quoting of Khayyám is singularly inappropriate,' Rahul warned, in a low voice.

'I see!' Rashid said, the smile fading from his cheerful face. 'But your impulse to turn educator begins to become comprehensible, regardless. Forgive my poor understanding!'

I joined my hands in a namaskar, not sure what to make of this strange foreign youth who seemed to be on such familiar terms with Rahul.

'We travelled together on our last voyage,' Rahul explained.

'You mean you extended the protection of your fleet to a poor horse trader and his defenceless ship,' said Rashid.

'Only in exchange for the finest mare in your cargo,' Rahul smiled. 'I will argue I had the better bargain. Did you say you brought Kalyanee?'

'No, I did not,' Rashid said. 'The Prince regent has taken a liking to her. I told him she's been spoken for, but one doesn't refuse a request from Prince Bhimdeva Solanki for long.'

'I'm sure you have much to discuss with your friend,' I said, gathering up my work. 'And Amma will be waiting for me.'

My youngest aunt had woken up from her nap and was frozen with horror at the sight of a foreign man in the room. Rashid saw the shock on her face and withdrew tactfully. 'Please take your time,' he said. 'I'll have a word with your father meanwhile, Rahul.'

'You receive Turkis in your home?' my youngest aunt breathed, scandalized.

'He is from Baghdad, not Turkey,' Rahul said easily, 'and an old friend. His king is Salah-al-din Ayyub, not Ghori.'

'Nevertheless, it isn't wise to be seen in the company of Arabs nowadays.'

It was the Sethani, who had come quietly to the door.

'You have been far away too long, Rahul. As Ghori casts his eyes towards Anhilwara, the memory of Ghazni has been refreshed in the people's minds. We cannot be seen doing business with them.'

'Ghori just decimated what remains of Ghazni's kingdom, and killed his descendents,' said Rahul. 'And the prince of Anhilwara himself is doing business with "that Arab".'

'Our rules don't apply to royalty, Rahul. Remember that,' the Sethani said, and turned to go.

Rahul looked at me quizzically. 'You may as well add your voice to the chorus, Leela. Apparently I should have that mleccha thrown out of the haveli.' The way he said mleccha—impure foreigner—drew my attention.

'What we've seen of Turkis is only plunder,' I said, 'and the wanton destruction of a peaceful and prosperous land. Have you forgotten?'

'I haven't forgotten,' he said and I could see that he was serious. 'The reason why my father and I returned early was to stand with Anhilwara and Malwa at this time of crisis. I don't disagree with her. Ghori is bent on following Ghazni's example—all signs point to it. But Rashid has no part in it. He's only interested in breeding the perfect horse and selling as many as he can to anyone who's interested. If anything, he can help us win if it comes to war.'

'I hope you're right,' I said. 'Your friend seems harmless enough, but I've never heard any good of them from anyone.'

'I have read their poetry,' Rahul said. 'No one who writes of love the way they do can be all bad.'

Love—where did that come from? We both fell silent, the chasm opening once again between us. Had he been reading love poems to send to Roopmati?

'We've done enough for today,' I said at last.

'Same time tomorrow, then,' Rahul said quietly.

11

I WAS MAKING STEADY PROGRESS, AND ENJOYING THE NEW world that was opening up through language. And yet, it was difficult, so difficult. Alongside the rules of grammar and calligraphy, I had to teach myself the rules to spending time in Rahul's company:

Keep to learning the language.

Minimize physical and eye contact.

Never mention his betrothal.

But what did you do when someone else broke the rules?

'I hate to interrupt,' the Sethani said one day while I was learning a new brush stroke from Rahul, 'but I have something for Rahul.'

'What is it?' he asked, looking up. I had never heard him address her as Amma, or any other word for mother.

'A portrait of Roopmati,' she said smiling.

His face turned stony. 'Can't it wait?'

'It's a good likeness,' she said. 'I can vouch for it because I have seen her.'

'Later, please?' he insisted, more civil this time.

She looked to me for support.

'He is being bashful since you are here, Leela,' she said. 'Why don't you see it and tell him what you think?'

She unrolled the scroll and held it up before my horrified eyes. My mind scrambled for an excuse, but there was no escaping the moment.

The girl portrayed in the picture was a vision of beauty. She had large brown eyes, with eyebrows that were etched into perfect arches. Her lips were delicate and fine. She wore a rich silk dress and plenty of gold jewellery set with glittering gems. One slim hennaed hand rested confidently on a book.

What had I expected? That they had lied about her beauty and wealth?

A part of me that had secretly hoped for a flaw in his wife-to-be died. She was suitable for Rahul in every way—beautiful, learned, rich. I couldn't even find fault with the excess of gold on her person, it was in perfectly good taste, complimenting instead of overwhelming her. My hand crept up to my own earlobe where Ajji's tiny drop earrings still dangled.

'She is…' I dropped my eyes, trying to find the words to describe her to Rahul. 'She is…'

'Perfect,' the Sethani finished smugly.

When I looked up she was gazing at the painting with satisfaction and Rahul was staring at me, his expression unreadable. I collected my books hastily, mumbled an excuse, and fled.

I did not care what they or my youngest aunt thought about my abrupt departure. I did not care what Baba would say about the lessons. I had had enough. There had to be a way to end this torture.

My leaving early that day had unintended consequences for Loky. I barely recognized him that day, so dirty was he, when my aunt and I passed him in the marketplace.

A knot of boys were playing with some puppies. They were the same ones Loky and I had seen before, but they had grown since then, pouncing and playing with one another instead of wobbling around blindly. The white pup with the speckled coat that Loky had admired had a silk cord around his neck. A boy led him along, a boy who looked like Loky.

It *was* Loky!

'Loksamudra!' I said sternly. 'What is this?'

Loky jumped at the sound of my voice. He tugged the gambolling puppy towards me.

'This is Moti,' he said sheepishly. 'I've been bringing kitchen scraps for the dogs since the time you were sick. The shopkeeper says I can keep him.'

'Moti?' I tried not to laugh. 'He's no pearl. He's a common street dog. You know Amma and Baba won't let you keep him. And how will we take him back to Ujjayani?'

'He's white, like a pearl,' Loky said, picking up the wriggly thing. 'Can I take him home?' He opened his eyes wide in entreaty.

'Does he have ticks?' I examined the pup gingerly. Oh, he assuredly did. 'Amma is not going to stand for this.'

Amma had once mentioned a herbal infusion that would take care of ticks, though... The pup licked my hand hesitantly, getting bolder when I didn't push him away.

I looked to my youngest aunt, who was the adult after all. Let *her* take a stand against the pup. But she patted the puppy and fussed over the mother dog, a black and white creature with soft brown eyes.

'We have a guard dog at my mother's place,' she said at last. 'It lives in the cowsheds with the cows and goats—a useful animal.'

'Can I keep him? Can I, can I?' Loky begged, sensing an ally.

'It is not for me to decide,' she stalled.

'Please, please, please,' Loky wheedled. 'I'll take care of him. I'll do everything he needs, you'll see.'

She was softening. You could tell by the way her hand stroked the creature. 'You can bring him home and ask your Amma. I think he's old enough to leave his mother now,' my youngest aunt said. She loosened the strings of her coin purse and gave the shopkeeper a silver piece. Loky gave a whoop and danced a little dance. Honestly, I thought, she needed to learn to be stricter before the twins grew up. If she caved like this to their every demand they would walk all over her.

I bent down and patted the mother dog and her remaining brood. 'We'll take good care of him,' I promised the mother dog. She thumped her tail. I thought she looked relieved to have one less pup to worry about.

I laughed as the little speckled mutt trotted ahead of us on his silken cord. It was the first time I laughed since the day the monsoon had arrived.

It was soon clear that the cleaning woman was Moti's favourite person. She arrived every morning with her basket and stick broom. Everyone cleared a path for her, because she was an untouchable, leaving her alone to do her work. Everyone except Moti, that is.

Stomach cramps had given me an excuse to skip my class, and Amma left me alone in the women's room, where girls in the household spent that part of the month. I watched through the barred window as Moti frolicked around the woman in the empty courtyard and she scratched behind his ears, clucking lovingly. She reached into her basket and Moti sat up, front paws raised, begging for something.

I must have made a movement because the cleaning woman glanced up and saw me. She froze, and hastily shut the basket. Moti whined and pawed at her but she busied herself with sweeping the ground and ignored him. Moti nosed her impatiently and when she didn't respond, he caught hold of the end of her sari and shook his head playfully.

'Stop that, Moti,' I cried through the bars, but he seemed to take it as encouragement, almost pulling the woman's garment loose. I ran out the room and tried to pry his teeth off her.

'No, no,' she cried. 'I can manage.'

'He might bite you.'

I grabbed him around the middle and tugged. 'What's wrong with you, you silly dog?' A shiny white tooth fell out of his mouth and landed next to me, surprising me into letting go.

We all fell into a heap; dog, woman, basket and I.

'What was that?' I asked, winded.

'Only a baby tooth. Puppies lose them all the time,' said the cleaning woman, but I noticed that she had quickly covered something on the ground with her basket.

'No, what is *that*?' I asked and lifted her basket.

Was that a...*bone*? With flesh attached to it, no less. I recoiled instinctively from the unclean thing. It was no less than a crime to bring such a thing into a Brahmin's home.

The woman started rocking on her heels and babbling softly.

'He reminds me of my Kalu, the dog I had when I was young like you. He loved bones, did Kalu. And so does this one. What was the harm I thought, if nobody found out?'

I studied the woman, fascinated, like I had never seen her before. I knew her from my visits to Ajji's house but I had never really paid any attention to her. She was old but spry, beautiful even. Dark blue tattoos covered her arms and her cataract-clouded eyes were lined with kohl.

'Shh,' I hushed, aware that she feared reprisal. 'It was kind of you to do so.'

'If they find out, I will be punished,' she wailed. 'It was foolish to put my family at risk for a dog.'

'No one will find out,' I soothed her. 'Let him enjoy the treat, he fought like a lion for it.'

Moti was gnawing away, looking blissful, his gum bleeding slightly where his tooth had fallen out.

'And I have made you unclean with my touch,' she said.

'Nothing the river can't purify,' I said lightly, dismissing her concern.

Her eyes softened. 'Only one other have I known as kind as you,' she said. 'The Nagarseth's son.'

I froze. 'What do you mean?' I asked, astonished by this insight.

'He hugged me, didn't he, when he returned from Java,' she said. 'Remembered the time I cared for him when he missed his dead mother.'

'Rahul hugged you?' I asked. Jains may not follow caste rules, but they could be as prejudiced as anyone.

She nodded. How like Rahul to disregard stupid rules!

'Then I will too,' I said, and wound my arms tight around her. She recoiled instinctively at my touch, before relaxing enough to endure my embrace. She felt no different than my own Ajji. She pulled back and looked at me, and I smiled at her. But her face grew troubled as it read the emotion on mine. No one knew the dictates of caste better than her. What could she see?

'You tread a difficult path, dear,' she said, passing a wrinkled hand over my hair. 'Have a care.'

She picked up the tooth Moti had lost and suddenly grinned, showing the gaps in her teeth.

'Now, do you want the lion's tooth as a keepsake, or shall I throw it out?'

The next morning I rose early and went to bathe in the river. Birds called loudly from the edge of the bank as I walked down the stone steps of the ghats. The Ujjayani ghats were far more beautiful, lined as the riverside was with temples and crossed with bridges—with the temple dedicated to Surya glowing on an island midstream. But the Narmada was much wider, especially here, where it was close to the sea.

I waded into the cold water, my sari swirling around me, feeling the sand at the bottom of the riverbed between my toes. The calm surface of the river reflected the morning light as I turned my face eastward, eyes closed. I poured water from my cupped hands and silently chanted the Gayatri Mantra, an invocation to the sun, the highest of all prayers.

But when I opened my eyes, the horizon was dark. The monsoon clouds had obscured the sky, blotting out the sun, the fading moon and any lingering stars.

A thought occurred to me—anyone could step into this river. Maybe upstream, an atheist, a foreigner, an untouchable, perhaps even Rahul, was stepping into it at this very moment. Why then these rules about caste and creed, whom it was permissible to touch or marry, when we were all made from the same earth and water?

'Do you understand?' I asked Loky.

Both his cheeks were stuffed with the sweet mithai I'd bribed him with.

He nodded, chewing away.

'Say Amma needs me *urgently* at the herb shop,' I repeated. Amma's herbs were as much in demand in Bharuch as in Ujjayani.

Amma did not charge for treating patients, though many grateful families sent us presents if they were able, but she did sell her medicinal herbs, since they took time to grow and prepare. 'And don't go playing with the dog and forget.'

He shoved another mithai into his mouth and nodded again.

'Leela,' my youngest aunt called. 'Let us go, I have to be back in time to feed the twins at noon.'

I shook a final admonishing finger at Loky to emphasize the seriousness of the task I'd assigned him, and followed my youngest aunt out into the street.

Let it work, I prayed, at least for today. I'll think of something else tomorrow. I couldn't bear any more lessons with Rahul.

Perhaps because of my plan to end my lessons with Rahul was it bittersweet to see him again. I was distracted throughout the lesson, listening intently for Loky's arrival to fetch me away. Ten minutes later, I was relieved to hear his high-pitched voice at the door.

'I think Amma needs me,' I said to Rahul, and started to gather my things, congratulating myself on my foresight. My plan was working out rather well.

'Awwwoooo,' came a plaintive howl, giving me pause.

Moti? Oh no, this couldn't be good.

Then there was pandemonium. Moti howling, Loky yelling, followed by screams, squawks and crashes, all coming from the direction of the courtyard.

'What is the meaning of this?'

The Sethani, it seemed, had joined in. I rushed to the courtyard to do what I could to control the damage by boy and dog.

What a sight—Moti running amok amid the flapping pigeons and the pet peacocks that lived in the courtyard, with three men and Loky chasing after him as the Sethani shrieked from the edge of one of the doors that opened out on to it. Was she actually afraid of dogs?

'Moti!' I said. 'Come here! Now!'

The craven cur dropped at my feet, cowering between my legs as if he was the one being terrorized, not the birds. I held on to his rope with a firm grip.

'Why did you bring the dog?' I hissed at Loky.

'I didn't,' he protested. 'He *followed* me.'

'Get that smelly, filthy mongrel out of here,' the Sethani demanded.

'He's not dirty,' Loky said. 'Leela bathed him in a herbal infusion to get rid of his ticks. He smells nice.'

'Ticks!' screamed the Sethani, throwing up her hands in horror. Behind me, Moti was beginning to dig a hole in the manicured grass of the courtyard. Clods of dirt flew everywhere.

Why, I thought suddenly, this might be enough to get me out of my lessons permanently!

'I'm sorry,' I said, trying to sound contrite. 'Perhaps we should go home before he destroys anything else. It sounds like Amma needs me at the herb shop, anyway.'

'I know,' Rahul interrupted unexpectedly. 'We can all go down to the herb shop. It's right beside the shipping docks. Some of our ship hands speak Mandarin.' Moti was licking Rahul's hands now, the traitor. 'Leela might pick something up from hearing a conversation between native speakers. And Loky would like to see a ship, wouldn't you?' He smiled at Loky.

'A generous offer,' I said, between gritted teeth, 'but there is no need.'

'I insist!' said Rahul, picking up Moti and draping him over his shoulders. He seemed delighted, and slavishly licked his ear.

'As long as that...that thing leaves immediately,' the Sethani said, looking revolted at Rahul's proximity to the dog. 'I do not care where you go.'

'I've never been on a ship,' my youngest aunt said unexpectedly.

'Me neither!' said Loky, excited. 'Will you show me where the pirates attacked?'

'A doli or palkhi for you, perhaps?' Rahul enquired, turning to me with an amused glitter in his eyes. 'It's a long way off.'

'I'll walk,' I said, and followed them out mutinously.

The winding alleyway to the herb shop was crowded with shoppers. Amma wasn't there, of course, but I had to make a show of asking for her. The nice old vaid, a former teacher of Amma's, looked a little perplexed by the whole thing, and Loky had guilt written all over his transparent face.

Rahul didn't comment on our quickly disintegrating excuse. Did he guess I had tried to get out of our lessons?

'Shall we visit the ship, then?' he asked.

There was no distracting Loky from the promised trip, so we wound our way to the riverfront. The ghats along the river were bustling with activity—women bathing their children, laundrymen washing clothes, priests performing rituals.

And the ships! The ships lay anchored further out, in the deeper waters of the river. Arab dhows with lanteen sails, massive Chinese junks, small local fishing boats, ferries and pleasure boats, and, of course, the Nagarseth's enormous fleet. The fleet was a mix of the larger Chinese junk style vessels, looming over us like floating forts, and smaller native dhows. All of them flew pennants of crimson and white, the colours of Anhilwara and Malwa, emblazoned with a blazing sun in the shape of a wheel—the Nagarseth's trademark.

Moti had jumped into the water, swimming strongly alongside the boat that carried us to the fleet. Loky ordered him back, fearing the crocodiles that swam in the deeper waters, and Moti finally climbed back, shaking himself and spraying everyone around him with water. Then he stood at the prow of the boat like a captain—exuding a powerful smell of wet fur.

We were rowed to the largest ship, a three-masted junk with a hull like a mountain, and were raised up by the few crew members who were still on the ship. They seemed happy to see the 'young master', and called to Rahul in a strange mix of languages that was inevitable with a varied crew on board. He was well liked, I could tell.

'This is the flagship of our trading fleet,' Rahul said. I could hear the pride in his voice as he looked over the clean lines of his ship. 'It was built right here, by Bharuch shipbuilders, with Malabar teak. One of the largest they've ever made—one hundred and twenty feet long and forty feet wide.'

'But the style,' I said. 'Isn't it a Chinese design?'

'Certainly,' Rahul said. 'Cantonese design, Malabar teak, Arab captain—'

'Arab captain?' I interrupted.

'The finest we've ever had,' Rahul said, smiling at my surprise. 'He's not on board now, or I'd introduce you.'

'Where do the passengers and crew live?' I said, looking around. 'Where does the cargo go?'

'We have three decks below,' Rahul said. 'Private cabins and cargo decks—I'll show you!'

'It must have cost a fortune to build,' I said, following him.

'We've just commissioned an even larger ship,' Rahul said. 'When it is ready we'll sail it back to Srivijaya. Yes, they're expensive, but this time we have a partner, though my father is still the majority holder.'

'It is Seth Oswal, I suppose,' I said resignedly. It was best to stay grounded in reality.

'It is,' Rahul said, and lapsed into silence.

Loky and Moti had run off with the ship hands to see how the huge bamboo sails were operated. My youngest aunt looked a little sick and refused to go below deck with Rahul. 'I didn't think it would feel this way. The sensation of standing on water is most unpleasant,' she said.

'Then we'll leave soon,' Rahul promised. 'Do we have time to show Leela the lower decks and introduce her to a Chinese man on board before we leave?'

She nodded.

'Come, Leela,' Rahul said and opened a hatch that led a steep set of stairs into the cool interior of the ship. 'There's someone I want you to meet.'

Rahul went on ahead down the stairs and I followed, looking around me with interest. The great wooden walls of the ship curved around us like the belly of a giant beast. Rahul held out a hand at the bottom of the stairs and I took it. Without meaning to, my hand memorized this fleeting touch, tucking it away carefully, to bring out and examine later like precious treasure.

A hallway with doors on either side stretched before us. Rahul led me to an opening with benches and a carpet at the end of the hallway. An open porthole let in some light, even though no lamps were lit.

'Baba,' he called. 'Are you there?'

'Rahul, son,' a thin voice said, and a tiny bent man emerged from a cabin door and walked towards us in slippered feet. In the dim light, I could see that he had almost no hair. His face was wreathed in wrinkles. His eyes were almost lost in them but

I could tell that they were twinkling. He wore a Chinese tunic, as Rahul had on his first day back.

'Baba, this is Leela,' Rahul said. 'Leela, Baba worked at the monastery, back home, where my grandfather teaches. I've known him since I was born. He comes to India on pilgrimage to Bodh Gaya.'

Rahul's family belonged to the type of nanadeshi merchants that were citizens of many lands. But even with family roots generations deep in Bharuch and Ujjayani, he still considered Srivijaya his home.

'Namaskar.' I folded my hands in greeting. The old man grabbed them with both his hands, soft like old leather.

'Leela?' he said. 'Leelavati!'

He looked at Rahul and started talking quickly. It was not Mandarin, the formal Chinese that I had been learning, I think, but a dialect spoken by Chinese sailors. Anyhow, he spoke so fast that I could not follow what he said. I shook my head at Rahul, signalling that it was too difficult. He just laughed.

'Slow down,' I said. 'I can't understand when you talk so fast.'

'Don't blame yourself,' Rahul said, confirming my suspicion. 'It's a different dialect.'

'He knows my name?' I asked, curious.

'It was a long voyage,' Rahul said, flushing a little. 'We talked of many things.'

'In monastery too,' Baba said, switching to Hindi, 'when Rahul was apprentice to grandfather.'

'What did you learn from your grandfather?' I asked. 'Dhyan meditation?'

'You could call it that,' Rahul smiled.

Baba broke into a long dialogue in Mandarin aimed at Rahul. Rahul said something to him in a warning tone, but he paid no attention.

What was he saying? I wished desperately that I could understand. Concentrate, Leela. I caught a word here or there that sounded familiar. 'Beautiful', I think, and 'home'. Then Baba said something clearly and slowly. Aha, this I could probably make out, I thought.

'Love has no jati, son,' he said deliberately.

What? Why would he say that? Jati was the word for caste.

'Baba,' Rahul interrupted. 'Not now!'

But he rambled on, smiling and senile. 'We should take her home, where no one cares about these things, so that you can get married.'

I blinked.

Love has no caste... What did he mean?

My eyes flew to Rahul. His face was startled, unguarded, vulnerable. I read everything that was written there. It took my breath away.

I must have looked faint because Baba slapped me bracingly on my back.

'The ship's movement...' he said in broken Hindi. 'I get... ginger root. Settle her stomach. Have her sit now.' He slowly climbed up the stairs.

Rahul grasped my hand and drew me to a bench by the porthole. 'Leela...' he said. 'Breathe.'

I sucked air into to my lungs with a gasp, and held tightly on to his hand.

'He said...' I finally managed to stammer. 'I thought he said...'

Rahul dropped his head and his hair fell over his forehead, hiding his face. But not before I could glimpse the expression on it.

I had a desperate urge to run my fingers through his dark hair, smoothing away the worry and sadness on his face. Instead,

I put my other hand into his. He looked up and saw the urgent question in my eyes.

'He knows my heart,' he said softly. 'He spoke the truth.'

The chasm between us was gone, and there was no need for words.

Suddenly I was in his arms, my face pressed into the hollow of his neck. How did I get there? It didn't matter, because in that moment, everything felt right in the world.

'I didn't know about the betrothal,' Rahul murmured into my hair. 'You must believe me. I will take the robes of a monk if they insist on marriage.'

His words were like the monsoon rain falling on parched earth. I drank them in.

'I don't know how things work here,' he continued. 'It's so complicated. And I didn't know what you felt...'

Sanity returned. What was I *doing*? I pushed him away.

'There is something I have to...' I had to tell him.

'What?' he asked.

'My birth chart...' I whispered, and closed my eyes. Tears were threatening to spill out.

'I can't hear you,' he said, leaning closer.

Conflicting thoughts raced frantically through my mind. What could I say? That anyone who marries me is doomed to die within a year? That Baba has been trying to calculate a mahurat, an auspicious moment, where some of the ill effects of my terrible fate could be countered? That, even if that was possible, Rahul's father, the rich and powerful Nagarseth, would never consent to such a marriage? And I, who loved him, how could I let the shadow of my ill fortune fall on his promising life? The dizzying happiness I felt only a moment earlier turned to despair.

'What?' Rahul asked urgently, clasping both my arms. 'You're not telling me something, Leela.'

Perhaps he loved me enough to marry me nonetheless.

But how well did *I* love him?

12

SOMEONE WAS COMING DOWN THE STAIRS. RAHUL LET GO of me.

My youngest aunt looked even greener than before when she reached the bottom of the stairs. But she was no fool. As soon as she saw us sitting by the window, she grew serious.

'Leela?' she asked. 'You are unwell?'

My mind had already been made up, so I didn't hesitate.

'I need to go home,' I said, heading for the stairs without a backward glance.

The bright light on the deck hurt my stinging eyes. I kept them cast down. It was easier to stop them from tearing up that way.

My youngest aunt had followed me very quickly for someone who looked that green. She put an arm around me to steady me.

'Did anything...' she hesitated, choosing her words carefully, '...*happen* down there?'

I shook my head.

'Hmm,' she said quietly. 'I've not been a good chaperone, Leela.'

I sensed that Rahul was right behind us, though I didn't look back.

'I think Leela finds the movement of the boat unsettling, as do I,' she said to Rahul. There was a new firmness in her voice that I hadn't heard before. 'Why don't you finish showing Loky the ship and then we will head back home.'

I heard Rahul walk away. His every footstep echoed in my heart.

I stared at the flat expanse of the river. The grey skies that had seemed so cool and life-giving before now felt suffocating and dark. I wished the sun would break through and finally light up the world.

'Rahul is engaged to be married,' my aunt said eventually. 'You will do well to remember it.'

I winced at the stern tone. Would she say something to Amma? But when I had the courage to look at her, she did not look unsympathetic. I realized she would say nothing. But I also knew that she would make an excuse to stop chaperoning me. I had been granted my wish after all. There would be no more classes with Rahul.

I could hear Loky's voice getting closer. 'Do we have to go?' he was complaining. 'I want to climb the mast.'

'Yes, we have to go Loksamudra,' my youngest aunt said firmly.

We boarded the boat and were rowed back to shore in no time. As the ship receded from our view, I thought I could make out the man Rahul had called 'Baba' looking down at me from the upper deck with distress writ on his wrinkled face.

When we reached the shore, I stepped out of the boat without taking the hand Rahul held out to me. We retraced out steps through the narrow streets of the busy marketplace. The crowds swirled around us, chatting, bargaining and examining the exotic wares on display; everyone was talking all around us. Their noise and bustle only made the silence between Rahul and me more deafening.

I had been looking at the river, the dog, the sparkling glass bangles on sale—everything, in fact, except at Rahul. But in a flash of lucidity, I recalled that it was possible that I would never see him again, ever. We were going back to Ujjayani as soon as the rains ended.

My eyes searched him out. His were fixed on me. He was not bothering with any pretence, the tenderness in his eyes unimistakable. For once, I didn't care if anyone else saw it as well. Of all the people in the wide world he had travelled, it was me he wanted. *Me!* The world faded away until only we remained. I didn't hear the clatter of horses, though it must have been loud, so the yelp that came after it took me by surprise. It was the scared yelp of a frightened puppy—Moti.

'Watch out!' Loky's childish voice piped up, indignant, but the undertone of fear in it brought me sharply back to my surroundings.

There was a loud curse. A war horse ridden by a horseman in armour reared high above Loky, who had rushed to help Moti. The steel in the horse's hoofs glinted sharply in the afternoon light. Any minute they would land on my brother and crush him.

I sprang before Loky, pushing him behind me, and glared at the intruder.

'Someone get rid of that urchin and his mutt!' a harsh voice said. 'You, wench, get him out of my way!'

The horse neighed loudly, rearing up again, its hooves inches from us. What kind of idiot rides a war stallion through narrow crowded alleyways without any regard to the safety of the passersby? Who was this hulking madman?

I covered Loky with my body and ducked my head under my arm, bracing for the heavy hooves to land, but they didn't. I opened my eyes, surprised.

Rahul had grabbed the reins and yanked the horse away. He was talking calmly to the frightened horse, soothing it down.

The hefty horseman leapt off the horse and grabbed Rahul by both shoulders.

'Who are you, sir, to have the audacity to stop the prince regent of Anhilwara in his own kingdom?' he demanded. Too late I noticed the insignia on his breastplate. It was Bhimdev Solanki, the prince regent of Anhilwara. The one they called 'Bholo Bhima' behind his back, for he was a reckless simpleton who lived to fight, gamble and carouse. He could have Rahul's head for this behaviour.

'Rahul Nagarseth, a faithful subject of this realm,' said Rahul evenly. 'I only seek to stop your majesty from unintentionally hurting the light of Ujjayani—the beautiful and virtuous Leelavati. She is the learned daughter of the noble and saintly Bhaskara Acharya, the teacher, a jewel of the kingdom of Malwa.'

The prince took off his iron helmet and stared at Rahul. He was handsome in a florid, muscular way, with a good-humoured face. He smelled strongly of perfume. I recognized the ingredients—I had smelled them many a time in Amma's herb workroom—sandalwood, aloe and camphor, if I wasn't mistaken.

'The light of Ujjayani, eh?' he said. 'Let's have a look.' He turned to the mounted party that accompanied him. 'Subhrata, as the prince of Malwa, I trust you can verify the truth of this claim.'

Another young man jumped off the horse behind the prince regent's and handed his reins to a groom. It was Subhrata Varman, son of King Vindhya Varman of Malwa. I knew him from the annual Magh mela that the royal family always attended in Ujjayani. I had been presented to them more than once. But would he recognize me?

Prince Subhrata was slighter than Bhimdev, but just as tall, with a sensible air. I could tell right away that he remembered me from Ujjayani.

'It is Bhaskara Acharya's daughter, just as he said,' Prince Subhrata said. 'And as you can see for yourself, the merchant was right to boast of this young woman's beauty.'

Suddenly all eyes were on me. I blushed pink but kept my gaze level with Bhimdev. He had no business almost running down small children in a busy marketplace.

The prince regent raised his arm in a gesture of awe.

'You spoke the truth, merchant!' he said. His eyes swept over me appraisingly. 'But she is yet a child. Give her a year or two, I say, and she will be the light of the country...'

How I itched to flatten this patronizing man with that Flying Tiger move Loky was always talking of! Anger flashed in in my eyes.

'Feisty, too!' The prince had noticed my anger and chuckled. He thumped Rahul on the shoulder. 'Oh, I approve, young merchant. You did right to stop me from crushing such a treasure.'

Perhaps he wouldn't punish Rahul, after all.

'Your highness, this is the man I have promised the mare to,' said a familiar voice—Rashid Al-Hamdani, of all people. What was he doing here? I had not noticed that he formed part of the prince regent's entourage.

Rahul was still holding the reins of the horse the prince regent had been riding—no, it was a mare. She was dark brown with four white stockings and a white face—the colouring they called 'panch kalyani', the five auspicious markings, and had the distinctive curved-back ears of a native bred horse. I could see why both Rahul and Bhimdev Solanki had their eyes on Kalyanee.

'*This* is the man?' Bhimdev said. 'It cannot be! He's only a boy! You said you had promised her to a warrior worthy of her.'

'He is the best warrior I know,' Rashid said without hesitation.

'That's impossible,' Bhimdev said.

'If you can beat him in unarmed combat you can have the mare,' Rashid said.

'Why, that's easily done!' Bhimdev sounded delighted. 'A fight for the mare, young friend?' It wasn't really a question, though he phrased it as one. He was already dropping his sword, shield and armour, stripping down for a hand-to-hand combat. People moved away, forming a circle around them. Rahul bowed stiffly. 'It will be my honour,' he said.

I fixed Rashid with a venomous glare. 'What have you done?' I hissed. 'The prince regent has at least a foot and a hundred pounds on Rahul. He'll kill him!'

Beside me, Moti gave a sad, wolf-like howl.

'I hate to disagree with one so lovely,' said Rashid smiling. 'But you're mistaken. I bet ten to one Rahul wins.'

'Forty gold pieces at five to one,' said Prince Subhrata immediately, sizing up Rahul expertly. 'He looks quick, but he's no match for Bholo's weight, I reckon.'

'That's the spirit,' Rashid said. 'Anyone else willing to put money on the prince regent?'

'Leela, come!' my youngest aunt said, tugging hard at my hand. 'This is no place for you.'

'No!' I replied fiercely. *No!*

If the prince regent intended to see this through, Rahul could be badly injured, or worse. At least the herb shop was close by. The old vaid could fix up Rahul's wounds if I brought him there quick enough.

The prince regent advanced menacingly, slapping the rippling muscles on his arms. 'On guard, merchant boy,' he said. Then he rushed at Rahul.

Rahul did nothing, simply watching him come. Surely, he would be crushed like a coconut. I squeezed my eyes to shut out the horrible sight. A surprised roar went up from the crowd.

I opened my eyes a crack. The prince regent lay flat on his

back in the dust. I unclenched my fists. How did Rahul do it?

'Told you,' Rashid whispered in my ear. 'In the words of the incomparable Khayyám: If I myself upon a looser creed, have loosely strung the jewel of good deed, let this one thing for my atonement plead, that one for two I never did misread!'

His joking words made my fears lighter.

'Your poet sounds like a mathematician,' I said.

'He was,' Rashid said. 'I'll send you his book on arithmetic if you like!'

But the prince regent had already jumped up, shaking himself like an injured lion. This time I kept my eyes open.

Rahul was crouched in a ready stance. When the prince regent rushed towards him, he moved swiftly, blocking the prince's fist, striking under his guard and whipping around to deliver one fluid, powerful kick to his back.

How good it felt to watch the Bholo Bhima land on his royal seat.

He looked furious. 'So you know how to fight, huh?' he said. This time he tackled his legs, trying to lock Rahul in a wrestler's hold. Rahul slammed his elbow into his opponent's gut and freed his legs, pinning the prince regent to the ground with his arm twisted around his back.

But when Rahul sprang back, his stance still at the ready, ten soldiers had surrounded him, their swords drawn and pointed at his neck.

Bhimdev looked mad enough to kill him. 'Get him!' he ordered.

'Enough!' said Prince Subhrata. The soldiers stopped, looking uncertain. The prince of Malwa was a respected guest in Anhilwara, but Bhimdev's word was law.

'You're from Malwa, are you not?' Prince Subhrata asked Rahul.

'I was born in Java,' Rahul said, panting. 'And we have homes and businesses in Anhilwara. But my father and his fathers before him were all Ujjayanis.'

'That makes him *my* subject, Bhimdev,' Prince Subhrata said, standing firm. 'Not yours.'

Bhimdev looked furious, but then a reluctant smile broke across his face. 'Your subject, Subhrata,' he conceded. He turned to Rahul. 'You beat me fairly, merchant. I suppose you should have the horse.'

'Refreshments for everyone at the Malwa camp,' Prince Subhrata intervened smoothly. 'We'll see you later, your highness.'

Rahul was on Kalyanee in a flash, and the next thing I knew the Malwa horsemen had wheeled around away from the dockside. We followed them slowly.

'Here's your money,' Prince Subhrata said to Rashid, who had come away with the Malwis. 'Why do you Turkis always have to make trouble?'

'For the last time I'm Baghdadi , *not* Turki,' Rashid complained.

'Fine,' Prince Subhrata said, without much interest. 'Where did you learn to fight like that?' he asked Rahul.

'From the Chinese scholar monks in Java,' Rahul said. 'And from my Chinese grandfather. It's called kung fu.'

And I had thought his grandfather taught him meditation!

'Can you sword fight?' the prince asked.

'Yes,' Rahul nodded.

'And ride a horse?'

'You think I'd give Kalyanee to someone who can't?' Rashid cut in, aggrieved.

'An elephant?' the prince continued.

'No.'

'Can you handle a bow?'

'Yes.'

'And a mace?'

'No.'

'You must train my men!' the Prince suddenly exclaimed. 'It is a royal order!'

'I owe you my life,' Rahul said humbly. 'I'm yours to command.'

He seemed distracted, twisting in the saddle to search the crowded lane. Was he looking for me?

'Where is...' I heard him begin, but my youngest aunt pulled me into a narrow lane.

'Come,' she said firmly. 'He will be fine now. We must head home.'

I lost sight of Rahul as the Malwa party thundered away.

'What a fighter!' someone in the crowd was saying.

'Like the young god Krishna fighting his evil uncle Kamsa,' said another.

I threw a last lingering look at the retreating Malwa soldiers, and turned in the direction of home. It was a good thing my youngest aunt was there to steer me, for I was dazed enough to have walked into the eastern sea.

13

BEFORE LONG, WORD CAME THAT RAHUL HAD BEEN formally invited to join the legion of Prince Subhrata Varman of Malwa. They were to leave soon. Malwa's army was heading home to Dhar, the capital of Malwa.

The monsoon season—and with it the fear of bad roads and flash floods—was almost over, and so we were to leave for Ujjayani soon, perhaps within the fortnight.

'But after Janmashthami,' Amma insisted. The festival celebrating the birth of Krishna, a favourite with women, was almost upon us.

I stayed away from Rahul. Twice, he had come to the house, and both times I had managed, somehow, to evade him. He even sent a message asking me to collect the lesson books we had worked on together. I sent Loky to the haveli to pick them up. Each time I was tempted to meet him, I reminded myself that it was for *his* safety, for *his* happiness, that I stayed away.

My only consolation was the rare, beautiful secret I held close to my heart—Rahul loved me.

So what, my head reasoned. Remember the laws written in our shastras? Women must marry men of equal caste. You are a Brahmin and Rahul is a Vaishya. He may be richer than your entire clan, but he's beneath you in caste. The families would never allow it.

But kings marry whoever they please, I argued back. They

are *kings*, my head said.

Rahul may be a Vaishya, but he is also a Jain. They do not believe in castes. All are equal to them, I said again.

Even more reason for the families to disagree. We deem them atheists. They consider us ritual-bound traditionalists. And they may not believe in caste, but they do believe in wealth. Is Rahul not engaged to the daughter of the wealthiest merchant in the land?

And besides, my head said finally, there is that other thing— your star chart. Even Jains believe in the stars, and there is no denying that yours are unlucky for everyone, no matter what their caste.

There was no arguing with that. Still, the thought that Rahul loved me back comforted me.

'What are you dreaming about?' Ajji came up to me. 'Help me string these flower garlands for the temple.'

The festival of Janmashthami was held at midnight, for that was when Krishna had been born—in a prison, under the watchful eyes of the guards set on his parents by his evil uncle Kamsa, who, it was prophesied, would be killed by Krishna. But as the monsoon rains crashed over the prison that night, the guards fell into a deep sleep. When Krishna was born, his father Vasudeva smuggled the child out in a basket of reeds, across the river Yamuna, swollen with monsoon rain, who parted her waters for the father and son to cross.

So, at midnight on Janmashthami, a lovingly crafted baby Krishna was rocked in his cradle in homes and temples across the country, songs were sung and stories were told of his miraculous escape and eventual triumph over the tyrant Kamsa.

I sat on Ajji's wide swing and threaded strand after strand of jasmine and rose garlands for Krishna's cradle and thought back to the day at the market when Rahul had wrestled the prince regent.

Everyone would be at the temple tonight, even the Jains. Would Rahul be there too?

I could not face him before Amma, Baba, Aajoba, Ajji—would they not see in my face how I felt, and what he felt, in his?

The festival was to be held at the temple. The main hall and the grounds would be full of people who would come for the service and the songs. Perhaps if I stayed in the lamp tower…there would be fewer people there. And I had a convenient excuse. Baba had said he wanted to make star observations since the clouds were finally clearing. If I volunteered, I could away from the crowds.

'You're needed at the temple,' I told Baba. 'Let me make the observations. They'll want you to officiate in the ceremonies. And no one else knows how to note them correctly.'

'Won't you miss the ceremony?' Amma said.

'Amma, you know I prefer watching the stars to any ceremony,' I said. 'And you hardly let me do it anymore. This is the last chance I have before we leave.'

Amma nodded. 'As you wish, but you mustn't go alone. Have Ajji's maid go with you. She hates the noise and the crowds at the main temple.'

While all the other girls and women dressed in their finest clothes and jewels, preparing for the midnight service, I spent my day writing notes and studying tables so I would not ruin Baba's careful observations.

But all the same, I shook out the dress Brinda had sent me. It was custom stitched, a long gathered skirt instead of a sari. It fitted me perfectly, as I knew it would. Brinda had an eye for such things. Fashioned from a delicate spring-green silk, it was the finest thing I'd ever owned. A heavy border of silver and gold weighed it down at the hem, making the fabric swing as I walked. A fitted blouse that ended well above my navel went with it. Amma arranged my hair in an intricate braid and laid a translucent green silk scarf across my chest.

'That Brinda,' she said fondly as she arranged my scarf. 'This scarf alone must cost over a hundred nishkas. You look like a princess tonight.'

Like the other women, I carried with me a silver platter laden with offerings to the gods, covered with an embroidered cotton kerchief. Flowers, grass, coconuts, dry unbroken rice and fruits. The butter lamps in our platters flickered as we made our way up to the temple.

Half the countryside around Bharuch, as well as the soldiers who had arrived with the king and the prince, had poured into town for the festival. The traditional pyramid of young men was forming on the temple grounds, with the boys at the highest level reaching for the pot of butter that had been tied just out of their reach.

The temple was lit with hundreds of lamps. The lamp tower glittered with more. Drumbeats rhythmically punctuated the air. As we went up the stone steps into the main pillared hall, Loky pointed excitedly. 'It's the king! Why, he's no bigger than I am!'

Mulraj, the young king of Anhilwara, did indeed look no older than Loky. He was accompanied by his widowed mother, Queen Naikidevi, a tall woman dressed in white with a careworn but kind face, and of course, his uncle, Bhimdev Solanki. The prince regent had cast off his armour for silks and gold, but the reckless gleam in his eye remained undiminished. I decided to steer clear of his path.

King Vindya Varman of Malwa was also present, along with his son, Prince Subhrata, and some of their most trusted generals.

There was a good chance that Rahul would be with them, so I ducked behind a column, though I attempted to look for him regardless. No Rahul. But there was someone else staring at me—a tall young man whom I did not know. He smiled slightly and he came towards me and greeted me with folded hands.

I responded in kind. He had fine features and a warrior's bearing. He was accompanied by a boy who looked much like him, but with an open, cheerful face. Despite his bold behaviour, the tall man had a shy manner.

'I am Ranveer Singh,' he said humbly, by way of introduction. He looked disappointed at my lack of recognition and added, '*Kanwar* Ranveer Singh. I have heard much about you from... from...'

Oh! How many hours I had spent listening to tales of the Kanwar from Brinda! So this was the Kanwar, my best friend's intended husband!

'I have heard much about you too,' I assured him.

'I trust you left everyone in Ujjayani well?' he asked next. He was too shy to ask after Brinda by name.

'Very well,' I replied. 'And they will feel even better when I mention that I met you, Kanwarji, and that you asked after them.'

He blushed and added, 'This is my brother Randheer,' gesturing to the boy next to him.

Brinda and the Kanwar had been engaged last spring, but it would be a while before their wedding. The Kanwar's father was an invalid, grievously wounded in battle. It was now his responsibility as the eldest son of a warrior clan, to ensure that all his sisters were wed before he could bring home his own bride. Brinda, I knew, would hang on to every piece of news of him I could bring back.

How unassuming he was, soft-spoken and serious in demeanour, just as Brinda had described. He would be a good foil to Brinda, with her sparkling, vivacious temperament. Somehow, seeing how perfect he was for Brinda made me feel even more depressed about my own fate.

'Amma will be looking for me,' I said. 'I must take leave of you.'

I could see the yellow of Amma's sari in the crowd. I had to find the old maid who was to go with me and set off for the lamp tower. But Amma had other ideas.

'Leela, you must sing,' she said.

'But I'm to do the observations,' I said. 'Don't you remember?' Why had she suddenly changed her mind?

'I think you should sing one song before you go,' Amma insisted.

There was no graceful way to refuse before all these people who now looked expectantly at us. I followed her to the front of the hall where a beautifully decorated cradle had been set up, and women were taking turns rocking it by pulling on the long silk rope that was attached to it.

Amma had me study the sixty-four womanly arts that well-born maidens were supposed to acquire. Singing, dancing, cooking, embroidery, writing poetry, making riddles and so many others. Truth be told, I was a dismal failure at most of these lessons, but I excelled at singing. Why did she want me to sing today?

I had never sung before so large an audience. My hands shook. Would my voice tremble too? I looked at the crowds and wondered if Rahul was out there somewhere. Someone presented a tanpura to me. I lifted its long smooth neck, settled the curve of the rounded wooden base next to me, and gently plucked at the strings.

'What song?' the accompanist whispered, snapping a deft rhythm on the drum with his quick fingers.

'Yashoda's lullaby in jhaptaal,' I whispered back and plucked the first note, its familiar drone settling my nerves.

It was easier to focus on the stone carvings on the tops of the pillars, so I kept my eyes there. My voice rang out pure and true, singing the haunting lullaby of Yashoda, the foster mother of Krishna, who raised him as her own child. The hall was silent when I finished.

'Another, another ...' voices cried. I pulled my gaze down from the top of a pillar and met the eyes of the boy leaning against it, standing above the seated crowd.

It was Mahendra, the suitor who had come to our house the other day. A shiver ran down my spine. He looked rapt and admiring, smiling a white-teethed smile at me. Too late, I realized that Amma wanted to showcase my best talent for the benefit of Mahendra and his family.

The echoing twang of the last plucked string faded into silence as I set down the tanpura. Passing the instrument to the next singer, I moved back to where Amma was seated. I wanted to be angry with her, but she looked so proud that I couldn't. 'Can I go now?' I asked instead.

I was tempted to let the maid sleep on where she dozed outside the temple, but I had promised Amma I wouldn't go alone. I shook her awake and she got to her feet, grumbling about her knees. She trailed behind me as I set off at a brisk pace. I looked back for a moment to search the crowd one last time and thought I saw the Nagarseth. Rahul would also be there now. Had he heard me sing? Suddenly I couldn't wait to get away. I lifted my skirt and ran.

I didn't stop running until I reached the lotus tank. The temple shone in the distance, its lights shimmering on the mirror of the water, music and laughter wafting from its crowded halls with every gust of wind. The lamp tower soared above me, quiet, inviting, deserted. I pushed open its heavy door and started to climb.

High up in the tower the sounds from the temple faded, leaving only the echo of my footsteps, and the tinkling of my silver anklets as I climbed. The steep, curved staircase could be treacherous in the dark, but tonight every niche in the tower was lit up in honour of the festival. I pushed the door open at the top and walked to the railing. There was someone there.

The clear night sky ablaze with stars framed his lithe form. His face looked serious in the glow of a single flickering lamp. I could see that the tender light of the other day still shone in his eyes—Rahul.

He'd been waiting.

My mind went blank. I was breathless from the exertion of the steep climb and shocked at finding him there. How had he known where to find me? Perhaps he knew I would try to avoid him, and guessed I might be here.

'Leela,' he said, coming towards me. 'I beg leave to speak with you.'

I looked away, trying to think of a way to stall his words.

'I've wanted to thank you,' I said, buying time, 'for saving Loky.'

He would not be distracted. 'I came to see you,' he said. 'But you weren't home. I sent a message through Loky, but you didn't reply.'

I couldn't deny it.

'I don't know if you are avoiding me of your own will or if you were compelled to do so...' He took both my hands in his. 'We started something on board that ship,' he said, 'and I'm determined to finish it. I can't go away like this, not knowing.'

My lungs were burning before I realized I had forgotten to breathe.

A hand under my chin lifted my face to his ardent gaze. 'You know how I feel, Leela,' he said, 'but do you return my affection?'

His question hung in the air unanswered.

Behind Rahul, the red glare of Mars winked at me like an evil eye, holding my tongue fast. But even its malevolent shadow could not stop my heart from pounding, *yes, yes, yes.*

Far below I could hear the maid panting loudly as she climbed up the stairs. Still he waited.

'I know it's a fine mess, with my betrothal, and you being a Brahmin and me a Vaishya, and a Jain, and a mleccha,' he said. 'But if it doesn't matter to you, Leela, I promise I'll find a way. Just say the word...'

None of that mattered. What mattered was Rahul. How could I put *him* in danger?

'Shall I ask my father to speak with your Baba?' he looked into my eyes and said, so softly I could barely hear him.

'No!'

The word burst from my lips before I could stop it, stunning us both. I pulled my hand away and covered my lips, but it was too late.

He looked stricken.

'Leela...' he said. 'you can't mean it.'

I shook my head silently.

The maid had finally reached the door. She saw Rahul there and glared at him, but he was still staring at me disbelievingly.

'In that case,' he said at last, in a voice that broke my heart, 'I apologize for...misunderstanding.' He bowed stiffly, 'I wish you every happiness. Always,' he added. And then he left, taking all hopes of my happiness with him.

'Rahul,' I whispered, but he was gone.

But I couldn't shake off the look on his face when I had

said no. I had to stop him, I had to explain. I paced back and forth on the narrow space on the observation deck. But how could I? Should I even try?

I stopped and smoothed a piece of birch bark I had carried for my notes under the light of the lamp. With my iron stylus I drew a rectangle and divided it with diagonal lines into twelve diamonds. Within them I wrote the names of the planets in the positions they had been in when I was born. I dipped my finger into the black ink, rubbed it over the bark, and then wiped away the ink so the lines stood out stark, etched against the bark. I handed my star chart to the maid.

'Find him and give him this,' I said. 'Go quickly.'

'Give who?' she asked.

'Rahul Nagarseth,' I said. 'Please, I beg you.'

She studied the desperation on my face for a moment, and left quickly.

I settled down on the cotton mat on the tower and started to write the observations, my hands shaking. Would Rahul be able to analyse the chart and realize my dilemma? I wanted him to understand, but what purpose would be served by telling him, when there was nothing he could do? My stars were what they were. I should not have sent it.

The maid came back soon enough, with the news that she had not been able to find Rahul. Did I want it delivered the next day? I did not.

I had refused him; that was all he knew. He would probably go ahead with his engagement now. I tore the bark up silently and threw the tiny scraps from the edge of tower, watching them float slowly down to the crowds below while the conches blew and the temple bells rang, signalling that Krishna had been born.

Part Two

Though a person may know astrology and that part of the science of Jyotisha which is known as Samhita, and deals with auspicious moments to be prescribed for various functions, etc., he may not be able to answer intricate problems pertaining to astronomy. Such a person, who does not know the astronomical part of science, which abounds in innumerable reasonings, is one like a king depicted in a drawing, or a lion fast tied to a pole.

—THE CREST JEWEL OF ASTRONOMY,
BHASKARA THE TEACHER

14

RAHUL RODE AWAY TO DHAR WITH THE PRINCE AND HIS men the day after the festival. We left for Ujjayani four days later, the grief of parting with Ajji, my youngest aunt and all my cousins made even sharper because I was leaving Anhilwara, with all its memories of Rahul. But perhaps it was for the best.

Two bullock carts and three horsemen made up our company. We were to meet with a caravan of traders, who were also headed for Ujjayani, later on. With Turki raids becoming bolder each year it was wise to be prepared for the long journey.

The first caravan stop was a day's journey from Bharuch. It was a bustling place, full of travellers and their animals—horses, bulls, even elephants. There was a constant din of many languages swirling about, mingling with one another. Cooking fires dotted the encampments; dinners had to be cooked, the bedding set up and the valuables guarded. We slept out in the open, it being a clear warm night. Moti played guard dog, barking at the distant howls of jackals and other wild beasts.

But I couldn't sleep. I looked at the stars, sleepless, unable to get the look on Rahul's face out of my thoughts. What must he think of me? Was he looking at the night sky as well? Would he be married the next time we met?

It was a long night.

When the day dawned it was back to the slow road again. Baba collected information about our route from the other travellers at the caravan stop. Which roads were flooded? Which villages had pestilence and were to be avoided? Where had bandits struck last and looted other travellers?

Ten days later we reached the outskirts of Ujjayani. My heart soared when we glimpsed the Kshipra river ahead of us, winding and clear, unlike the full muddy waters of the Narmada. The flags on the spires of its famous temples and pavilions fluttered in the breeze. The wide stone steps of the familiar bathing ghats led invitingly to the riverbank. The bridge of boats that spanned the river's calm waters creaked underfoot as our bullock carts jingled across, bringing us home.

How cosy our house looked, swept clean for our arrival! The maid and the steward unloaded boxes and baskets from the bullock carts. Gomati, my brown cow, lowed a greeting from the cowshed, and Loky and Moti ran about exploring everything.

Amma opened the shrine room and lit a butter lamp, thanking the gods for our safe arrival. After she was done, I knelt in front of the incense-perfumed shrine, the light of the lamp flickering softly over our household deities, and felt my troubles ease. I touched my forehead to the altar—

Mother Saraswati, your counsel helped steer my path in Bharuch. May you always bless Rahul with your protection. May he be happy in his marriage.

Feeling better, I went up to my room and started to unpack.

'Leela!'

A cyclone of silks and silver threw itself at me. 'How long you were away!'

Brinda's arms were wound tight around me, and suddenly I was sobbing, my head on her shoulder.

'I got your letter,' she said quietly. 'There's more to tell?'

I nodded miserably.

'I want to hear everything,' she said.

'Rahul...' I said, my voice catching on a sob, 'he wanted to marry me.'

'Of course he did,' Brinda said soothingly, ignoring the fact that Rahul was engaged to someone else. 'And what did you say to that?'

'What could I say?' I wept. 'I can't marry anyone without killing them!'

'Did you explain?' she asked. I shook my head.

'But he won't care for his safety,' she said, catching on. 'Is that what you're afraid of?'

'He won't care *now*,' I said, 'but what about later? Imagine living with such a prophecy? I couldn't do it...'

She patted my back like a mother burping a child. 'Do you know what you have to do?' she said at last. 'Run away and live together regardless... If you don't have a marriage ceremony, you won't have a problem.'

I snorted through my tears at the absurdity of the suggestion. Brinda could always make me laugh.

'And what will we tell our children?' I asked, playing along.

'That might be awkward,' she admitted. 'How about you marry him after Roopmati? If you are his second wife, it might break Mangal's influence.' Her eyes flashed anger for a second. 'Maybe it will kill *her* instead!'

The mention of Roopmati brought the sorrow rushing back. 'You know it doesn't work that way,' I said miserably. 'And besides, I could never be a second wife.'

'There's something not right about that woman,' Brinda said darkly. 'I can feel it.'

'No, there isn't,' I protested. 'I've seen her picture and heard stories about her. But can we not discuss this anymore? Please?'

'Fine,' she said, taking my hand. 'But don't you worry about it. You're meant for great things, Leela. If not Rahul, then *something* else.'

'I missed you,' I said, smiling through my tears. 'Especially when I met Kanwar Ranveer Singh,' I added casually. I had kept the best for last.

She screamed with delight. It was good to have something pleasant to share with her. I gave her every detail about the Kanwar I could remember. Brinda sighed and clutched my elbow, drinking in every word.

'I knew you would like him,' she said. 'Did he tell you when the next sister is getting married?'

'This winter, he said,' I replied.

'Two sisters wed,' Brinda said dreamily, 'two more to go. I wish he could just marry them off in a herd, instead of one at a time.'

I felt almost my usual self by evening. Amma's medicinal herb garden was in full bloom after the monsoon rains; Gomati had had a new calf; I had examined the library room at the observatory and satisfied myself that the rains didn't do too much damage this year; and even Brinda proclaimed Moti to be the most handsome dog she'd ever seen.

As the sun set over the temples of Ujjayani, I looked out from my window at the peaceful scene below. The sound of the temple bells, the arching circles of light from the evening lamp ritual at the riverbank, the flocks of green parrots winging across the twilit sky, all melted the misery in my heart.

But then my eye caught something closer to me. There was someone—a young girl—curled up beneath the tall neem tree in Amma's garden. She was crying, just as I had been this morning.

Who could it be?

I ran downstairs and tiptoed to the weeping girl. She didn't even notice me.

'What's the matter?' I asked, laying a gentle hand on her shoulder.

The girl looked at me, startled, and then wiped her red eyes with her scarf.

'So sorry, I came with my mother,' the girl addressed me as mistress, a term I associated with my mother, not myself. 'She brought fresh vegetables for your kitchen. I'm just waiting for her to be done so we can leave.'

Oh, she must be the vegetable vendor's daughter, I thought.

'But why are you crying?' I persisted.

She dropped her head on her knees and started to sob again.

'Is she bothering you?' another voice asked. I looked at the woman who had spoken, the girl's mother, I presumed.

'Oh no, I was just asking her what the matter was,' I said.

'It is a long story...' she sighed. 'You would not want to concern yourself with it.'

'I like long stories,' I said firmly.

The woman squatted by her daughter, and put a gentle arm around her. 'This is my daughter, Bittan. We had a marriage proposal for her this week,' she confided. 'A good family, but they wanted to match horoscopes and check for compatibility before fixing the match. What an idea! All this astrological matching, it's for the rich. For poor people like us it's good enough that the girl be healthy, hard-working and good humoured. And really, who remembers when girls are born?'

'And then?' I prompted.

'I told them the time of her birth, as best as I could remember it. They had a chart prepared to check for astrological compatibility.

The next thing I know...' she shook her head and fell silent.

'They sent back my birth chart and rejected the proposal,' Bittan said, her voice breaking. 'They said it was unlucky, and that no one in our community should be allowed to marry me. Especially not *h-him*.'

15

JT MUST BE FATE, I THOUGHT, THAT BROUGHT HER TO ME today. Who else could understand her pain? And maybe, just maybe, I could help.

Bittan started to wail softly. It was enough to make up my mind.

'You're guessing her time of birth anyway,' I said. 'Then why not pick the best possible time? I can help you there, if you bring me her chart.'

The older woman gaped at me, confused.

'I can calculate another time, close to it, that is better astrologically,' I explained. 'For all we know that might be her actual time of birth. Tell the boy's family that you had given them wrong information, and have a new chart prepared for Bittan.'

'The astrologer who drew the chart will not change the time. I already begged him to. It is a matter of principle, he says. Nor will any other astrologer in Ujjayani. They all know each other.' She dropped her head in her hands. 'And it is also very expensive to have it redone.'

'Will no one redraw her chart then?' I asked.

'Well, word is that the drunken astrologer across the river might do it. For a fee, that is. But he is expensive...'

'I'll make it for you,' I said calmly.

'You? But...' she looked at me carefully. 'You *can* do it, can't you? You must have learnt it from your father.' She clasped my hands gratefully and tears shone in her eyes. 'I thank you!'

Bittan raised her red eyes to me with hope; and something else—respect.

I brooded over my offer after they left. Would the fates punish me for meddling with the girl's chart? I'd done it once for Asha, so this couldn't be worse. That girl would die of a broken heart otherwise by the looks of it. What was the harm in giving her a chance at happiness?

The chart arrived in a basket of brinjals the next morning. Bittan's mother handed it to me secretively as Amma picked out the day's produce. I smiled reassuringly when Amma's back was turned, and promised to have an altered chart ready the next day.

The palm leaf was not the best quality, but the chart had been drawn with care and accuracy. Yes, there were definitely problems—both Mars and Saturn were in the wrong houses. It wouldn't be possible to modify the chart she had given me, since the writing was so deeply etched into the palm leaf. I would have to make a new one.

I examined the palm leaves Baba had in his room—the best, as always, even if we could afford nothing else. I would have to age one of them by rubbing ash on it. I chewed on my metal stylus. There were two possible times I could pick that were still reasonably close to the date in the chart. Which one? I picked the one which was most auspicious, although it was further from the original date than I would have liked. But I had to give the girl the best start I could.

I had never actually made a complete star chart before, but I knew how it was done. I worked quickly to finish before Loky came back from his lessons, trying to match my more feminine hand to the plainer etching of the previous scribe.

A nagging guilt ate at me as the chart took shape. What was I doing? Faking her birth time would not actually change it. Even if no one knew about it, the obstacles to happiness caused by the planets would remain. Shouldn't I warn her about the worst possible effects of her fate and help her take precautions?

But I didn't know what precautions needed to be taken.

I had to find out.

How? Where? Who could teach me?

Suddenly it struck me. The observatory, of course! The library at the observatory always had all the answers.

I needed no excuse to go to the observatory. Unlike schools in other cities, where the sight of a young girl would likely cause chatter, most teachers at the Ujjayani observatory paid me no mind. I had grown up there—ever since I could walk I had spent most of my time at the observatory; as much a part of the school as the walls. Lately Baba had put me to use copying astronomical texts and commentaries in the library. There were usually fewer errors if the scribe understood the material, but people who knew advanced astronomy were usually not copy scribes—except for me. I was, of course, happy to help. The library was my domain. The best part of coming home was being back there.

It took me longer than usual to get there. I took a circuitous route—one that took me past the Nagarseth's Ujjayani haveli. I knew Rahul was away in Dhar, yet it drew me like a lodestone. His presence radiated from the building, like the warmth of the sun from sandstone long past sunset. The haveli stood quiet and empty, the only sounds were of the birds and squirrels at the chabutro bird feeder at the outer gates. It was the only one in

Ujjayani—the resident staff must have orders to keep it stocked. I tore a piece of roti from the lunch I had packed for Baba and threw it to the stray dogs who were eyeing the birds with hungry eyes. Seeing the chabutro had brought back such bittersweet memories.

Still, there was the observatory. I turned my steps towards it, thinking of plans for my future. My work at the library was not enough—I would have to talk to Baba about teaching. Money was still tight. It was becoming hard to find good teachers or keep the old ones for the paltry sum they were paid. What was the use of wasting my talents on ferrying lunch and copying old texts when they paid good gold for teachers who knew less than I did?

I walked down the stone steps that lined the riverbank, and along the narrow causeway to the familiar old building set midstream in the river Kshipra—part sun temple, part school and part observatory.

Boys with freshly shaven heads that denoted their student status played on the steps of the ancient building, their books forgotten. Loky was one of them. He was lucky that he didn't have to leave his home to go study, since Baba himself was his teacher.

'What's for lunch?' Loky skipped down the steps and tried to grab the carefully packed basket I had brought.

'Hold on,' I said, holding it out of his reach. 'Let's find Baba and we will eat together.'

Baba was surrounded by his honour students; serious-looking boys, some of whom had been in my class when they were younger. Their instruments lay by their side. The sundial, the plumb line by which the degrees of declination were to be calculated, the star chart on which the position of the nine grahas, or planets, were to be marked in relation to the twenty-seven asterisms. I knew them well. But now there were no girls left in the class, although Baba had not neglected to continue my advanced lessons privately.

'Here she is!' Baba seemed annoyed with his class. '*She* can explain this in no time.'

'Explain what?' I asked.

'I asked them how one can tell, by observing an eclipse, whether the object causing the shadow is larger or smaller than the moon or the sun,' Baba said.

'By the duration of the eclipse and the shape of the horns,' I replied, confident.

'I don't understand,' a student muttered.

'Draw them a diagram,' Baba said, and handed me his chalk.

Luckily, living with Baba had prepared me for such sudden challenges. I was used to having explanations demanded of me without warning.

The north-facing wall was painted a dark colour so that instructors could write on it. I drew a circle each for the sun and moon and drew a curved shadow on each.

'Observe that the horns of the moon during an eclipse are very obtuse,' I began, and expanded the curved shadow into its own complete circle. 'From this we may deduce that the object causing the eclipse is larger than the moon.' I expanded the curve on the solar disc. 'The object covering the sun on the other hand, is smaller than the sun itself. Even during a total eclipse a bright ring may sometimes be seen around the circular shadow causing the eclipse. Any questions?'

Baba scanned his students. 'Apparently not!' he said, with satisfaction. 'Thank you, Leela.'

I inclined my head in acknowledgement as the students burst into applause.

'Lunch?' I asked.

Baba waved off the boys and followed Loky and me to a sunny terrace outside the hall. '*You* should be teaching this class,' he muttered, half to himself. I should, I thought irritably, but who will let me?

I poured out some water for them to wash their hands before laying the food out for us. Baba still looked worried and distracted.

'The west wall is crumbling away,' he said eventually. 'There are so many things to be done and they all need money.'

'Aren't things better with the Nagarseth back?' I asked.

'He's funding both the Malwa and the Anhilwara army,' Baba said. 'Until the tax revenues are collected and the state treasuries return his loan, he can promise us nothing more.'

'The treasuries of Malwa and Anhilwara are hardly a credit risk,' I said.

'He's still short of money until his rear fleet arrives from Srivijaya,' Baba said. 'We can have nothing until then.'

'We'll manage, Baba,' I said soothingly. 'We always do.'

'This is the city of King Bhoja, who fought Ghazni, rebuilt Somnath and was the most learned king in history,' Baba said sadly. 'The city of Kalidasa—crest jewel of poets—and now, Ujjayani has no funds for her best school.'

'We'll think of something,' I repeated. This would be a good moment to broach the subject of teaching. I knew he wouldn't give permission for me to teach the advanced class, where most of the boys were older than me, but perhaps I could teach the younger ones?

'I nearly forgot,' Baba said, reaching into his cloth bag. 'I've a letter for you. It's from Rahul.'

I took the tube he handed me without comment, and opened it with remarkable composure. It held a scroll bearing my name in Sanskrit, but the letter itself was written in hanzi characters. Why, unless it was meant to be private?

'I'm not sure I will understand it,' I said, reluctant to read it before Baba.

'You will soon,' Baba said, smiling. 'I have arranged for a new tutor for you: an old Chinese monk. He should arrive in a few months and you can start working with him.'

'Won't that be expensive?' I said, putting the letter away to examine later.

'You can pay me back by doing translations for the library,' Baba said, waving it off.

I should have talked to Baba about the teaching. I should have borrowed texts to study remedial procedures for Bittan. I should have stayed and attended the advanced lecture Baba was scheduled to give that afternoon. But I could think of nothing but the letter.

What did it say? I started to head home, but stopped at a deserted spot by the river, where I could read the letter in solitude. I sat down on the sun-warmed stone of the ghats and brought the scroll out. My heart pounding hard, I unrolled it and smoothed out the birch bark gently.

I had lied to Baba. I could read the letter perfectly well.

Perhaps it is unwise to write this, but I feel I must. I know that of the many things consulted when contracting a marriage— family, honour, health, possessions, star charts, caste and faith—love is not considered to be of much importance. Yet to me it is paramount. You know I love you. I had felt, or rather hoped, that you were not indifferent. I assume, based on our last exchange, that other considerations take precedence over your affection. I fervently hope this may change. I know the difference in our faiths is a serious obstacle. I know it is difficult to flout the norms of society. My parents did, and although they paid a price, they never regretted it. If you reconsider, I will do all I can to ease our way.

Know that I shall wait. That I shall not change. That I shall not marry until after you do. You are all I have ever wanted.

I may be wrong in my assumption. Perhaps I have seen only what I wanted to see. In that case, forgive me. I will only cross paths with you again if it is your will. You know where to reach me. I will wait for your reply. Until then, goodbye.

16

'AND YOU WAITED *THIS* LONG TO TELL ME?' BRINDA SCOLDED, her face rigid with indignation. For all her ladylike airs, her grip was like an eagle's talons. I winced.

I had been avoiding music lessons. It was becoming harder for Baba to pay for them, but Nishikantji had somehow come to know of our financial constraints and had insisted I continue at no charge. So here I was, even though there was hardly any music left in my world.

'It's only been a few days. I just haven't seen you...' I said.

I didn't want to mention the problem about the music lesson fees.

'...because you have been skipping classes to save money,' she said. 'I know.'

'Did you tell Nishikantji?' I asked, surprised. Of course. It had to be Brinda.

'Stop changing the subject,' she countered. 'Out with it. What did the letter say?'

'Shh!' I hissed. 'Nishikantji will hear you.'

'He begged you to change your mind, he said he'll wait, didn't he?'

How did she know?

'Yes,' I admitted.

'Did you write back?' Brinda asked.

'I don't know what to say.' The weight of all my recent worrying lay heavy upon my voice. 'I've tried…and I do want to explain, but…'

Brinda slipped an arm around me. 'Start writing,' she said, 'and the words will come.' She gave me a squeeze. 'We go to Dhar next month. Finish the letter and I will carry it for you. I'll make sure he gets it safe.'

'Silence, girls!' Nishikantji thundered from across the room. 'Enough gossip. I don't hear any scales being practised by either of you. You neglect your practise, and my name is sullied because of your bad singing.'

Brinda rolled her eyes. She knew that like storm clouds out of season, Nishikantji raged mightily, but it always came to nothing.

'Start with the alaap,' he instructed. 'Leela, begin! Let us see what your voice sounds like after months of disuse.'

I cleared my throat. My voice was strained and weak at first, but gained in confidence with each rising note. Nishikantji closed his eyes and listened to me, rapt. There had been a time when he considered me his best pupil, but that was before I started skipping classes.

'Hmm,' he muttered when I had finished. 'A little rusty.' But he didn't look too upset. 'Join in, Brinda.'

The accompanist added his rhythm to our melody and suddenly the music poured from my heart. I threw myself into it, tackling even the most challenging ragas that Nishikantji asked of us. My voice soared.

The clouds have gathered, my love
Thunder shakes, lightning falls
I wait all night by the window
Listening for your silent flute

As I sang the last song that Nishikantji had set us—a love song by Radha about the sorrow of parting from Krishna, her childhood sweetheart—Brinda stopped singing, listening to me instead.

> *The moon is hiding, lost and moody*
> *Rain weeps softly into the streets*
> *On the pathways you walked*
> *The clouds have gathered, my love*

There was silence when I finished, followed by applause.

'Your voice has reached a new level, child,' Nishikantji said gently. Were there tears in his eyes? 'You have mastered the viraha ras, the emotion of parting, in your singing. And I am not ashamed to be called your teacher.'

If Brinda was to deliver the letter, I didn't need to write it in my beginner's Chinese. I could write in Sanskrit and be assured that it would not fall into the wrong hands. Brinda knew everyone in the royal court at Dhar, the new capital, kin as she was to the Parmar warrior clan that ruled the kingdom of Malwa. She had been raised in Ujjayani, but Dhar was second home to her.

But what would I write? I tried to think of a way to have Rahul put me out of his mind once and for all. Perhaps if he thought I didn't care for him...

> *Rahul,*
> *I thank you for the sentiments expressed in your letter, but I*
> *cannot return them. I regret leading you to believe otherwise.*
> *I wish you every happiness in your marriage. I remain your*
> *friend always.*
> *Leelavati*

I stared at my neat, crisp letter, hating every word. I could not send him this. It was a lie and he deserved the truth.

A crash brought me out of my reverie. Loky had burst into my room with Moti at his heels. I covered up my letter hastily.

'Look at the trick I taught Moti,' he said. 'Watch for a minute. Watch!'

'Will you please leave me alone, Loky?' I said, on the verge of tears.

Loky scowled at me. 'What's wrong with you nowadays?' he said, and stomped out. I stared after him remorsefully, and jumped up to latch the door behind him. I was never going to get this letter done in time. I tore up my last attempt and brought out a fresh palm leaf.

How about the bare facts? I could try and explain my situation while making it clear that I was reconciled to my fate. If I stated it dispassionately, surely he would understand, without being moved to press his suit anew?

Dearest Rahul,
I am a Manglik. According to my birth chart, anyone I
marry faces an early death. I could never bring such a fate
upon you, whatever my sentiments. I wish you every success
in your marriage. I remain your friend always.
Leelavati

Abrupt, but truthful. Partly truthful, anyway, though carefully devoid of all emotion. But Rahul was not a fool. He would easily guess the rest. Even with so little said there would be consequences. I crumpled the letter. May as well write down everything then...

Dearest Rahul,
No considerations could ever weigh against you in my eyes.
I knew you for my own since before you went beyond the
seas. But fate has ruled against it, and though I will hold

you in my heart always, I cannot ever endanger you by marrying you. I love you...

And always have, and always will. Hot tears splashed on to the palm leaf page as I crumpled the letter between my fingers.

'No letter, then?' Brinda asked. 'You're sure?'

'It's for the best,' I said. 'If he doesn't hear from me he will perhaps start to forget me little by little. What can I achieve by reminding him? It will get in the way of his relationship with Roopmati. He must marry and settle down. That's the only way he can be happy...and safe.'

Brinda pursed her lips. 'What makes you think he'll be happy with her?'

'I've seen her picture,' I said. 'She's beautiful, well-read and rich. Why wouldn't he be?'

'Because she isn't you,' Brinda said. 'I'm going to keep an eye on Rahul. He was so reedy when I saw him last, I can't imagine why he interests you. And I'll bring back a full report on Roopmati. Even if she isn't in Dhar, someone will know her well enough to provide all the information I need. When I come back, I'll tell you what I really think.'

'And I want to hear everything about the Kanwar,' I said. 'About the sister's wedding, too. I'm sure he will have arranged the next sister's marriage by the time you return.'

Brinda glowed with happiness. 'I'll sure he will.'

I smiled back at her. 'And now, to send you off in style, let me delight you with a fine performance by Loky and Moti.'

She rolled her eyes. 'It will be my honour.' Brinda had brothers too.

I stuck my head out of the window. 'Loky, will you please, please show Brinda Moti's new trick?'

✧

'Leela, where are you?' Amma called.

I pushed the text I'd been working on under the basket next to me, just as she came to the verandah.

'Yes, Amma?' I asked.

'Honestly, I don't know what you're up to these days,' Amma said.

'I'm copying manuscripts,' I lifted a finished manuscript from the basket to make my point. 'See?'

'A commentary by Lalla?' Amma said. 'Baba does not agree on much with that particular astronomer.'

'Nor do I,' I said. 'But that's no excuse for letting his texts vanish from the world!'

'That's all well and good,' Amma said. 'But these days, you don't go anywhere, you don't talk to anyone, you don't even dress properly...' her voice trailed off. 'I'm worried about you.'

I smoothed my hair down and tried a smile. 'Amma, I'm fine.'

'No, you're not,' Amma said. 'Now, I want you to get dressed and go help at Urvashi's wedding.'

Urvashi? She was our neighbour's daughter, but...

'Is she really getting married?' I asked. 'Now?'

'Yes, and wear this,' Amma took off the gold chain around her neck and put it carefully around mine.

'Amma, where is your other chain?' I asked looking up surprised at her bare neck. She looked away, uncomfortable. 'I sold it,' she said finally. 'The teachers' salaries have to come from somewhere.' She put her hand over mine. 'Don't worry, Leela. Your Baba's sure the funds promised by the Nagarseth will be here soon, and then I can buy it back.'

I frowned, remembering the lavish jewellery the Sethani wore. How dare she delay the payment and make life harder for my Amma.

'The Nagarseth has loaned a fortune to King Vindhya Varman and to Queen Naikidevi of Anhilwara,' Amma reminded me, guessing my thoughts. 'Education must wait when war is upon us.'

'Education is important too,' I retorted. 'I'll go help at the wedding, Amma, but only if you promise to talk to Baba about my teaching at the observatory. What's the point of paying money for new teachers when I can do it as well as anyone else?'

Amma held my gaze for a moment and then nodded. 'I'll talk to him,' she said. 'I know he worries about you teaching the older boys. They're so susceptible to youthful attachments. But you could easily teach the younger class basic arithmetic without causing comment. I think it may be best for everyone if you have something to occupy you.'

'I'll get dressed,' I said, smiling.

'And Leela,' Amma said, 'at the wedding you might meet a new teacher Baba has hired. Be sure to talk to him.'

I looked deep into the flames of the wedding altar, my vision blurring for a second. Fiery golden sparks rose up from it every time the priest asked the couple to pour butter into the flames as he chanted their rights, duties and wedding vows. The pictures I saw in the holy fire were of happier times. Kites, ships, a boy leaping in the rain, a face still sharp in my memory, even though it had been months since I had seen it.

I sat on the bride's side. Little Urvashi—all grown up and moving away from Ujjayani. I could barely believe it. Soon I would be the only old maid left.

Someone poked me with a sharp elbow.

'No one's looking,' Urvashi's young sister Uma hissed. 'Let's steal the bridegroom's shoes.' She gave me a meaningful look and vanished into the crowd.

I sighed. I was in no mood to help them steal the groom's shoes, tradition or not. The other girls thought it was fun, but it was a lot less fun when you had done it dozens of times and were starting to become the oldest of the shoe thieves. Still, I'd promised Amma I would help.

I moved away casually, mingling with the crowd at the outer edge of the altar. A giggle from behind a flower pot alerted me to the presence of allies.

'Any idea where they are?' I whispered to my young accomplices.

'In the basket behind that boy, I think,' said Uma.

It was the task of the groom's friends and brothers to guard the shoes from the bride's sisters and friends.

I took stock of the enemy. They were all from out of town, having travelled with the groom's party from Suryapur. The one guarding the basket had his back turned to me but he looked familiar. Did I know him?

'I'll distract that boy while you sneak the shoes out,' I told Uma.

I picked a platter of sweets, tender milky morsels flavoured with honey, cardamom and rose water, topped with nuts, and walked towards the basket guard.

'Greetings!' I said. 'May I offer you some of Ujjayani's famous mithai?'

I could see the little girls creeping towards the basket under cover of the crowd.

The familiar-looking boy turned around, and the smile vanished from my face. It was Mahendra.

'Leelavati,' he said. 'Namaskar. I am Mahendra. We met in Bharuch?'

He looked less awkward, even attractive, I admitted grudgingly. He had grown into his arms and legs, but his bold flashing smile was the same. My impulse was to turn and run, but I had to cover for the girls who were nearing the basket.

So I smiled sweetly at him instead. He blinked in surprise.

'Imagine seeing you here!' I said politely.

'I had hoped to see you,' he said frankly. 'My sister Asha was married two months ago. Did you know?'

'I did not,' I said. 'Congratulations!'

'It would not have been possible if it hadn't been for you,' he said quietly.

I was astonished. Surely Asha and her mother hadn't told the men? They might not have agreed to tweaking her time of birth.

'Baba doesn't know,' Mahendra added, guessing my thoughts. 'But Amma had me draw up Asha's chart with the time you had suggested. I want to thank you for your quick thinking that day.'

For the first time, I began to like Mahendra. I smiled warmly at him.

'I have been reading up on the Samhitas to see what precautions and remedies can be prescribed for the worst possible alignment of her chart,' he continued. 'I want to make sure we do all we can, just in case.'

'Which ones?' I asked, curious. We had probably been reading the same books.

I was right. He named the Brihat Samhita, the classic text on the subject. From his conversation it was clear that he knew it well. He is intelligent, this boy, I'll give him that, I thought to myself.

'I've taken up a teaching post at the observatory,' he said after a pause. 'I have decided to make my home in Ujjayani.'

So this is what Amma meant when she mentioned the new teacher.

'Ujjayani is lucky,' I said. 'Baba must think very highly of you to appoint you. In fact,' I hesitated, 'I may actually be teaching at the school myself.'

'*You?*' he looked shocked. 'Really?'

'Yes,' I said, a little stiffly. 'Don't worry, I can keep up with the rest of you.'

He looked unconvinced, and my temper started to fray.

'You don't believe me, do you? Well, how about a test? Ask me anything you want.'

He folded his arms mock seriously and quoted, 'Tell me, dear woman, the cube of nine, the cube of the cube of three and the cube of the cube of five and the cube roots of these cubes, if your knowledge be great in the computation of cubes.'

'Elegant verse,' I said. 'You *do* know that it was composed by Baba especially for me when I was little, do you not?'

'The answers, my lady!' he demanded.

It was hard not to laugh at his expression when I gave him the correct answer to Baba's problem.

'Astonishing!' he said.

'Thank you,' I replied, trying to hide a smile, for behind his back, the girls had removed the shoes from the basket beside him and were sneaking away.

One of the other boys realized this sooner than we had hoped.

'We've been robbed!' he cried out. 'Mahendra, you fool, you've been tricked. What kind of a guard are you?'

Mahendra's jaw dropped as he looked from the empty basket to me. I just raised an eyebrow and smiled innocently at him.

'See you at the observatory,' I said airily and stalked off.

We did well that day—silver bangles and a bag of coins from the groom before we gave him back his shoes. The little girls were thrilled. They stuck their tongues out at the groom's friends, who sat around scowling at Mahendra. He, however, gazed into the distance contemplatively, strangely unconcerned about letting them down.

17

'NAME THE SIX SEASONS,' I ASKED THE CLASS. 'STARTING with spring.'

Fifteen little boys sat around me, cross-legged and alert, in the hall that served as my classroom. It wasn't a master class, but at least these young students were officially mine. It felt good to be a teacher.

'Basant, Grisham, Varsha, Sharad, Hemant, Shishir,' they chanted.

'And who can name the two halves of the year,' I asked, 'and tell me why they are so divided?'

A round-faced boy raised an eager hand. 'They are Uttarayana, when the sun moves north and daylight increases, and Dakshinayana, when the sun moves south and daylight decreases.'

'Very good,' I said. 'And can you identify the two halves of a month?'

'Krishan-paksh, the dark half of the waning moon, and Shukla-paksh, the light half, when the moon waxes,' he said.

Perhaps I had found my calling, I thought, pleased with their performance, for they remembered all I taught them.

The gong sounded, signalling the end of class. As the boys started to get to their feet, I picked up the posy of kadamba blossoms—perfect golden globes with their enchanting fragrance—that had been left on my low wooden desk.

'Before you leave,' I said. 'I want to say that I appreciate the thought, but no more flowers, please.'

There were often flowers at my desk when I came to class, a gift from a student, I assumed. I always tucked one of each in my hair, not wanting to reject a present from a child. Jasmine, kutaja, champa. But kadamba? They only bloomed for a week every year and were very expensive out of season.

But why did they look so puzzled? Then one of them said, 'It's not from us.' The rest of them giggled.

'What do you mean they're not from you?' I asked. 'Who are they from?'

'Him…' the child pointed. I followed his gesture with my eyes, a horrible suspicion creeping into my mind. And to confirm it, there was Mahendra standing at the door of my class, smiling affably at all of us.

'Thank you,' I said. It wasn't their fault, after all. 'That's all for today, students.'

Mahendra was waiting for me in the hall. 'How was your class?' he asked. His proprietary attitude annoyed me. Why did he have to appear every time I stepped outside my class?

I held up the flowers accusingly. 'Are these from you?'

He flashed his dazzling smile. 'I've been discovered.'

I resisted the impulse to stomp the delicate bouquet to a pulp. To think I'd been wearing his flowers for days and he hadn't said a word.

'Flowers such as these are best offered to Saraswati,' I said curtly, stopping before a small niche with an image of the goddess of learning and laying the lovely blossoms reverently at her feet.

He waited until I was done. 'But you are Saraswati incarnate,' he said.

The cheek of him! 'I will be Kali incarnate if you don't stop fooling around,' I said, fixing him with a stern eye. 'Or perhaps I need to speak to Baba?'

'No need for that,' he said smoothly. 'No more offerings, if you so wish.'

'Here's a painting for you from Brinda,' Amma said when I got home.

'A painting?' I asked. I hadn't heard from her at all in the months she'd been away.

Amma nodded. 'And a note to go with it, but it's not very long.' I looked at the note first.

Leela,

I know I haven't kept my promise to write, but you'll forgive me when you see the painting I've made for you. See anyone familiar in it? I don't mean the Kanwar, though I'm well pleased by how his likeness turned out. Leela, they are friends! Who would have thought that my warrior would befriend a merchant? But truly, a merchant with such valour has never been seen before. Their legion is away on a joint exercise with Anhilwara's Bhimdev, so it's very lonely here. I cannot wait to see you and Ujjayani. I have so much to tell you! Brinda.

'What is the painting of?' Amma called from the kitchen. We no longer had a maid—the size of our household had been shrinking along with the endowment for the observatory.

'The Kanwar, of course,' I said, more calmly than I felt. I unrolled the cloth and spread it out. The painting was large. It showed a training ground of the Malwa army—horses, elephants and soldiers, all alive in colourful detail—a beautiful piece of art.

Three archers stood in the foreground. One of them, the

Kanwar, was leaning on his bow, the second, who looked much like him, stringing his, and a third with his bow up, string taut, arrow nocked and ready to release. My heart raced—surely, I thought, *surely* that was too tall to be Rahul?

She had painted him in heroic profile, nearly as high as the Kanwar. His stance was sure, his bare arms and shoulders thick with new muscle—a pleasing contrast to his lean waist. The picture was so vivid you expected to hear the sharp sound of the arrow cutting through the wind any minute. But Rahul's face—long hair pulled back, brow knit with concentration—was worryingly stern.

He looked focused and unsmiling; not a dimple in sight.

Oh, Rahul! I placed my fingertips on the page, my chest tightening with unshed tears.

Amma's voice made me jump. 'Leela, you have a visitor.'

I rolled up the painting and put it away. What could have brought Bittan here? I hadn't seen her since her wedding, although her mother talked of her often.

'I have to pick up a sack of flour from the mill,' Amma said. 'Mind you don't tarry too long chatting with the girl. The water needs to be drawn from the well before dark.'

'You look like a happily married woman!' I said, smiling as I came to the door where Bittan stood. She was the perfect picture of a newlywed bride, with her pretty anklets, toe rings, bangles and sindoor.

But Bittan hadn't come alone. As soon as Amma left, there was a knock on the door and Bittan hurried to let in a young man with a stubbornly set jaw.

'What is the matter?' I asked them, although I had a fair idea.

'This is my cousin Viru. He was going to see the astrologer across the river,' Bittan said hastily, 'but I talked him into coming to see you instead.'

'What about?' I asked.

'He is my mother's sister's sister-in-law's son,' she explained. 'He wants to marry my second cousin on my father's side. Only, her birth chart—it is disastrous! But they still want to marry. His parents will never allow it if they know what her chart says. I told them you may be able to help.'

I thought about it, trying to decide whether to help them or not. 'I can examine her chart and give you my advice,' I said. 'Have you brought it?' Viru handed it over without a word.

I studied the chart carefully, and looked at their hopeful faces, feeling torn. There was no way to soften the blow.

'Based on this, I would not advise her to marry at all,' I said finally. 'It is too risky to her spouse.'

'Can you not change the chart?' Viru asked. 'If I have no objection to the risk, why should it concern you?'

'Hold your tongue, Viru,' Bittan hushed. 'She's only being honest.'

She searched my face. 'Is there any chance you might be able help them?'

'Bittan, I redid your chart because you did not know *for certain* what day you were born,' I explained. 'I did so for another girl who was also unsure of her birth day. You were both guessing anyway, so it made sense to pick the best time and hope it was correct. But this,' it was hard to look at the couple as I said this, 'I cannot do this in good conscience.'

I grasped her hand. 'But believe me when I say that I have *great* sympathy for your situation.'

'I'm not giving up,' Viru said, stubbornly. 'If she won't help us then I will go to the astrologer across the river.'

'But you said he was greedy and incompetent!' I looked from Bittan to Viru.

Viru fixed his fiery eyes on me. 'We have no choice.'

I was not easy in my mind afterwards. I waited for a glimpse of Bittan for weeks so I could know how Viru and his love had fared. When I finally managed to talk to her it was to find that Viru had indeed sought out the astrologer across the river.

'He gave Viru a new chart—a neat one, thankfully, since he happened to be sober. He didn't bother explaining the risks and remedies, as you had tried to.' Bittan frowned. 'We were lucky. There are people who have paid him his dues and received nothing. But my cousin is not easy to double-cross.'

'Received nothing?' I said, outraged. 'Is he not afraid of the gods that he cheats people so?'

'He's afraid of nothing,' Bittan said. 'Except running out of wine.'

'Tell your cousin that if he's set on this course I will explain the possible precautions to him,' I said. 'He must guard against the dangerous implications of this marriage. At least, go into it with eyes open.'

I made a note in my mind to be sure to pay attention to the rumours and whisperings about that rogue astrologer. If I ever ran into him I wanted to give him a piece of my mind. What did he mean by peddling his fake charts to desperate young people? That boy was stubborn and in love—why would anyone responsible encourage him in a course of action that could result in his doom?

'Do you think I could speak to Kumarilla Mishra?' I asked Mahendra. 'I have a Phalit question for him.'

Mahendra taught in the Phalit section of the school. Jyotish, Vedanga, Phalit—whatever you called the predictive art of astrology—was a popular subject with a large student base and held good employment prospects for graduates, but it wasn't Baba's favourite branch of study. He much preferred the pure mathematics of Ganit, and so my private education had been biased accordingly. But I had been catching up.

'You want to speak to the head of the Phalit section?' Mahendra asked. 'I can help you if it is something simple,' he permitted himself a small smile. 'Some people consider me quite knowledgeable.'

'Thank you, but the question is for him,' I said as civilly as I could.

'As you wish,' Mahendra shrugged. 'I believe he has a break between classes soon. Would you like me to bring you to him?'

We found Kumarilla Mishra warming himself in the spring sunshine by the river, his white hair lit up like a halo around his birdlike face.

'Acharya,' Mahendra said, 'Leelavati had a question for you.'

I touched his feet in respect and he motioned us to sit beside him. 'Sit, sit, both of you. Of course I have time. What is it, my child?'

'Acharya,' I asked. 'Are people truly helpless under the sway of bad planetary influences? Can the remedies you teach ever reverse the effects completely?'

From the corner of my eye I saw Mahendra raise his eyebrows at my question. I wished he would go away.

'Ah, the most important question of all, Leela,' the old man replied. 'Are we pawns in the hands of fate or can we rise above it? A difficult question, very difficult indeed.'

'What is your opinion?' I persisted.

'Well, we know that the stars and planets affect the world. The sun controls the seasons and life in this world. The moon controls the tides. The other planets work in more subtle ways. No one can deny their handiwork, and no one can work against their will. Take the sun, for instance. If you sow seeds in winter, when the sun is weak, will you have a harvest? The planets work on the same principle.'

'But if you shelter seedlings from frost, some of them may yet grow in winter,' I countered.

'Is this question personal?' Mahendra interrupted.

'Yes,' I snapped, eager to hear the Acharya's response.

'True,' the old man said. 'But it is difficult. Why would anyone put in ten times the effort for half the harvest?'

'Because of love...' I answered stubbornly. 'What if a couple's star chart is not compatible, yet they want to marry. Through the remedies prescribed in the texts, can it be made possible?'

'Ah, love!' said Kumarilla Mishra, with a twinkle in his eye that was clearly directed at both of us. 'Well, that depends.'

'On what?' I asked. 'The nature of the remedies?'

'On the quality of the love,' he replied. 'Is it attraction, is it infatuation, or is it true love? Like I said, it depends.'

'Say it *is* true love,' I said.

'True love may, and I say *may*, do ten times the work that growing wheat in winter demands. And it may even be that this winter wheat tastes better than the easy wheat harvested in autumn. But attraction and infatuation will let the wheat wither and the farmer shall die of hunger.'

'So the remedies do not really matter?' I asked.

'They do; they can help, certainly,' he said. 'Wearing red coral and pearl will balance the partners' energies, for example. But in the end, it is the quality of the bond between the two that will determine the success of the marriage.'

The gong went off for the next class.

'Thank you for your advice, Acharya,' I said.

'Come anytime, Leelavati,' he said, laying a gentle hand on my head.

Mahendra fixed me with a questioning look as we walked away.

'Leelavati? It is rumoured that you remain unwed because your birth chart presents a problem. Is it true?'

I shrugged.

'I knew it,' he said. 'That's why you helped Asha.'

He wouldn't go spreading it around, would he? 'Please do not speak about this, Mahendra,' I begged.

'You have my word,' he said. 'And Leela, it is possible to counteract negative influences of planets in a spouse's chart. Especially for people who know the field of astrology well,' he smiled smugly. 'Someone like me, for example.'

Oh, now the stupid man thought I wanted to marry him! I stared at him in disgust. 'It was *truly* a hypothetical question, Mahendra,' I said. 'I was not asking for myself.'

'I understand,' he said, with a meaningful gleam in his eye. 'Of course it was.'

'*Uff!*'

Infuriated, I walked away from him as quick as I could.

Brinda! She was back!

I rushed to her house as soon as Amma told me of her arrival.

'Namaskar!' I greeted Brinda's mother hastily, as I burst through the gate into the courtyard of their haveli. 'Where is she?'

'Slow down,' she smiled. 'Let me look at you! Why, you've grown up, Leela.'

'Thank you,' I said, blushing. 'But where's Brinda?'

'All right, all right,' she said. 'She's up on the terrace, see?'

There was Brinda, leaning over the carved handrails, looking as fresh and fashionable as ever. I ran upstairs two steps at a time. The screaming, the laughing, the hugging!

'Leela, you're no longer a freak of nature!' she said, looking at me appreciatively. 'You have proper curves!'

'So how was the Kanwar?' I asked. 'He looked well in the painting you sent me.'

Brinda gazed into the distance, a smile on her face. 'I made sure I spent time with the sister that was getting married, didn't I? But the family was always there. We did not have a moment alone, but his brother and sister carried messages for us. Guess who is a good friend of his now?'

My heart began to beat faster.

'Rahul Nagarseth! You didn't tell me how handsome he had become! So tall and strong and muscled...not reedy at all. Did you recognize him in the painting I sent you?'

'He's changed,' I said, 'but not by much. Thank you for the painting, Brinda. Can I,' I hesitated, 'can I keep it?'

'It's yours,' she waved airily. 'I kept an eye on him, like I said I would,' she continued. 'It wasn't hard because the Kanwar and his brother and all my cousins trained with him. He fights hard and fears nothing, they say—a real leader. He's a favourite of King Vindhya Varman and Prince Subhrata, and with the women too, from what I hear.'

'The women?' I asked. 'Why?'

'Because he's been everywhere and seen everything, and he's more of a poet than the rest of them put together.'

I bit my lip.

'He's been given his own legion,' Brinda continued. 'He's the youngest commander of a cavalry troop in the history of Malwa.'

'Is he happy?' I asked. She tilted her face, considering.

'He hides it well. But I feel he still nurses a broken heart.'

I couldn't decide if that made me feel better or worse.

'Did you meet Roopmati?' I asked.

'She wasn't there. All I heard was that she's pretty as a picture if she doesn't open her mouth. No sense or learning, and terrible teeth besides, from chewing paan. But I do have some other news,' she paused for emphasis, 'news that changes everything. Word is that the last fleet the Nagarseth was waiting for was lost to pirates off the coast of Malabar. Leela, the Nagarseth could be facing bankruptcy, considering the amount of money he has recently loaned out.'

'Oh, no,' I whispered. Facing bankruptcy! No wonder our endowment money had not been forthcoming.

'My feeling is that, given the situation, Rahul might go through with the wedding to Seth Oswal's daughter,' she said. 'It's the only way they can recover their losses.'

My heart sank. Rahul would do anything to help his father.

'But if they are no longer wealthy,' I asked, 'why would the Oswals want to honour the match?' I asked.

Brinda snorted. 'Because everyone knows that the Oswals are bloodsucking moneylenders, but the Nagarseth is an honourable man. He may have no money, but his good name in a score of countries and his vast network of accquaintances in trade are reason enough for an alliance between their houses.'

It made sense. I knew the deep bond Rahul had with his father. He wouldn't hesitate to marry Roopmati if it meant saving the Nagarseth's business and reputation.

'Before this, he had threatened to become a monk if they forced him to marry her,' Brinda said. 'Or so I heard. Pity. Imagine if he became a Digambara,' she smiled dreamily. The Jain monks were of two sects—the Shvetambar, the white-clad, and the Digambara, the sky-clad, who did not wear any robes at all. 'Why, he'd cause riots everywhere he went.'

I blushed. 'Brinda!'

She gave me a hug. 'I was only trying to put a smile on your face, Leela. Now, are you going to tell me about the young Brahmin who is teaching at the observatory or not?' she asked.

'How do you know about Mahendra?' I asked, surprised.

'I have my sources,' she replied mysteriously.

It was better to tell her about Mahendra than to hear more about Rahul, I decided. I had to reconcile myself to the idea of Rahul married, happily or otherwise.

'I have to let Baba know,' I said. 'If there's no hope of funds from the Nagarseths, we have to make other arrangements.' I sighed at the hopelessness of it. 'He may have to shut down part of the school.'

'I know my father will do what he can,' Brinda said. 'It'll be nothing compared to what the Nagarseths might have done, but nevertheless...'

'Thank you,' I said warmly. 'Every bit is appreciated.'

I took my leave, my mind a mess of conflicting emotions. I had to calm myself before going home. I headed to the riverbank.

'Don't mind me, my lady!' The man reeked of alcohol. 'I'd leave if I could, but my legs won't cooperate at the moment. Apologies!'

So much for the peace and quiet of the riverbank. I pulled my gaze away from the soothing waters. Was that tall, dishevelled and clearly inebriated man talking to me?

My nose wrinkled in disgust as I got to my feet and turned to go, but my foot caught on a stack of manuscripts and scattered them everywhere. I picked them up, and lifted them to my forehead in apology. All books and manuscripts were instruments of Saraswati and were not to be disrespected. But what could such a man be doing with the Jyotish Samhitas?

It took me the space of one breath before realization hit home.

'Stop!' I said to the man without preamble. 'You are the astrologer from across the river, aren't you?'

The man raised an eyebrow, with something like amusement on his drunken face.

'Guilty as charged,' he said merrily. 'One is obliged to cross the river now and then, especially when the creditors on the other side start being bothersome. Are you, er...' he looked a bit guarded suddenly, '...an old client of mine, perhaps?'

'No, I'm not,' I said hotly. 'And I think it's despicable that you take money from desperate young people and peddle your fake charts without any regard for their safety or future.'

'A believer in the fates, I see,' he said. 'Such youthful outrage! Go away, girl, you're making my head hurt.'

'Not until you answer me!' I insisted.

'Answer what?' he enquired. 'You just said you weren't a client of mine.'

'You made a chart for a friend of mine. His name was Viru,' I said. 'It was for a girl who is a Manglik. Not too long ago. Do you remember?'

'Who can forget the forceful Viru,' he smiled ruefully. 'He confiscated my wine while I worked on the chart.'

'Good thing he did,' I said. 'I saw her original chart. And if he marries that girl you know as well as me that he's doomed to die!'

'Is he? Is he, indeed?'

I stared at him perplexed. 'You *saw* the chart!'

'I saw the man!' he retorted. 'Good health, no ill habits, devoted to the Manglik girl, capable of keeping secrets.'

'We're not talking about him!'

'Aren't we?' he asked musingly. 'No, we're not. Nothing is ever as it seems. We could be talking of me. We could be talking of you. Tarry a while my girl, and I'll tell you a story.'

'I have no wish to hear your lies and justifications...' I began, but he cut me off. 'No lies. Just listen!'

I was curious, I had to admit, so I sat quietly as he settled down on the ghat and looked into the middle distance, his red-rimmed eyes suddenly aglint with tears.

'I loved a girl who was a Manglik,' he said. 'And they married her off to an old man, a disgusting dried-up grandfather.' His face contorted into a sneer. 'He thought he'd enjoy his last days with a young wife. Except he didn't...'

'Didn't what?'

'Didn't die!' he said bitterly. 'He enjoyed his young wife for a long, long time.'

My hand crept up to my face in horror.

'She gave him two fine sons, and would have given him more had I not...'

'Not what?' I cried.

'Tried to kill the old bastard!' he replied savagely. 'Oh, don't look like that. I didn't succeed, although, I admit, I wanted to. But at least I made sure that he was in no shape to bother his wife any more. But I digress.' He raised a shaky finger. 'The point is...the *point* is that he shouldn't have lasted six months according to the charts, and yet, he lives—to this day!'

He looked so broken-hearted that I didn't want to question

him further, but I had to know. 'Are you sure she was Manglik?' I asked.

'I'm an astronomer, aren't I?' he said. 'Yes, I'm sure. And his chart offered no protection from Mangal either.'

'What happened to her?' I asked.

'She knew, of course,' he said. 'Knew that I had tried to kill him. She begged me to spare his life so she wouldn't be widowed on top of everything else. She asked me to go away before anyone found out.'

'She cared about you,' I said, my voice catching in my throat.

'Very much,' he said, a small smile dawning on his face. 'The last son that decrepit old buzzard thought was his...well, never mind. He's growing up strong with his mother.'

'I didn't hear that,' I told him firmly.

'It was unfair and unjust to both of us,' he said, eyes blazing again. 'Things would have been different had they disregarded the charts. So very different.'

'That's why you change the charts of others?' I asked.

'What else can I do to drown my sorrows?' he said. 'Do you still believe in the power of the planets, my girl?'

I twisted the bangle around my arm, my head in turmoil. 'I have to go...'

'Not convinced, eh?' He laughed mirthlessly. 'I'll not argue with you, for whatever you might say, I can see that you're already arguing with yourself.'

Without realizing it, my steps turned to my well-trodden route past the Nagarseth's haveli.

The haveli was bustling with sound and activity. Horses, bullock carts and servants thronged the front gate.

They were home.

18

JT TOOK ME ONLY A MINUTE TO REALIZE THAT SOMETHING was wrong. This was no joyous homecoming. There was an underlying sense of fear and confusion in the bustle. People stood well clear of a carriage—a three-domed rath with a powerful team of bullocks, hot and exhausted, harnessed to it—and masked men carefully bore a litter from it to the open gates of the haveli. It wasn't apparent if the person they carried was dead or alive.

If the masks raised fears, the red flag hoisted from the high roof of the haveli—to the surprise and confusion from the crowd below—confirmed it. It was the warning flag; the flag that by law every household must fly to warn the town that its members had a case of the deadly disease—the smallpox.

Not Rahul, I prayed, merciful goddess, not Rahul.

'Who is sick?' I asked. 'Please, can someone tell me who it is?'

It was no use asking, for the crowd didn't know. They stood grim and silent, watching the spectacle. But the carriage driver jumped off his place behind the tired-looking bullocks and spoke up, 'It is the mistress. We were two days' journey away from Ujjayani when she was taken sick. I drove through the night to get her here as soon as possible. My beasts are spent, and I don't know if we reached in time.'

I laid a hand on the sweaty brow of one of the bullocks. They needed a rub down and a long rest after being unhitched.

'Have you had the teeka?' I asked him. He nodded. 'The whole party had had it, by God's grace, except for the poor mistress, of course.'

I remembered that she had not approved of the teeka the day they had visited us in Bharuch.

'Has a vaid been sent for?' I asked.

'I don't know,' he said, leading the tired oxen towards the stables at the back of the haveli. 'It is difficult to find anyone who's willing to treat the disease, you know.'

I did know. Amma was one of the few healers in the city who would treat a person with smallpox. Most people did not want to be anywhere near it, and who could blame them, with the disease being as contagious as it was?

Hoof beats signalled an incoming horseman, riding hard. Could it be Rahul? No, I recognized the grey hair and heavy build as the stallion pulled up. It was the Nagarseth. He must have been behind the Sethani's party, but he would have made up the distance between them as soon as he got the news about his wife.

'Where is Padma?' he asked the main steward. I realized that Padma was the Sethani's name. I had never heard him speak her name out loud before. Respectable men did not utter their wives' names in public, but this was not the time for social niceties.

The crowd was dispersing, some of the servants, too, were walking away with them. I had seen it happen before—servants, even family members, abandoning the diseased, leaving them to die alone.

From the side door, I saw a group of women leave. The Nagarseth saw them too.

'Ten bags of gold coins for anyone who stays and helps nurse the mistress!' he declared in a carrying voice. Most of the women kept walking, but an old maid, with pockmarks on her face that indicated she had survived the disease before, turned around. His shoulders slumped with relief.

'Go to your mistress and try to make her comfortable,' he ordered.

'It will not be easy, master,' she said. 'She is burning with fever, and the rashes are everywhere—the size of lentils.'

I winced at her description.

The Nagarseth clutched at her arm, 'Can anything be done?'

'I am a maid, not a healer,' the woman said. 'I don't know how to treat her.'

I stepped forward. 'You must use cold compresses to bring her fever down and give her a tonic of neem oil,' I said, unable to stop myself. 'Oh, and apply a paste of turmeric, gram flour and milk to soothe and disinfect the rashes. Then wash it off with water infused with neem leaves.'

'Leela!' the Nagarseth said, hope returning to his voice as he recognized me. 'Will your mother come to her?'

I shook my head. 'Amma has gone to visit the temple of Ambadevi at Mandu. She will not return for four days.'

'Is there anyone else capable of treating her before that?' he asked.

'I don't think so...' I said.

The Nagarseth looked old and beaten. 'I have already lost a wife. I cannot bear to go through this again.'

I remembered what Brinda had said about the lost fleet. He had not hesitated to offer gold to anyone willing to nurse the Sethani. Was it the last bit of gold they had?

A Brahmin's curse is potent, child...

Ajji's words suddenly came back to me. It was I myself who had once wished the pox upon her.

'If you give me permission,' I said, 'I will treat your wife.'

'You?' the Nagarseth was astonished. 'No…you are so young. I cannot let you risk your health.'

'I am trained in Ayurveda,' I said. 'I have learnt by my mother's side ever since I could walk. And I've had the teeka every year since I was a child. I believe myself immune. Amma would have treated your wife, and I know Baba will not stop me. Time is of the essence if you wish to save her. Grant me access and a pair of hands to make the medicines she needs.'

He hesitated, but only a moment. 'Come,' he said, flinging the door open. 'I will send word to your Baba.'

We hurried through it.

Every limb and muscle in my body throbbed with pain. I had been prepared for vigilance and care, but not for the sheer physical effort of nursing a desperately sick woman. I had only nursed children like Loky and my younger cousins before, and had no experience of nursing a full-grown woman.

The house was deserted. No one would help us for fear of the disease, so everything had to be done by the pair of us. The old woman did not have the strength for many of the tasks we had to perform—drawing water from the well, tending the fire to boil the neem-leaf infusion, cooking a simple meal to keep our strength, lifting the fever-wracked frame of the Sethani so that we could apply the poultice and the cold compresses she needed. It was hard physical labour of the kind I wasn't used to.

The bitter smell of neem leaves was everywhere. We burnt neem leaves to purify the air, and boiled a vat of water with neem leaves to bathe the round, pus-filled rashes that had appeared all over the Sethani's body.

We had to work constantly to keep her fever down. Cold water from the basement well had to be drawn for the cold compresses to her forehead. I mixed a paste of turmeric, sandalwood, gram flour and other cooling ingredients to soothe the irritation from her rashes.

We applied it carefully on the Sethani and held her hands down to stop her from scratching and infecting the sores.

'Can you hear me?' I asked her gently. 'You must not scratch the pox or it will get putrid.'

She could not speak, but her eyes showed a flash of recognition. She held her hands still. For the first time, we felt we had a chance. Our patient could hear us and follow our commands.

Worse than the exhaustion was the struggle to keep my wits about me, and not lose my good judgement to weariness and worry. It was hard to look on this disease without fear and revulsion. The pustule-filled pox had transformed the Sethani's body into something of a nightmare. But though I did not think at first that I could, somewhere within me, I found Amma's clear-eyed focus and resolve. The old maid and I fell into a silent rhythm, taking turns to feed, sponge and watch over the Sethani in the days and nights that followed.

A week later, or less perhaps, I do not know for sure, I walked up to the terrace of the haveli and looked at the city spread below. What I saw filled me with dread. There were red flags on nearly two dozen buildings. Three in the Brahmin tola, our own neighbourhood! The markets were quiet, the town deserted. Funeral pyres burnt on the banks of the Kshipra. Loky's face flashed before my eyes. No, he would be fine. Amma had made sure that he had had the teeka, and she would be home by now. That must be why Baba and Amma had not come for me. The entire city had been infected and they were needed elsewhere.

The next day, as I dozed by the Sethani's side, she sat up by herself, opened her eyes and spoke.

'Leelavati,' she said, soft but clear. She knew it was me.

I nearly cried when I heard her speak. She had suffered our ministrations without complaint, although she must have been in agony. Amma always said that you could tell much about a person by the way they bear pain and illness. The Sethani had had courage and patience and fortitude. How wrong I had been in my shallow dislike of her.

That was a turning point. After that, it was a slow but steady recovery, no longer a fight between life and death. And we had another ally on our side, the Sethani herself.

The part of the haveli where her apartment was located had been quarantined off from the rest of the house so the disease would not spread. Slowly, as news of the Sethani's recovery spread, the servants returned, and our work became easier. When Amma finally came to see me, she was equal parts furious and proud.

'The teeka is not infallible, foolish child. You have had some protection but you may yet get the disease. Since you have already been exposed to it and the damage is now done, you may as well stay. It is not as if the rest of the city is safe.'

I learnt of the other outbreaks in the city from her. She was much needed there, so she had let me continue to nurse the Sethani. But she had found other maids who had survived the disease, so we now had extra hands to help with the actual nursing.

It was nearly a week more before the Sethani could leave her bed. It felt longer. Because of the help we now had, I did not have as much to occupy my time. I missed my usual routine of studying and teaching. Instead, I spent my time practising my singing since there was nothing else to do in the apartment, isolated as we were from the rest of the world.

I was in the middle of one of the songs Nishikantji had been teaching us when I realized that the Sethani was on her feet, listening as I sang. I stopped and turned to look at her.

'Beautiful,' she said softly, her voice still weak. 'You have a singular voice.'

'You look better,' I said gently. I was used to her now, the awkwardness between us had long vanished.

'Thanks to you,' she said humbly. 'You have taken good care of me, Leela.'

I had done it for Rahul, and for the Nagarseth.

'You must send for your clothes,' she said. 'And anything else you need. It seeems we are to be confined here for some time.'

The old feeling of inadequacy made me conscious of the tired cotton sari that hung limply around me. I raised my chin. 'These *are* my clothes.'

The Sethani was quiet. I did not say anything about the grant money that the Nagarseth had been tardy with. I remembered what Brinda had said about the pirates and the lost fleet, but I also remembered the bag of gold that the Nagarseth had offered the old maid a week ago. How different our circumstances were! Difficult times for us meant that there was no sugar to make rice pudding for Loky, or new clothes to replace torn ones for me. Difficult times for *them* meant that they had to choose between giving gold to the temple they were constructing in Ujjayani or giving gold to Baba's observatory.

'I know the funds we had promised the observatory have not been forthcoming,' the Sethani said, as if hearing my thoughts. 'There have been downturns in our business, and…liquidity issues, which have forced us to hold back on our endowment promises. I have always respected the Acharya's dedication to education.'

Respect wouldn't buy back the jewellery and household items Amma had had to sell off to put food on the table.

'There is no need for explanations,' I said, trying hard not to let my indignation on Baba's behalf show in my voice.

'And was there need to stay and nurse me?' she asked.

'I didn't do it for gain!' I said.

'The more reason for me to be in your debt,' she said. 'Things have been…difficult. And they continue to be so, but there are promises made by the Nagarseth that need honouring. We may not be able to remit the full amount promised immediately, but we can make a start.'

'Thank you,' was all I could think of to say.

She waved if off. 'It is nothing but an investment for the future. Half our accountants come from your Baba's school.'

That much was true.

'I'm sorry you have been cooped up here with me. It must be so tedious for a young girl like you.'

'I've been keeping busy,' I reassured her. 'My teacher says I need to practice my singing. But I miss my class, and Baba needed help with his new book on arithmetic.'

'I remember that you teach now,' she said. 'Why don't you test my knowledge of Ganit? It'll keep our minds active.'

'All right,' I said. 'Would you like to solve a verse from Baba's book on arithmetic?'

'Certainly,' she said affably.

'A traveller engaged in pilgrimage,' I started, 'gave half his money at Prayaga, two-ninths of the remainder at Kasi, a quarter of the residue in payment of taxes on the road, six-tenths of what was left at Gaya; there remained sixty-three nikshas with which he returned home. Tell me the amount of his original stock of money.'

She listened with evident pleasure. 'A clever riddle!' she said. It took her a minute but she worked it out.

'Would you like to try another?'

She was an intelligent woman, I had to admit. Even her voice didn't sound so very nasal any more.

The scabs over the pox scars were starting to peel. The neem-infused paste I had applied over it must have stung, but the Sethani took her treatment with her usual fortitude. But she looked at her scarred reflection with sad resignation.

'I was never pretty,' she said. 'And now these scars have ruined whatever appeal I possessed.'

She was wrong. Her personality was like a force of nature. It would take more than a few scars to dent it.

Perhaps it was the isolation, but she opened up to me in other ways. 'It is not easy to try to fill the shoes of a much-loved wife and mother. It is not easy to compete with a ghost,' she said one day. 'I compensated by managing my husband's business. At least there, I was useful.'

More than useful from what I'd heard.

'I married too late to have children of my own, and it was not easy for Rahul to accept me. I was never much good with young children. But now that he is grown, we understand each other better. For that, I am thankful.'

It touched me to hear her speak with such affection of Rahul. But it was also uncomfortable to be her confidante when she spoke of him. But since she was determined to unburden herself, I kept quiet and listened.

'It was a mistake to rush him into the betrothal with Roopmati as soon as he returned,' she said. 'It made sense from a business perspective, our families own complementary interests. And I thought if he married a local girl, it was less likely that he would go back to Java.'

So *that* was why Rahul had been betrothed in such a hurry.

'He is not happy with the engagement, though I can find no

fault with the girl,' she continued. 'But it is so difficult to retract a promise once given. Especially since the Oswals have been so good to us during our time of need.'

Rahul, then, had still not come to terms with his betrothal.

'You have known Rahul since childhood, have you not? He spent two years here in Ujjayani, didn't he?' She frowned a little. 'I really don't understand why he avoids coming here.'

He avoids coming here. The words hurt. Hurt physically, like a blow to the stomach. The floor tilted unnaturally in a slow way and I took a hasty step to gain my balance. I felt sick.

It couldn't be... I raised a trembling hand to my face.

'What is it?' the Sethani asked, rushing to me.

Beneath my fingers I felt a small raised bump.

I had the pox.

Amma came immediately. She handled it well, although she must have felt anxious.

'It isn't uncommon,' she said, 'to have a reoccurrence. Your body has been weakened with all the demands you made on it. You need rest, sleep, nurturing. With luck it will be mild and easily treated.'

The Sethani was beside herself with remorse.

'If there is one mark on her because of this, I will never forgive myself. Her face, her beautiful face! Oh, it is my fault!'

19

AMMA TOOK ME HOME IN SPITE OF THE SETHANI'S insistence that I stay at the haveli until I recovered. I was glad of it. It was a comfort to be home in my own bed. Baba and Loky kept away until the fever broke and the rashes were dry, but Moti kept me company, and I had my books. I was vain enough to weep over the scars marring my once-smooth skin, but they were far fewer than the Sethani's.

'Only a couple on your temple,' Brinda said, scanning my face carefully when she was finally allowed to visit, 'and a few on your neck and wrist. You've been spared, Leela, thank the gods. Why you had to stay and nurse that woman, I don't know!'

'She isn't that bad, really,' I said. 'And you shouldn't have come so soon.'

I was still afraid for her safety.

'Nonsense,' she said. 'Your Amma says it's safe now. You'll be back to normal in no time, you'll see.'

I had to be. I was determined to be well in time to attend the meeting Baba had been preparing for at the observatory. I had not told him of the Sethani's promise yet, for fear that she would not honour it and I would get his hopes up for nothing. Instead, I had been his sounding board for new ideas to raise funds. He would need all the support he could get.

The assembled teachers and senior students formed a crowd of white and saffron robes around Baba. It was rare for him to request the presence of the entire teaching staff, so they knew the announcement had to be important. We waited quietly for him to speak.

'We need new patrons desperately,' Baba said in a carrying voice, so all could hear. 'I have been thinking this over for some time, and I believe we must do something to raise the prestige of our school. And I have decided that we shall challenge another school to a debate.'

This led to an outbreak of murmuring amongst the crowd. It had been decades since a major debate had been held at Ujjayani. Baba raised his hand for silence.

'I have sent an invitation to the best astronomical schools in India—Nalanda and Vikramasila,' Baba said. 'It is my hope that one of them will accept. I know that they are worthy rivals, even though we have differences in opinion on several subjects.' He smiled. 'But I am confident that we can argue successfully against them.'

'What if we lose?' Kumarilla Mishra asked. 'Nalanda has lately acquired a reputation of unfair tactics.'

'I have heard this as well,' Baba said, 'but that is a risk we must take. Our largest donors are in difficulties. We are, unfortunately, not their first priority. The king is obliged to spend the treasury on maintaining the army in fear of the threat from Ghori. How is the next generation to be educated if all the schools close down?'

The murmuring this time hummed with positivity. He had them convinced. Baba had always been a good orator.

'I will start to prepare our best acharyas for the contest,' Kumarilla Mishra said. 'The Phalit section will not let you down.'

There was a buzz of excited chatter as the assembly disbanded.

Mahendra would be picked to represent the school, for sure. But what about me? I was out of practice, it was true. I had missed many classes in the month I had been sick. I flicked my braid forward to cover the pox scars on the side of my neck. But who was I fooling? Even if I were fully prepared they would never pick a girl to represent the school.

I found a quiet corner on the southern terrace of the observatory and sat down to practise my much-neglected Chinese calligraphy. I had missed many classes with my new teacher because of my illness. As I wrote, a tall shadow fell over my palm leaf.

'Why are you so intent on learning this language?' Mahendra asked.

I looked up from the neat characters I had painted. I was getting quite good at it. It was not only because of the connection with Rahul that I valued the language, but I could not deny that that formed part of my interest.

'I don't know,' I said. 'I enjoy learning how people from other lands think. What they value, honour and consider important. It's fascinating.'

'They're foreigners,' Mahendra said. 'What does it matter what they think?'

'You say that because you haven't read their texts,' I responded, surprised at his easy dismissal. 'I have translated astronomical treatises for Baba, as well as many Buddhist works for the library. There is some difference in their interpretation of the scriptures, but their reasoning is sound, and the language, poetic and beautiful.'

'Those are naastik texts,' Mahendra said. 'You should not be reading such atheist doctrines.'

I fumed at his authoritative tone. Who was *he* to tell me

what to study? Jain and Buddhist texts were freely available in our library. Many of their basic subjects were common to all traditions and written in Sanskrit, the common language of the educated. Baba said it didn't make sense to separate books according to the faith of their authors.

'It is not for you to say what I should be reading,' I retorted sharply. 'I believe I can decide that quite well for myself.'

He flushed. 'I didn't mean to tell you what to do, Leela,' he said. 'I just wonder why you are so interested in foreign texts.'

'You didn't complain when I showed you the translation of the star catalogues,' I pointed out.

'They confirmed our observations...' he said.

'...so they're not useless after all,' I finished. 'Now if you'll excuse me, I have a language lesson with a foreign barbarian!'

He had the grace to look a little shamefaced as I left. He did respect my new Chinese teacher, who, with his simplicity and patience, had won many hearts in Ujjayani.

Things were getting worse at home. The financial difficulties were thrusting hard choices upon us.

'Not Gomati,' I cast my arms around the brown cow's neck. 'Amma, I won't let you sell her.'

'Not Gomati,' Amma said. 'But Dhanno is full grown now.'

Dhanno stood beside her mother in the cowshed, chewing placidly, unaware that she would soon be taken from the only home she'd ever known.

So far, I had told no one of the Sethani's promise of funds. What if she didn't keep her word? But with Dhanno's future at stake, I had to tell Amma.

'I know something you don't,' I said. 'The Sethani is going to send money to the observatory very soon,' I caught the free end of Amma's sari, the way I used to when I was a child. 'Please wait a while before you sell the calf?'

Some of the tension drained from Amma's eyes, but she didn't look completely convinced. 'It is not wise to keep creditors waiting,' Amma said. 'We have never done so before and we will not begin now.'

I pulled off the drop earrings and the armband that Ajji had given me and handed them to Amma. 'Then sell these,' I said.

Her lips tightened. 'You value the cow more than your Ajji's jewellery?'

'Yes, for she lives and the gold does not,' I retorted. 'Amma, it's only for a while. When the grant money arrives we can buy it back. It is mine to give, isn't it?'

She took it, only because she had believed what I had said about the Sethani's promise. When I hugged Dhanno that night, I held back tears as I remembered Ajji's soft hands lovingly pressing the band around my arm. But I would get it back. The Sethani had to send the grant money. She *had* to.

A week later we had summons from the Nagarseth. At last! The Sethani had invited Amma and me to lunch. I hoped she had done so to make good on her promise to forward funds for the school. I hurried to get dressed in the best of my shabby clothes, and spent a few delicious minutes anticipating better days. We would buy Loky a new pair of shoes, replace the brass thalis Amma had been forced to sell and get back my Ajji's jewellery.

'And they are entertaining visitors she wants you to meet,' Amma said.

'What visitors?' I asked as we hurried to the haveli.

'Someone wealthy by the look of their cattle,' Amma said, eyeing the pair of matched white bulls yoked to a richly decorated rath chariot—double domed, with silk curtains and pennants—that waited in the lane outside the haveli.

'Leela!' the Sethani embraced me warmly. The pox scars had healed completely. She examined my face closely. 'You look lovely! I'm so thankful you were spared disfigurement,' she said.

'We heard that you have company?' I asked.

'Yes, Sethani Oswal,' she swept a hand towards a richly dressed woman of middle age seated in the hall, 'and Roopmati, my daughter-in-law to be, have been on a pilgrimage to the Jain tirthas and break journey here before proceeding home.'

Rahul's fiancée. I remembered her face from the portrait I had seen once, months ago. If seeing the portrait had been a jolt, seeing her in person was much worse. I clasped my hands together tightly. Yes, it was her.

I knew she would be beautiful; she didn't disappoint. She was slender and small, with flawless skin and arch eyes. Even her eyebrows looked perfectly painted. How did one achieve that? Her hair must have taken two maids five hours to arrange, and her dress, a master weaver half a year to craft.

'We're very glad to meet you,' Amma said. 'Rahul is like a son to me, and I wish you both happiness together.'

Roopmati arched an eyebrow at Amma before murmuring her thanks. Did she think it presumptuous on Amma's part to speak of Rahul as a son?

'You girls probably have much to chat about,' the Sethani said brightly. 'Leela can tell you about Rahul when he was younger. They were classmates, you see!'

Roopmati patted a seat close to her, gesturing me to sit there. 'You're the tutor's daughter we were just hearing about,' she said, her manner openly condescending. The sight of my scars and shabby dress disgusted her, I could tell.

'Yes,' I acknowledged. 'How were your travels? Did you see much of interest?'

'Temples, mountains, temples on mountains,' she said dismissively. 'Lots of fasting and praying and travelling. We had no chance to shop for anything decent, or meet anyone interesting.'

'I have heard so much about the temples at Palitana, Girnar and Arbuda,' I said. 'If I had the means to visit them, I would.'

She stared at me. 'They're Jain temples. Why would a Brahmin bother going there?'

'Oh, I've heard they are beautiful,' I said. 'Anyone can appreciate that.'

The places they had visited were extraordinary—three of the five holy mountain peaks of Jainism, covered in rich foliage, crystal lakes and countless exquisitely carved temples.

'Roopmati is fasting for Rahul's good health today,' Roopmati's mother said, suddenly changing the subject. 'Isn't that sweet?'

Roopmati smiled cloyingly at the Sethani. 'It is my duty, after all.'

My throat tightened with envy and emotion. What I would give to have the things she took for granted. And if Amma so much as glanced at me she would catch me visibly upset. I had to get away to calm myself.

'Excuse me a minute,' I said hurriedly. 'I dropped an anklet in the courtyard, I think.' It was a lie, of course, but I didn't care who I convinced. 'Pardon me while I go look for it.'

'Wait, I can send someone to look for you...' the Sethani began, but I had rushed away before she could finish.

Alone in the courtyard, I tried to stop trembling. I had to get my composure back. But it was unbearable! She was the luckiest woman alive, and I, the most wretched. I could not look at her, talk to her, without feeling my misfortune bearing down upon me.

I squared my shoulders and berated myself mentally. How foolish I was being! Baba needed the grant money, and I had to make sure I was there to remind the Sethani of her promise, whatever it cost me.

'I thought that was you!'

The happy voice sounded familiar. Bittan was standing next to me, holding a large basket of flowers.

'Oh, you surprised me!' I said, wiping away my tears on the back of my hand. I seemed to run into her everywhere.

'Are you all right?' she asked, looking concerned.

'My anklet...' I said. 'I thought I dropped it here.'

She raised my worn sari with one hand and said in surprise, 'But they're both on your feet.'

No fool, this one, I thought wryly.

'Why, you're right, Bittan,' I said. 'I was mistaken.'

'Did you see the fine young lady upstairs?' she asked in a hushed tone.

'Yes, I did,' I said. 'She is a very lucky girl.'

'Empty up there, that one,' she said, tapping her temple. 'She gave me the wrong change.'

'She did?' I asked, surprised. Maybe the rich didn't care about the change.

Bittan pulled me into a hallway, talking fast and low. 'She cheated on her fast too. Asked me to smuggle in sweet cakes with her flowers. And she can't even write. How is it possible of someone that rich? Even I can write...a little.'

I was shocked at the disclosure. 'She really can't write?'

'They ordered flowers to offer at the Jain temple. My husband and I,' she blushed prettily, 'our flower business is prospering, thanks be to the gods. But you should see the order she wrote for me. Shocking it was, full of mistakes and misspellings. And then she shortchanged me by two nishkas.'

'Oh no!' I said. I remembered the portrait they had sent for Rahul in Bharuch; Roopmati with her hand resting confidently on a book. If the vegetable vendor's daughter was telling the truth—and she had no reason to do otherwise—then they had lied about Roopmati's education! Unless the Sethani knew of it, and had disregarded it? No, I could no longer believe that of her. How could Rahul be happy with someone who had no learning whatsoever?

They couldn't hope to fool them long, but by then the wedding would be final. What an outrageous, underhanded trick. Having met Roopmati, I did not doubt her part in it, and my heart ached for Rahul. I didn't care how, but something had to be done.

'Is something the matter?' Bittan asked.

'No, everything's fine,' I said. 'Only, if you trust me with the order that she'd written out, I'll try and make things right.'

'I'd trust you with anything,' she said. I smiled at the sincerity in her voice and took the order she handed me.

I looked at the uneven writing in disbelief. If you had all the wealth in the world, why would you choose to be so ignorant?

I ran up to the terrace I had fled from only moments before.

'Found your anklet?' Amma asked when I reappeared.

I nodded, my mind racing. How best to reveal the truth to the Sethani?

'I lose ten such a month,' Roopmati said airily. 'Who cares about trifles like those?'

She did not intimidate me now. I studied her face. Brinda's

sources were right, she did have bad teeth, stained red with paan juice. Mine were perfectly straight and white, thanks to Amma's ruthless extraction of every loose tooth I had ever had, and her insistence that I brush twice a day with a twig of neem.

I couldn't let Rahul be saddled with such a woman. One of the reasons the Sethani had mentioned for arranging the match was that she shared Rahul's interest in language and literature. Surely if she knew, she would reconsider their betrothal in spite of the debt they owed to the Oswals?

'Baba has been busy composing more of the arithmetic verses we solved together,' I said to the Sethani. 'Would you like to hear some?'

'Yes, I would love to,' the Sethani cried, not at all disconcerted by my abrupt change of subject, though Amma looked a little surprised. 'They were so diverting. You must hear these, Roopmati.'

I tried to think of something that the Sethani could not easily solve. Something she might need help with. She was quick at arithmetic, but what about mensuration?

'In a certain lake swarming with ruddy geese and cranes,' I began, 'the tip of a bud of lotus was seen a span above the surface of the water. Forced by the wind, it gradually advanced, and was submerged at the distance of two cubits. Compute quickly, mathematician, the depth of the water.'

The Sethani laughed delightedly. 'Excellent!' she said. 'But, oh, it has been so long since I worked with such problems... I forget how to. Roopmati, would you like to try to solve it?'

My plan had worked.

'Oh, I'm not good with numbers. I can never calculate anything,' Roopmati said sulkily.

'Oh?' The Sethani looked disappointed, and Roopmati's mother seemed a little worried.

'Oh, the flower vendor's wife is waiting for you in the courtyard,' I said. 'She says you gave her the wrong change for her order.' I brought out the order.

'Let me see that…' The Sethani took the palm leaf out of my hand.

'Did you write this, child?' she asked Roopmati.

'Yes,' Roopmati said slowly, casting a sidelong glance at her mother.

'Interesting,' I remarked. 'I've heard so much of your love of writing. Poetry and drama, in particular.'

Amma looked askance at me, shocked at my behavior.

Roopmati glanced at her mother, who took it as a cue to defend her.

'She has had the finest education,' Sethani Oswal said. A stout statement, but would it bear examination?

The Sethani's eyes had narrowed slightly.

'Refresh my memory,' the Sethani said to Roopmati's mother. 'Who was your daughter's teacher? Rahul is fluent in six languages. I distinctly remember your assurance of Roopmati's own interest in learning before we finalized the betrothal.'

There was silence.

'Her teacher…' her mother said at last, 'was Acharya Krishnadas, was it not? He is highly renowned in Anhilwara.'

'Acharya Krishnadas?' the Sethani asked, taken aback.

'Yes, of course, he is a most excellent teacher,' Roopmati gushed.

'And you have learned from him recently, these past few years?' I asked relentlessly.

She threw a poisonous glance my way. 'Of course I have,' she said, her voice filled with scorn.

Amma took my elbow and squeezed it tightly in warning.

'And here I thought that Acharya Krishnadas has been deceased these past six years,' Amma said to no one in particular. 'Well, we should leave. It seems that you have much to discuss.'

✧

The Sethani handed Amma a generous advance on the grant as we took leave of her. We had money! That, along with my exchange with Roopmati, made me a little giddy with pleasure. I kissed Dhanno on her wet brown nose when we got home. Then I ran all the way to the goldsmith's shop, jumping over a small goat, pushing through a crowd of elderly pilgrims, stopping only to buy some laddoos for Loky from the sweetmaker.

'The earrings and armband I brought last week,' I said, bursting into the goldsmith's shop. 'Please can I have them back?'

My excitement seeped away as he shook his head.

'I'm sorry,' he said. 'They were sold only yesterday. If I had known you'd be back for them I would have held on to them longer.'

He tried to lessen my distress by offering to waive his fee on other ornaments. But what could replace Ajji's earrings? I loved them ever since I was a baby, pulling on them when I played in her lap. The day she had taken them off her sagging earlobes and given them to me, I had felt as rich as a princess. Nothing could make up for the loss I felt.

20

'MAKE WAY!'

Bells jingled, warning of the approaching untouchables. People parted to avoid even their polluting shadow.

'Stay back, lady!'

I shrank back, but couldn't help smiling at a bright-eyed boy who formed part of the group. He reminded me of Loky when he was younger, but, of course, my brother was a Brahmin, and the bells the child wore marked him as the lowest in the social ladder, the value of his life lower than that of a working ox. A great pity, I thought, for he looked like a smart little boy, just like the ones I taught at the observatory. But it was strictly forbidden to touch his kind, let alone teach them.

The streets were especially crowded. It was close to Deepavali, and people thronged the seasonal fairs and markets that preceded it. All over the city, potters were busy making the clay oil lamps for the festival of lights.

We were busier than ever at the observatory. Nalanda had accepted Baba's challenge, and the debate was to be held right after the festival.

I stopped to look up as I passed the Jain temple commissioned by the Nagarseth. It was not the largest of the many splendid temples lining the ghats, but even unfinished and shrouded in scaffolding, it was the most beautiful. The sandstone it was built from had been brought all the way from the quarries of Makrana and carved by the finest sculptors in Malwa. When had they started work on it again? It looked nearly complete.

'No slacking off,' I heard a master sculptor scold an apprentice. 'There isn't much time left.'

I turned around, intrigued by the comment. 'Pardon me,' I asked the sculptor, 'but wasn't the date of completion pushed back? I though the Nagarseth was no longer funding the temple construction because of setbacks in business?'

'Oh, we're working all hours now, lady,' the sculptor replied, smiling with satisfaction. 'Don't you know? The ships came in safe after all!'

'The fleet was not lost, then?' I cried. 'The house of Nagarseth is still in business?'

'The house of Nagarseth is finished,' he said and grinned broadly. 'It's the house of Jagatseth now. The master has been given a new title by the king. Jagatseth—banker to the *world*.'

'Oh,' I breathed, relieved.

'We have orders to finish work by Deepavali. I believe he wants to perform the ceremony of consecration in thanks for the honour,' he said. 'There will be a big show, bhavati.'

I smiled a little at the 'lady'. More and more people were starting to call me bhavati, lady, instead of bala, girl.

'I'd best let you get back to work,' I said.

Jagatseth! What an honour, I thought as I walked on. The title was hereditary, so one day Rahul would inherit it. Would he be here for the ceremony at the temple? Yes, he had to be. And on Deepavali! That was only two weeks away.

At home, Amma confirmed what I had heard. 'Yes, it's true. All of it—the fleet, the new title,' she said. 'King Vindhya Varman is to formally present him with a maanpatra in Ujjayani. The whole court from Dhar will be here for the consecration of the temple, for the presentation of the title and for the debate as well. And there will be royal guests from Anhilwara and Ajmer too.'

This would be more excitement than our city had seen for years.

'I can think of no one more deserving,' Amma continued. 'While other traders are happy to stay close and safe to the cities they know, he has built an empire with his enterprise. And he has brought more wealth to the coffers of Malwa and Anhilwara than anyone before him.'

I had stopped paying attention to what Amma was saying. My stomach clenched into a tight knot with a new realization. Rahul would be in Ujjayani, and soon. The words from his letter swirled in my head. *I love you... I will wait... I will not change...*

How much of it was still true?

Brinda came to visit. She had known as soon she heard the news that I would be dreading the thought of facing Rahul.

'We must prepare,' she told me. She was almost as excited as I was since most of the noblemen of the court, the Kanwar included, would probably attend the ceremony. 'We have to look as fine as all the girls from Dhar.'

'But I have nothing suitable to wear,' I wailed.

'You will,' said Brinda, confident. 'We have a couple of weeks, don't we? Believe me, Roopmati will not be able to hold a candle to you when I'm done.'

Brinda's maid advanced upon me, armed with a twist of thread pulled taut between her hands. I viewed her with trepidation.

'It won't hurt?' I asked.

'Not a bit,' she said.

It was a bald-faced lie. By the time she had finished shaping my eyebrows my face felt like it had been stung by a thousand ants.

'Look in the mirror,' Brinda said. 'Was it not worthwhile?'

I was right to trust Brinda. Thankfully, my eyebrows had not been shaped into the pencil-thin lines that Roopmati favoured. Instead she had tidied the natural arch in a way that emphasized my eyes. I looked...pretty.

'Now for the arms,' she said.

'What about my arms?' I asked, alarmed.

The warm honey and lemon mixture felt soothing against my skin until the maid pressed a strip of clean cotton firmly down upon it, and ripped the hair off my arm.

'Stop howling,' Brinda said bracingly. 'Honestly, you're such a baby.'

I tried to cooperate, I did. And I had a newfound respect for the bravery needed of people like Roopmati to look beautiful every day.

'Clothes,' said Brinda after my torture was complete. 'This one, I think.'

The skirt was a turquoise blue with delicate lotus blossoms woven into it with sparkling silver thread. It caught the light as Brinda shook out its silken folds and held it up for me to see. The scarf and the blouse were shades of the same blue.

'I couldn't,' I said nervously. It was scrumptious, but the low-cut style of the blouse made me uncomfortable.

'The scarf covers you up, see?' Brinda said, understanding my unease. 'Unless you *let* it slip...'

Roopmati had worn something in the same style, hadn't she?

'Perhaps I will,' I said, feeling braver.

'Good,' she said. 'Just promise me you won't get ink under your nails again after my poor maid spent all morning removing them. It will look awful with the henna.'

'How am I supposed to write then?' I asked. 'We have so much work to do before the debate.'

'Who cares about the debate?' Brinda said. 'Rahul's coming! And the Nagarseth can take care of all the needs of your school now.'

'But the reputation of our school, our city and our land is on the line,' I said. 'There's so much at stake.'

'Well, you can look lovely as you watch them fight it out,' said Brinda. 'If Rahul doesn't appreciate your beauty, I guarantee you that Mahendra will.'

I made a face. 'Why did you have to mention him?'

'It's wise to keep an open mind, my love,' Brinda replied with a sage smile. 'Just in case.'

'Bhavati bhiksha dehi!'

A voice called from outside the door, begging me, the lady, to offer alms. I picked up a pot of cooked rice from the kitchen and opened the gate.

A group of monks stood outside, their eyes modestly averted. Barefoot, clad in white and carrying only a fan of peacock feathers to sweep away insects from their path, and so keep them safe from injury. Some of them wore a white cloth mask over their mouth and nose, so they might avoid harming the smallest of creatures in the air with their breath.

They were Jain monks. There were many more of them on the streets recently, knocking on the door to ask for daily alms; they had all gathered to attend the consecration of the new temple.

The monks moved on. One of them stooped to leave a few grains of rice by an anthill. How gentle they were, I thought, and felt blessed to have given them alms, even though they were not of my faith.

The monks were not the only recent arrivals in the city. There was also a sudden influx of nobles and rich merchants, who wanted to socialize at the ceremony, as well as the poor, who knew that the new Jagatseth would certainly donate generous alms at the ceremony.

And then there was the group of haughty scholars from the city of Nalanda who had come to Ujjayani for the debate between the two schools. They were boarded at the guest house next to the observatory, and gave me disapproving looks every time they glimpsed me at the school.

I dressed modestly, as always, but since Brinda and her maid had taken over my hairdressing, I was more conspicuous than before. The monks from Nalanda clearly thought I had no business teaching or learning in the company of men. I did my best to avoid them, even missing the mock debate held between them and the Ganit section of the observatory that morning even though I was sorely tempted to attend it.

One person at the school clearly appreciated my new look though.

'I know you don't accept offerings,' Mahendra said glibly, 'but such loveliness cannot go without homage.'

I made no move to take the lotus he offered me.

'No?' Mahendra said.

'No,' I replied firmly. 'Can I ask what you think of the competition? I heard there was a practice debate this morning. How well matched are the schools?'

'The Acharya demolished all their arguments.' He smiled smugly. 'We may be a small school compared to theirs, but the quality of our scholars is far superior. And well they know it too.'

✧

Finally, the guests of honour, the Nagarseth, who had been away on business again, his extended family, and the royal party all arrived in town. Baba brought the news as well as an invitation to a mango feast at the Nagarseth's orchard the next day. Only a few people had been invited, and our family was one of them.

'The Sethani insisted we bring Leela,' Baba said. 'She is very grateful to her for her care when she was sick with the smallpox.'

Rahul would certainly be there at the mango feast, surrounded by the beautiful people of the courts of Malwa, Anhilwara and Ajmer; and probably Roopmati as well. As far as I knew, they were still betrothed. At least, with Brinda's help, I wouldn't look completely out of place.

Amma twirled me around once I was ready, delighted to see me in the blue lotus fabric. She'd purchased new saris for me ever since the Sethani gave us money, but they were nothing compared to this shimmering, exquisite silk.

I felt breathless with anticipation, as if I had been running for miles. The moment I had been anticipating and dreading at the same time, was finally here—I would be meeting Rahul.

The entrance to the mango orchard was crowded. Rows of rath carriages with tall domes, silk drapes and beautifully decorated, perfectly matched white oxen, were lined in the wide avenue before it. We had walked, of course. The Nagarseth welcomed us warmly, touching Baba's feet and asking for his blessings. Even though they were roughly the same age, Baba had been his teacher once. I was glad to see the Sethani looking well. Her pox scars had almost faded; she wore them proudly, not trying to cover them up with a veil, nor hiding her face in a corner.

She clasped my hands in both of hers. 'Leela, it is good to

see you!' I was glad to see her too, though I scanned the crowd warily. No Rahul yet. Perhaps he had not come after all. Still, every nerve in my body was tense.

I tried to divert myself by studying the lavish decorations. Carpets had been laid out and low tables set up where the guests would be feasting on mangos carefully selected this morning by the head gardener. So many varieties—langra, dasheri, chausa— some from this very orchard, some brought from other regions just for the feast.

'When do we eat?' Loky said, hungry as usual. The mangos were making his mouth water.

'Soon,' I said. 'But you have to behave, Loky, remember the last time you met the prince?'

The royal courtiers surrounding us were dressed very elegantly. My pretty blue skirt, that I had thought was rich and fine, seemed commonplace in this assembly. Were these the people whose company Rahul enjoyed now? Where was Roopmati?

The Sethani solved that mystery.

'You are acquainted with Roopmati already, are you not?' she said, gesturing me towards Roopmati. And there she was, looking stunning in pale pink, rose-coloured rubies glimmering at her neck.

She stared at me for a moment. 'Well, you've improved since the last time we met,' she said finally.

Was I supposed to be grateful for such an observation?

'Ah, the light of Ujjayani!'

A familiar voice. Prince Subhrata Varman had not changed much physically, but his manner was more self-assured. Alongside him was another familiar face—Rashid Al-Hamdani.

'Your majesty!' I folded my hands in greeting to the prince. Then I turned to Rashid and smiled warmly. I had not seen him since the day Rahul wrestled Bhimdev in Bharuch. 'And you, sir,

I believe, still owe me a book!"

He did not look much changed. 'I have been remiss,' he replied, contrite. 'Accept my humble apologies. It will soon be arranged!'

'This lovely grove was missing its Shakuntala until you arrived,' the prince said. 'The light of Ujjayani still, Rashid? I think we have to revise that statement.'

'Assuredly!' said Rashid. 'The region illuminated by her virtues has vastly expanded.'

I smiled under the scrutiny, amused by their manner, but a little flustered by the compliment too. Prince Subhrata's comment did not make me furious like the bold stares of Bholo Bhima, but it was still uncomfortable to be scrutinized by royalty. Where was Brinda? She had promised to rescue me if I found myself in an awkward situation. Here I was, caught between the unlikely trio of Roopmati, Prince Subhrata and Rashid.

But Brinda was on the other side of the orchard, chatting animatedly with a girl I took to be the Kanwar's last single sister, and the Kanwar himself. No, I was mistaken, it was the Kanwar's younger brother. He had grown to resemble the Kanwar very closely, but still had his open, friendly stance. The Kanwar himself towered behind the two, watching Brinda with shy adoration. No, there was no possibility of help from her.

'You are too kind,' I murmured, blushing. 'I must go find my brother. I promised Amma I would keep an eye on him.'

'You *are* too kind,' said Roopmati to the prince, clearly annoyed at the attention I had received from royalty.

'You dispute my assessment and Rashid's! We need another opinion, I think,' cried the prince. 'Wait, here is just the man we need!' he exclaimed, looking behind me. 'Didn't we say, my boy, that in a few years she would be the light of the country?'

Roopmati's face had composed itself into a coy smile, and in a flash, I realized who the prince was talking to—Rahul. He must be right behind me. A hot flush crept up my neck and spread across my face, but I did not turn around. I mumbled an excuse, and without turning around, brushed right past the prince and walked quickly into the crowd. A sob caught in my throat. At the edge of the clearing, where the crowd thinned, I broke into a run. I had to get away.

✧

The mango orchard was endless. I ran further and further away from the sounds of the feast. When the tall stately mango trees started to disappear and the thorny scrub trees took over, I slowed down and stopped, leaning against the trunk of a tree to catch my breath.

'Leela!' It was Loky, buzzing after me, like a flea following a dog. 'Where are you going? Don't you want to meet Rahul? He's become as tall as a tree and as strong as a tiger!'

I glared at him. 'No, I do *not* wish to meet Rahul. Now go back and leave me alone.'

Loky stared at me. 'You're acting strange.'

'Go away,' I said through gritted teeth.

'*No*,' he was adamant.

'Loky, I don't...' I began.

'Help!'

I stopped. The voice was faint and far off, but we had both heard it.

'What was that?' Loky asked.

I was glad for the distraction.

'It's coming from there...' I hurried to the edge of the woods, listening carefully. There it was again; it had a strange echoing quality, as if it was coming from underneath the ground. I ran toward to the sound but suddenly I gasped and stopped. The ground fell away before me. I had nearly fallen into a hole. An open well, unmarked, with no wall around it. And someone was down there.

I sat at the edge of the well and peered into the darkness. I could see a man clinging to something two feet below the edge. By his dress he looked like a low caste, an untouchable.

'There's a man down in the hole,' Loky cried, as he caught up with me, panting.

My mind raced. There was no time to get help.

'Stay back,' I said, pulling off my scarf, and doubling it for strength.

Loky got on his hands and knees for a better look.

'Here!'

I threw one end of my scarf into the well. The man grabbed it tightly with one hand, his feet kicking against the yawning abyss. As I started to pull, the delicate fabric began to rip, and he slid back. 'No!' I cried out.

Think, I said to myself. If I lay down and leant into the opening, I could just about reach him. But I could never pull him out, even if Loky helped.

He began to slide down again. Whatever he was clinging to would not hold for long. He will die while I stand here pondering, I thought. I threw myself on the ground, ankles wrapped around the roots of a sturdy shrub, and reached out for the man's arm with both hands. And he an unknown man and an untouchable!

The weight of the man made my muscles scream. 'Loky, get help,' I yelled as soon as I got a firm grip on the man's arm.

But who, in that glittering assembly, would help the man? And not reveal my own role in the rescue?

'Loky, wait! Get Rahul.'

'But I thought you didn't want to see him...'

'Tell him I need help. Tell no one else!' I warned. 'And hurry!'

The man in the well had terror written all over his face. His palms, slippery with sweat, slipped a little from my grasp, and his grip tightened painfully. A rock was digging into my ribs. The root of the shrub was starting to give way, or maybe it was only my imagination.

'You will be pulled in...you should let go,' he rasped.

'No!' I ordered him. 'Stay still...'

I tried to think of a way to calm him down.

'Do you have children?' I asked desperately. 'No? How about... uh, buffaloes?'

'Three,' he said in a hoarse voice, 'Three animals. Finest buffaloes you've ever seen.'

'Do they have names?' I asked.

'Big One, Little One and Fat One,' he replied.

And so we carried on our strange conversation. Where *was* Loky? Oh, why didn't I tell him to get the first person he ran into? Was that him?

Yes! Heavy footsteps indicated that help had arrived. Someone knelt beside me. 'Stay away, Loky!' I screamed. 'I don't want you to fall in.' But it wasn't Loky next to me. An arm reached into the well, grabbed the man by his other hand and hoisted him out with ease, setting him back on his feet.

It was over.

Released from my burden, I rolled on to my back, breathless from the exertion, silently thanking Saraswati, Ganesh and all the gods. When I finally lifted myself off the ground, every bone and muscle in my body ached. I dusted off my dress and wiped my brow on my sleeve before taking stock of the situation.

The untouchable man was standing before a tall stranger.

No, it wasn't a stranger.

'Are you unhurt?' Rahul asked the man. The man nodded.

'Go quickly before you are seen,' Rahul continued. 'You must speak of this to no one! Loky, lead him to the road away from the carriages.' Loky and the man hurried away, leaving us alone.

Sunlight filtered through the thorny branches of the kikar trees, dappling the ground around us. Overhead, a koel called to its mate, and something, a monkey perhaps, scampered above. But beneath the canopy of trees, the very air sang with the presence of Rahul.

Was it really Rahul, grown so different? He was a foot taller than I, his chest wide and arms muscled, his waist narrow as a panther, the jewelled sword belt clasped snug around it his only ornament. The breeze stirred the long dark hair that fell to his shoulders. What did they make him do in Dhar these past two years to change him so? The fine white wrap draped over his shoulder did nothing to hide his athletic build.

Even his face had changed—his neck broader than I remembered, his dimples shadowed with the hint of a beard. His long hair had been pulled away from his wide forehead in a warrior's knot. It had been months, years, since we had talked alone on the lamp tower, but he still had the power to scatter my wits.

'You're not a child anymore,' I finally managed to say.

'Nor are you,' he replied.

What a picture I must make—Brinda's dress covered in dust and dried grass. So much for my borrowed finery and painstaking care in preparation for this moment! When I thought about the contrast I presented to the impeccable Roopmati, I felt like dropping into that well after my scarf.

The *scarf*! I realized now that I had been standing before him without it, and his eyes had certainly skimmed the curves

I had acquired since I saw him last. A faint blush spread over my cheeks.

He must have noticed my discomfort because he stepped forward and cast his own wrap about my shoulders, letting go of the ends so they draped over me, the soft linen still warm from his touch.

'I-I had the pleasure of meeting your...of meeting Roopmati Oswal this past summer,' I stammered out, to remind myself of our true situation.

'The betrothal was annulled this week,' he said quietly, looking intently at my face. 'Both families agreed to it.'

What? The announcement shocked me into raising my eyes to his and suddenly, there was only silence and light, as if a quiet radiant flame had formed a circle around us and there was nothing else in the world. We drank each other in. It had been so, so, long.

I love you... I will wait... I will not change...

Stop, my brain warned. What are you doing?

'Leela...' he began. His eyes rested on the three pox scars below my jawbone, the single one above my eyebrow, the one at the base of my neck. 'I heard about the smallpox...'

My face burnt with embarrassment. Did he think me ugly?

'I should go,' I said, wiping my still-throbbing hand on my skirt.

'Don't be ashamed of helping him,' he said, in that deep voice I was still getting used to. 'It was the right thing to do.'

'You mistake me,' I said with dignity. He must think that I wiped my hand because I thought it unclean after clasping an untouchable's arm. 'Only, it hurts...' I flexed my fingers uncertainly.

At least I had been right in guessing that he would help pull the man to safety no matter what his caste. Who else would have done that? Not Mahendra, not the Nagarseth, perhaps not even Baba.

'Your hand...' Rahul swore as he caught sight of it, bruised purple with the force of the man's grip, marked by his long, rough fingernails.

He dropped to his knees and raised my hand to his face, turning it over to tenderly kiss the bruise, and the pox scars on my wrist. I held very still, not breathing, fighting the urge to drop my other hand on to his head. Then he stepped back and up, my hand still held in his.

I was trembling, aware that I was only inches away from him, noticing his bare chest, sprinkled lightly with hair in intriguing patterns, and his arms that were twice as thick as my own.

'Forgive me,' he said. 'I had no right...'

He dropped my hand gently, turned on his heel and walked quickly away.

I pulled his wrap tight around me, rooted to the spot. I knew in that instant that I had been fooling myself when I had thought of Mahendra as a possible groom. There would never be anyone else for me.

21

J BARELY SLEPT FOR AN HOUR THAT WHOLE NIGHT, AND then, only with Rahul's wrap pressed to my face. How different he was! And yet, he was the same Rahul—the one who didn't hesitate to help a man regardless of his caste, the one who still loved me.

The words of the drunken astronomer haunted me. Was it true, what he said?

It was hard to explain my strange disappearance into the orchard to Amma. Luckily, the excuse that Loky had taken off to play in the orchard and fallen part way down the well, and needed me to rescue him seemed plausible. As Amma dressed my bruised arm, the injury seemed glaringly disproportionate, but she did not challenge our version of events. Loky kept the secret too, mostly because of the promise he had made Rahul.

Rahul would be busy at the temple consecration, and the public almsgiving that would follow. Thousands of people would assemble for the almsgiving ceremony. Even Baba would attend, as there was a large grant to be collected for the observatory. The Nagarseth, or rather, the Jagatseth—I would have to get used to that name—had always been a generous patron of the observatory, and he would not forget it during this occasion either.

But there was still work to be done, and of course the big debate to prepare for. Many of us still made our way to the observatory as usual. Besides, it had the best view of the almsgiving ceremony, as I discovered at lunch, when we broke from classes to find the entire tower crowded with students watching the show. A large platform had been built by the river where large amounts of grain, new robes and money had been stacked for giving away.

'You missed the king!' Loky said. 'He read the maanpatra, and made a big speech besides.'

The king himself! But King Vindhya Varman, a genial old man with bad knees, couldn't hold my interest long. My eyes were fixed on Rahul. Even from this distance, my eyes picked him out instantly—a tall, handsome figure in plain white robes. It seemed he had taken over the task of presenting gifts from his fatigued father. Rahul stood centre stage, an attendant stood next to him holding a large platter. As each recipient made their way to him, he touched their feet, placed a cotton robe around their shoulders and handed them a bag of grain. The Jagatseth and the Sethani watched as he repeated this task over and over, treating monks, beggars and widows with the same respectful courtesy.

Roopmati Oswal stood by the Sethani. I might have known. She didn't act like she was no longer the future daughter-in-law of the Jagatseths. She looked perfectly coiffed and dressed, as always. I smoothed back the strands of hair that had come loose from my own messy braids. A pointless exercise, as the river breeze simply whipped the tendrils across my face again, a moment after I had tucked them in.

It was impossible not to notice the way Roopmati kept her eyes fixed on him. Rahul was intent on his task, but once he smiled at her briefly, and I felt a stab of jealousy. I looked away, irritated with myself.

It is customary to fast before the almsgiving ceremony, and as the sun rose higher and higher, I grew concerned for him. But soon, after presenting the final gifts to Baba and the head priest of the new temple, it was over.

'Who's that?' Mahendra's voice interrupted my thoughts. I had not realized that he had been watching me. He pushed back his well-oiled hair with one hand. 'Do you know him?'

'The Jagatseth's son,' I said, keeping my voice matter-of-fact. 'I think you met him in Bharuch?'

'Oh, yes, I remember,' Mahendra said. 'Half-Chinese, isn't he?'

I winced at his casual dismissal. 'Aren't you supposed to be helping the Ganit students practice for the debate?' he continued.

'Yes, I am,' I said, and made my way back into the building.

It was a relief to return home after the long hours of practice with Baba's best students. Amma needed help with the decorations for Deepavali. I busied myself with drawing a symmetrical rice-powder rangoli around the sacred tulsi tree in the centre of the courtyard. The house looked clean and festive, with its freshly limewashed walls and swept courtyard—an oasis of comforting calm.

There was a knock on the door. I looked up. We weren't expecting anyone. Amma was busy preparing for the Laxmi puja in the evening, so I dusted off my hands and opened the door.

The Sethani stood in the doorway, an attendant holding a platter covered in silk next to her. Behind her loomed Rahul.

She wrapped her arms around me.

'I have something special for you, Leela,' she said, smiling. 'I never thanked you properly for your care when I was sick. I meant to give you this at the mango feast but you left in such a hurry.'

'Come in, please,' I said. 'Amma! Look who's here to see us!'

Amma came, her arms full of the mango-leaf garlands she'd been stringing to hang at each door.

'Rahul!' she cried. 'Oh, my word! Didn't I tell you, Leela, that he would grow?'

'As tall as his father now,' the Sethani noted with satisfaction.

The Sethani chatted on, but I didn't hear what she was saying, my attention was focused painfully on the quiet presence next to her. I studied Rahul's feet with my downcast eyes. They were large but well-shaped for a man's feet. Why was he here?

'Sit by me, Leela,' the Sethani said. 'Let me see how these look on you.'

She pulled the silk cloth off the platter and lifted up a gold necklace sparkling with rubies. It was typical of her taste—heavy, ostentatious and clearly worth a fortune. She reached over to clasp it around my neck and stood back to see how it looked.

'I was right, Rahul,' she said approvingly. 'Rubies *were* the right choice. See how well it looks on her? I know you said that it was too heavy, but the girl is worth her weight in gold.'

'It looks fine,' Rahul said. 'And I wasn't saying she's not worth it. I meant the style isn't her.'

I glanced up at him briefly, but he kept his face turned away, a furrow between his eyebrows. The Sethani rolled her eyes.

'He thinks he knows your taste because you've known each other so long,' the Sethani said. 'Why, you're practically brother and sister.'

How wrong those words felt!

'No!' we chorused together, Rahul's voice low but emphatic, mine high and shrill. The Sethani looked from my face to his with her sharp eyes.

'There can only be one Loky,' Rahul said lightly, trying to cover up this sudden outburst, while I dropped my eyes and stared at the floor, thankful that Amma had gone to fetch refreshments.

'Hmm…your Amma tells me that an auspicious date for your

wedding has been found at last, and they have a suitor in mind?' the Sethani asked. 'I bought this set of ornaments as a gift for your wedding.'

The furrow between Rahul's brows deepened.

'I know nothing about that,' I protested, blushing and confused. I turned a furious questioning look at Amma as she returned with rose-scented sherbet for the guests.

'Open up!' cried a cheerful voice from the door. Mahendra. Rahul flung open the door and scowled at him.

Mahendra didn't miss a beat. 'I see you have guests.'

'This must be Mahendra,' the Sethani said. She scanned him from head to toe with appraising eyes.

'What a fine young Brahmin,' Rahul said, his neutral tone failing to hide, from me at least, the scorn in his voice. 'I believe we've met once?'

'Yes, we have,' Mahendra said. 'And I've heard much about your generous and accomplished family since.' Nothing about his Chinese blood this time—the flattery was meant for a potential patron, I suppose. 'And Bhaskara Acharya was just saying this morning that you're not only a good trader and warrior, but also thoroughly acquainted with algebra and arithmetic.'

'He is too kind,' Rahul said. 'Please excuse us, we were just leaving.'

'The Acharya wonders if the almsgiving platform may be used for the debate? It's a better venue than the observatory. If you have no objection to it being used, that is,' Mahendra said. 'More people will be able to view it and it will be cooler out in the open.'

'Of course,' Rahul said. 'It will be good to put the structure to some use. I'll make sure the site is cleaned and prepared for the debate.'

'I know you are busy with the preparations for Deepavali,'

the Sethani said to Amma, 'not to mention the debate. I will take my leave. It is always a pleasure to see you.'

As Amma walked them to the door, Loky and Moti erupted into the courtyard and pounced on Rahul with equal glee. The Sethani cried out and shrank behind me.

Their arrival won a small smile from Rahul. 'This handsome hound can't be the same puppy I knew in Bharuch! Is it?' Rahul said as Moti pranced around, all pricked ears and proud tail, trying to shower love on Rahul with every bit of his dog soul. Rahul bent down to pet him just as I knelt to try to calm Moti down. For a moment, we were at the same level and our eyes met. He drew back instantly. He was hurt and angry; if only I could reach him somehow.

I took a deep breath. 'I appreciate your mother's gift very much. But you were right about my taste...' I said, as clearly as I could, in Chinese.

Rahul looked astounded. 'You continued your lessons then?' he asked in the same language. I nodded and rose to my feet.

He stood too. I had to tilt my face up to his now, unlike before. His expression softened as he looked down at me.

'Lady!' There was a junior student of Baba's at the door. 'Come quickly! There has been a terrible sickness at the observatory. The Acharya, the entire Ganit staff, they've all been taken ill.'

'What!' Amma cried out.

'How did it happen? Speak!' Rahul ordered.

'They had taken lunch and passed around the sweets sent by the delegation from Nalanda in honour of the festival,' the student said. 'Twenty minutes later, they were all vomiting violently. The sweets were tainted.'

'Foul play,' Mahendra said bitterly. 'They knew they were outclassed. Surely it was deliberate.'

'It doesn't matter,' Amma said. 'The important thing is to restore them to health. Quick, we must bring them here. If it is what I suspect, I have some medicine that will help. Leela, boil some water with the herbs I keep in the kitchen and clear the courtyard for them.'

Amma left with the student. Rahul, Loky and Mahendra followed her. To her credit, the Sethani stayed on and lent a hand as I prepared the antidote and had the courtyard cleared. The thought of someone deliberately poisoning my Baba simply to win a debate made me furious. I wished I could crush those responsible for doing this to him. I did not know I would soon have my chance, but not in the way I had imagined.

22

'THIS IS NOT HOW I THOUGHT WE'D BE SPENDING THE festival of lights,' Amma said.

Her new sari crinkled as she leaned her head on my shoulder—Amma, who never showed any signs of weakness. 'I wish I could make them suffer for hurting Baba,' I said, and gave her a fierce hug. I was still very angry.

Amma raised her head to look at me.

'I know, I know,' I said even before she could begin. 'We're not them. We should not be doing the same things they have done. Also, I have oil on my hands, and it's time to check on Baba.'

I washed the mustard oil off my hands at the well in the back garden while Amma went inside. It had taken hours to place oil-soaked wicks in the hundreds of diyas, tiny oil lamps made of clay, which now lined the perimeter of the house and the courtyard in a string of lights in celebration of Deepavali. The house glowed like devalok, but there was no light in our hearts.

Baba had been too sick to even lead the prayers at the Laxmi puja. Loky took his place at the home altar, his voice steady and serious, and afterwards blessed all the members of the household in Baba's stead, Moti and the cattle included.

I followed Amma to Baba's bedside and watched her sprinkle flower petals and Ganga water from the puja thali over him. Baba managed a wan smile before closing his eyes again. I could tell he was still dizzy and nauseous, but at least he was out of danger.

'He looks better,' I whispered. 'Will he be well enough to attend the debate?'

Amma shook her head.

'They will have to forfeit,' she said. 'With care they may be well enough in a day or two, but there's little chance the other delegation will agree to postpone the date. Not after they stooped to these measures to win.'

It was clear to everyone that it was no illness, only a dirty trick by the Nalanda scholars. But it went against the rules of hospitality to accuse a guest of wrongdoing. We just had to grit our teeth and bear it.

Amma stayed by Baba's side all night, feeding him medicated water to keep him hydrated. As the diyas died out one by one, I fell asleep thinking of ways to make the corrupt, conniving scholars from Nalanda suffer.

The crowd was enormous. I swallowed as I stood before the assembly on the platform by the river. It hardly felt real, but this was no dream. Amma had sent me to make a formal apology on behalf of Baba at the assembly. So here I was, in front of what seemed like all of Ujjayani, and the king and the royal court besides.

I wore the sari I had been given for Diwali, Amma's heavy gold bracelets, as well as the flamboyant necklace from the Sethani.

'Regal,' Amma had said as she kissed my forehead before sending me off. I did not feel regal, I felt overdressed and nervous. But when I saw the smug expression on the face of the head scholar from Nalanda, cold fury made me forget everything. I looked him in the eye as I spoke.

'My father sends his apologies, your highness. He and all the Ganit scholars of Ujjayani have been afflicted with a strange illness…after tasting the sweets so kindly sent to them by the delegation from Nalanda. He asks for the assembly to be postponed by a day. According to the doctors, at least some of the scholars may be well enough by tomorrow to attend the assembly.'

The people in the audience murmured angrily. The large Nalanda delegation was seated on one side on the platform, but a small group of Phalit students and teachers were the only ones representing Ujjayani on the other side. The king was seated on a wide throne in the centre, which was layered with silk bolsters.

'We are not foolish enough to believe that it was only chance that made our scholars sick at this precise time,' the king said. 'We feel there is treachery behind this sudden illness. We believe that the delay is justified and should be granted.'

The head scholar from Nalanda turned not a hair. 'Are you accusing us of wrongdoing, your majesty?' he asked innocently. 'The king of Kannauj will not be happy to hear of scholars from Nalanda being treated this way in Malwa. If some scholars from Ujjayani are sick, surely others can take their place? We teach thousands of students at Nalanda. There is no reason for a delay.'

I fumed at his brazen denial of their treachery.

'I am sorry that the honourable Bhaskara has been taken unwell. But we must leave tomorrow, your highness,' the moderator, a highly regarded Brahmin from Varanasi, interjected. 'It would be best if we proceed as planned today. Can no other scholars be found to represent Ujjayani?'

'The observatory at Ujjayani is a small school, not a large institution like Nalanda. We do not have very many teachers,' the king said.

'Then you've no choice but to forfeit,' the Nalandan noted smugly.

'We shall do no such thing!' the king retorted. His hand went to his sword and his cheeks flushed with rage.

'Your majesty, there may yet be another solution…' The even toned interjector was Rahul.

Even now, in the middle of such conflict, he could make my heart beat faster. He wore his trademark white robes, his tanned brown skin glowing in contrast, looking as handsome as ever. But that was unimportant. What was his solution to this problem?

'Speak, Rahul Jagatseth,' the king said. 'I will listen to your counsel.'

'Let us open the debate to all citizens of Ujjayani,' Rahul said. 'There are many learned people in the city. I am sure new champions may be found.'

The king considered before replying. 'I am tempted to expel these two-faced scholars and all the rajdoots of Kannauj.' He looked over the assembly. 'But you may be right—Ujjayani is the most learned city in Malwa. It might be possible to find replacements from among the citizens.'

'I must protest,' the Nalandan said. 'The challenge is between the two schools. Only a teacher of the school may represent Ujjayani.'

'How about the students?' Kumarilla Mishra asked. 'Surely we can ask our best boys to take the place of their teachers?'

Yes! I scanned the crowd looking for Baba's honour students. There was Digvijay, and Krishnakant. We could still have a chance. Rahul's voice close to me made me jump. He spoke in a low but urgent voice.

'For the love of Ujjayani, nominate yourself!'

No one else paid any attention. I realized with a start that he was speaking directly to me, and in Chinese. I was the only one who could understand him.

'*Me?*' I whispered back, also in Chinese.

'They won't allow students to participate,' he said. 'But you are a teacher. They will have to allow you.'

My heart started to race. 'I...couldn't.'

'I'm sorry,' the moderator said, consulting his rulebook. 'The rules of the debate clearly state that only a teacher may take part in the debate.'

Rahul kept talking. 'The king is angered easily, and heaven knows he has had enough provocation. He may break the alliance with Jaichand of Kannauj over this, and then who will come to our aid if the Turkis attack? He may even declare war on Kannauj. The lives of countless men can be saved if the assembly continues as planned. I know you can do this. You're the only one here who can.'

But I didn't know all the subjects, and I had had no time to prepare. I could probably hold my own on basic subjects, but not on the questions Baba had spent weeks preparing his team for. 'I don't know...I've not studied properly in months. I only teach the youngest classes and all we do is arithmetic and algebra. What if I lose?'

Rahul's eyes brimmed with confidence; confidence in my ability. 'They will begin with basic operations, followed by algebra. You know those, Leela. You know them well. Only then will they move on to trigonometry, planetary motion, eclipses, the nature of the world—you've copied more texts and commentaries on those than anyone I know. You will have retained the knowledge, I'm certain. I think it's likely that by noon some scholars will have recovered enough to take over, maybe even your Baba. Until then, you must carry on alone.'

The panic I felt subsided as I absorbed his certainty, but now I was furious at the cheating, double-crossing men that had hurt Baba. The vast crowd, the royal court, the assembled scholars that so intimidated me only minutes ago, all faded away.

'It isn't important that you win,' Rahul said, 'only that the debate is held as scheduled.'

Well, I'd always wanted a chance to prove myself. Maybe this was it. I took a steadying breath. 'If I'm to compete, Rahul Jagatseth,' I said. 'I will do it to win.'

Rahul smiled wide enough for both of us.

The king raised his hand and the whisperings of the onlookers died out. 'Does no one have a solution for this predicament?'

There was silence. Then I stepped forward.

'With your blessing, your majesty,' I said. 'I am ready to represent Ujjayani.'

There was a collective gasp from the assembly.

The king looked more puzzled than relieved. 'Stay out of this, child.'

'Your majesty,' I persisted. 'I have taught Ganit at the observatory this last year and more. I believe I fulfil the criteria required by the rules of the debate.'

The king looked astounded. 'Can this be true?' he asked no one in particular. 'How can you know Ganit, young woman? Who allowed you to teach at the observatory?'

'I've trained under Bhaskara Acharya since childhood, your majesty.'

'You are his daughter, are you not?' The king seemed to weigh the matter in his mind. 'I know the credentials of your family, but...can anyone vouch for your competence in the subject?'

'She has taught at the observatory this past year, your majesty,' Rahul said quietly. 'I can confirm that. And I was in class with her for two years, as a child, and never had the best of her.'

'Well, that is quite a testimonial!' The king, clearly, was impressed.

'But she must have the support of the delegation, not the king,' the moderator said. He looked at the small group of scholars from Ujjayani. 'Do any of the scholars from the observatory support the claim of this young woman to be your representative?'

There was silence as we waited. Not many in the Phalit section were familiar with my abilities. All they knew was that I taught the youngest classes arithmetic. Would they support my claim? Then a voice spoke up.

'I support the candidate, your majesty,' said Mahendra.

A cheer rose through the crowd at his words.

'But he is only a junior scholar,' the Nalandans protested. 'His recommendation carries no weight.'

'I second the recommendation,' said Kumarilla Mishra, much to my surprise. What did *he* know of my abilities? 'Leelavati teaches the junior classes arithmetic at the school, but her command of Ganit is unquestioned. I have heard that from Bhaskara Acharya himself. What do you say, moderator?'

'It is unusual, of course, but I will allow it,' the moderator said unexpectedly. 'In Mithala, we count the scholar Ubhaya Bharati, wife of Mandan Mishra, in our lineage of gurus. If this young woman has the training and the confidence of her peers, I have no hesitation in admitting her into the assembly.'

'Ridiculous!' the scholar from Nalanda spluttered. 'I will not stoop to disputation with a *girl*.'

'We have proclaimed our champion,' the king said firmly. 'Face her or forfeit.'

The head of the Nalandans laughed derisively. 'You have been reduced to nominating women. Very well, we are ready to face your so-called representative.'

As the moderator from Varanasi stood up for the invocation to Saraswati, the goddess of learning and patron of the arts, under whose auspices the proceedings would unfold, I bowed my head and prayed sincerely that I would uphold the honour that my city had placed in me.

✧

It had been hours. Sweat shone on the bald head of the monk from Nalanda as we waited for the response.

'The answer given by the representative from Ujjayani is correct,' the moderator from Varanasi said at last.

I could be at ease at last. Once again I had given my answer late, long after the delegation from Nalanda, but at least it was correct. It was noon and there would be a break soon. I needed it.

'Water?' offered Kumarilla Mishra. I took the copper lota and lifted it high to pour a thin stream of water into my parched throat. Handing it back to him, I contemplated the floor in miserable silence. I was trying my best, which was all I could do.

The other delegation worked as a team to solve the problems the moderator set us and took turns answering the questions, but I had to do everything by myself. My arms and legs hurt from standing at the blackboard writing figures. My fingers were covered in chalk dust. My head hurt from the fierce concentration with which I tackled the problems.

'You are doing well, child,' Kumarilla Mishra said soothingly. 'They have had three wrong answers already, while you have had none.'

'Really?' I was surprised. I had been so busy calculating my answers that I failed to realize that the responses of my opponents were not always correct. 'But they are always faster than I am.'

'There are six of them and one of you; it does not matter. But in any case, I think that is about to change.' There was a twinkle in his eyes. 'Has your Baba taught you the chakravala method?'

'Yes,' I said. The chakravala or the wheel method was the best way to tackle problems of varga prakriti, the multiplied square. 'The next session will have many of those problems,' said Kumarilla Mishra, 'and I do not think they know that technique.'

Of course! The chakravala method had been developed by Baba, and was a big improvement over the older kuttaka, or reduction method, that our competitors would likely use. Not many people outside Ujjayani knew how to use the chakravala. I could feel the tension in my body ease a little.

It was finally time for lunch. I could smell the delicious meal that had been served up by the king's special cook. Fluffy basmati rice, chapatis rolled as thin as kerchiefs, creamy lentils, crisp-fried lotus root and for dessert, rose-scented pudding topped with cardamom, honey and nuts. I tried to remember every detail of the chakravala as I ate my fill.

After lunch, as the king made a speech about the importance of peaceful debate as a means of resolving problems, I realized to my shock that the crowd had swelled to even larger proportions than what it had been in the morning. News of the treachery of the scholars from Nalanda and of the unusual candidate nominated for Ujjayani had brought many curious townspeople to the assembly. Yes, it was a holiday, being the day after Deepavali, but who knew that so many people would turn up for a subject as plain as mathematics?

I tried to put the size of the audience out of my mind as the moderator started presenting his questions again.

Kumarilla Mishra was right—this session covered varga prakriti. This time around, the scholars from Nalanda frowned in concentration while I raised my hand earlier than them. I was already ahead in accuracy, and now the time difference between our replies was shrinking as well. While they checked my method and results on the board, I could rest and prepare for the next question.

'Cheating!' the scholar from Nalanda cried after the third such answer. 'There is no way to solve this problem so quickly. This must be foul play!'

The moderator, an older man, stick-thin, with a strict but fair manner, looked intrigued. 'Through a most ingenious method, the results are correct every time, though I barely follow how you deduce it. What is this method called, young lady?'

'It is the chakravala method,' I explained. 'Baba developed it and it is not generally well known outside Ujjayani.'

'Impressive!' the moderator exclaimed. 'I rule the problem fairly solved.'

'You are going by the lady's charms, not her solutions,' muttered the head scholar from Nalanda in a low voice.

'Are you accusing me of partiality?' the moderator retorted. 'Do you dare call into question the honour of the school of Varanasi?'

'No, no,' one of the junior scholars from Nalanda hastily amended, looking shamefaced at his head's remark. 'We have no complaints.'

'Then I would advise you to finish struggling with the problem that the lady from Ujjayani has solved so elegantly,' the moderator said witheringly. 'Your time is still being accrued.'

The scholars immediately went back to the problem they had abandoned.

While they worked to finish the problem, I scanned the crowd anxiously. There was no sign of any of Baba's students or of Baba himself. The next phase of the debate would not be simple calculations but arguments and counterarguments on the nature of time, space and the cosmos.

I knew the theories taught at Ujjayani, but I knew only the very basics of the treatises that our rivals would be expounding upon, which meant that I was at a severe disadvantage in arguing against them.

The moderator announced the results for arithmetic and algebra. 'For arithmetic and algebra, I have great pleasure in announcing that the quickest, most accurate computations were by Ujjayani!'

Loud applause rang out from the crowd.

'Now we move on to the last segment—the theories of the spheres, the calculations of planetary motion and the description of the laws of the natural world.'

For the first time since the debate began I looked over to where Rahul sat. The approval in his eyes warmed my spirit. But he looked worried too. Then he spoke quietly to the moderator.

'Sir, perhaps we could have the Phalit section now instead of staying true to the original schedule? We might have a better discussion if our only representative from Ujjayani is allowed a chance to rest,' Rahul said.

'A sensible request,' the moderator agreed.

'We are ready,' Kumarilla Mishra said.

So it was decided.

I rose to leave the platform, walking off the stage to the roped-off area behind it. A part of me wanted to keep walking, running even, far away from here, where I wouldn't have to face the difficult questions that lay ahead. But I couldn't.

My head throbbed, the heavy ornaments I had on were digging into my skin. I pulled off the ruby necklace and earrings and tied them firmly in a corner of my scarf. Then I loosened the tight braids Amma had arranged that morning until my hair fell free over my shoulders. I coiled it into a knot at the nape of my neck and stuck a writing stylus through it. Ah, already I felt much better.

The sound of footsteps made me turn back to the stage. Rahul was descending the steps with an armload of books.

'Do you know their theories?' he asked, without preamble.

'No,' I said. 'Well, only a little.'

'Then start reading,' he said, putting down the stack next to me.

'Why didn't you nominate yourself?' I asked. 'You are as quick as I am.'

'No,' he shook his head. 'I used to be, but I've had my head in accounting ledgers and bills of sale for too long, and now, in a metal helmet. And I am not a qualified teacher at the observatory. You are.'

'You said they would get here,' I accused him.

'They still might,' Rahul said. 'But you have to assume they won't. Now study. You only have an hour or so.'

He walked away as if in a hurry, then stopped and turned back.

'Leela?' he said.

'Yes?'

'You shouldn't go on stage bare of ornaments.'

'It's just…they're heavy.' Had I offended him by removing the rubies his stepmother bought me?

'I know. But perhaps you'll wear these?' he pulled something from a small breast pocket in his tunic and dropped it on my lap. It look me a moment to realize that they were Ajji's drop earrings! How had he found them?

'Rahul…' I said, my voice catching in my throat. But he had already hurried away.

I hooked them on, feeling my strength return at the familiar weight on my ears, and bent over the stack with renewed focus.

But there was so much to catch up with that I had barely managed to glance through the material before it was time to go back.

'What is the nature of the world?' the moderator asked. I scanned the assembled crowd for Rahul, but there was no sign of him. We had reached the part of the debate where the reaction of the audience, as well as the judgement of the moderator, would determine the victor. I did not know the material well, but at least I had the advantage of a home crowd, but only if the people of Ujjayani were willing to support the arguments of a young girl over that of a male scholar.

'The world is enclosed in a cosmic egg with the Earth at its centre. The Earth is a flat disc, fixed, firm and still. It is supported from below by the cosmic serpent—time. At the centre of the Earth lies Mount Meru.' The voice of the Nalanda scholar was rich and sonorous, his words poetic. Unbelievably, his descriptions were based on the Puranas—the ancient Hindu texts. What was he playing at? Astronomers from Aryabhatta to Lalla had shown that those descriptions were more fantasy than fact. Yes, the beliefs were repeated in households everywhere, and astronomers often pandered to the public about them, but *this* was a serious debate! Wouldn't Baba want to state known scientific fact, even if they went against the Puranas? But even if that would perhaps convince the moderator, the people were more familiar with the Puranic view. Would they be able to accept it?

The Nalandan continued, 'Around the central continent lies the ocean. Beyond the ocean, in concentric rings are the other seven lands and seas. The stars, asterisms and the planets, including the sun and moon, circle the world in a wheel-like motion with its axle fixed on Mount Meru, driven by Pravaha, the cosmic winds. When the sun goes behind Mount Meru it is nightfall, when it comes out, it is daytime. Below the world are the seven hells. Above the polestar, the seven heavens. So it is written in the scriptures. So it is.'

As I feared, the crowd rumbled appreciatively. Here was a subject they could follow. The worldview described was one they could imagine; it agreed with the descriptions in the Puranas, popular amongst the masses.

I listened quietly. Soon it would be my turn.

'And according to Ujjayani, what is the nature of the world?'

I took a deep breath. Just say what you know. That will be the easy part.

'The world is a sphere, not a disc,' I said. 'It supports itself. The stars, the asterisms, the constellations and the planets surround it but do not circle it. The world rotates so it appears to us that they are circling it. These assertions can be supported by direct perception, inference from observations as well as comparisons.'

There was silence. I knew the crowd wanted to support our view, but it must have seemed preposterous to them.

'This is a newfangled, discredited theory adopted from foreign sources,' the Nalandan said. 'The Arya-paksha astrologers are the only ones that follow it, and mlecchas like the Turkis. Are you sure you speak for your father and your other eminent scholars, girl? Or are you making a mistake?'

'I speak for Ujjayani,' I said firmly. 'The other scholars are in agreement with this view.'

'If you are sure, then let the cross-examination begin,' the moderator said. 'Ujjayani will ask the first question.'

'Oh,' I cleared my throat, 'Er...what supports the cosmic serpent that you say the Earth rests on?'

'The Puranas say a turtle,' he replied.

'And what supports that turtle?'

'Another turtle,' he said.

'And that turtle?' I asked.

People in the audience were starting to whisper.

'I see what you are trying to do,' the Nalandan growled in a low voice.

'If the Earth rests on a support, then that must, in turn, have a second support, and then a third. Thus you have the absurdity of an endless series of supports. If the last of these needs no support, then why not the first—the Earth itself?' I said to the moderator.

He looked like he was trying to hide a smile.

The next question would be to me. It was just as well. At least I knew how to defend our theories. I knew so little about theirs that I had no idea what question to ask him next.

'Everyone knows the world is flat,' the head scholar began. 'You just have to look down. How can you prove that it is round?'

'I know that is how it appears. But that is due to the sheer size of the sphere of the Earth. But through careful observation it can be proved,' I said.

'Continue,' the moderator said. The audience would not understand latitude and arc minutes. I would lose them if I was too technical, and he knew it.

'If you travel south and look at the night sky, familiar stars in the north vanish and new ones appear on the southern horizon. This is because of the spherical nature of the Earth,' I said. 'I you pass below the equator at Lanka, you can no longer see the Dhruva Tara—the polestar.'

'We can't verify that!' the Nalanda scholar exclaimed.

I knew one person who could have verified it. Rahul had travelled beyond Lanka, and he could confirm the observation. But he was nowhere to be seen. I would perhaps have to demonstrate the spherical nature of the Earth through diagrams and calculations. And then I would lose popularity even if the moderator awarded me the point. How could I explain it in a way so that everyone would understand?

'I have other reasons as well,' I said. 'It can be observed anywhere that when a ship appears on the horizon, the top mast appears first, then the sail, then the ship itself. As if it is rising up along a hill. This can only be explained if the Earth itself is curved, like a sphere.'

'You have seen this yourself?' the moderator asked.

'Yes, at the port of Bharuch,' I said.

'So maybe the sea does slope away at Bharuch. But you said it can be observed anywhere,' the Nalanda scholar argued.

'The sea does not slope away because water finds its own level,' I replied. 'Yes, Bharuch is the only place I have seen it myself. But many people have reported seeing this in other places—on the east coast, the west coast, the southern tip, the coast of Bengal.'

'Is there anyone here who can verify your claim?' the moderator asked.

I looked around at the assembled crowd. Malwa was a landlocked kingdom, and Ujjayani itself far inland; not many people had seen ships come into port. And there was still no Rahul.

I tried to think of another simple proof based on the observations that Baba had explained once. One had to do with the shadow of a sundial in different cities on the same day. But that was nearly as complicated as the calculations I was trying to avoid. I picked up my chalk and walked to the board.

'Then let's prove it through calculations, shall we?' I said. I began by drawing a circle for the Earth and placing Ujjayani and Lanka and Rohitaka on the prime meridian.

But then, to my surprise, a young monk from the Nalanda

side stood up.

'I can verify it,' he said. 'I was born and raised on the east coast. Indeed, when a ship appears on the horizon it is not seen all at once but first the top and then the rest. Just as the lady described.'

The head scholar of Nalanda choked back his anger.

'The next question from Ujjayani, then,' the moderator said.

I had written down a few questions I had wanted to ask before we started, but my mind went suddenly blank. How could I question the Puranas before the people of Ujjayani without offending them? Would Baba want me to? Perhaps he had the respect and standing to do it, but not I.

'The next question, please?' the moderator repeated.

As my silence lengthened there was consternation on many faces. I had to do something. I opened my mouth to speak.

'Perhaps...' a voice interjected, 'Perhaps, it is time I joined the discussion?' I turned around and here he was. Baba! Wan but alert, he was being carried in on a palanquin by four bearers.

Rahul walked beside him along with four teachers from the Ganit faculty. The crowd exploded into applause, and tears of exhaustion and relief ran down my cheeks. The reinforcement had arrived.

So that was where Rahul had gone! It would be all right now. I sighed in relief.

'We are pleased to see that you have recovered, Acharya!' the king hastened down the steps and escorted Baba to the platform personally.

'Thank you, your majesty,' Baba said, walking slowly up the steps, leaning on the king's arm. 'I am sorry for the delay, but we are now ready to enter into discussion with our esteemed colleges from Nalanda.'

Baba clasped both my hands when he reached my side.

'Are you all right, Leela?' he asked worriedly.

'Am *I* all right?' I shook my head and laughed. 'I was not the one almost poisoned to death. Are *you* feeling better?'

'Well enough to bury these charlatans,' Baba said grimly.

I rose to leave as Baba and his students settled down at the podium.

'Where do you think you are going, child?' Baba said, leaning forward.

'You are here now...' I said.

'But we are not done yet. You are one of the best Ganit scholars of Ujjayani, and we need every one of us here today.'

Part Three

On an expedition to seize his enemy's elephants, a king marched two yojanas the first day. Say, intelligent calculator, with what increasing rate of daily march he proceeded, he reaching his foe's city, a distance of eighty yojanas, in a week?

—VERSE 124, *LEELAVATI*, BHASKARA THE TEACHER

23

So I stayed on. Relieved of sole responsibility, I only took the lead when Baba called on me, and call on me he did. I never imagined sitting by Baba's side, a Ganit scholar in my own right, having my opinions considered seriously in full view of the world. I was fatigued beyond anything I had ever experienced, but it was the proudest day of my life. And then finally, after four more hours of disputation, it was over. Ujjayani had won.

Something seemed to break within the ranks of the Nalanda scholars after Baba returned. Perhaps not all of them were happy with the way their superior had tried to sabotage the debate. When, as per custom, the opposing scholars admitted defeat and accepted Baba as their guru, many did so with humility and grace.

'It was an honour battling with you today, lady,' a quiet young monk from Nalanda said. He was the one who had verified my claim. 'I would be even more honoured to learn the excellent chakravala method you employed.'

'Baba is composing a treatise on the subject. It should be available soon,' I said. 'The method is described in it. If you wish, we can send you a copy.' I smiled at him. 'I am indebted to you for verifying my observation, even though it disadvantaged your side.'

'My only allegiance is to the truth, lady,' he said.

The king and his advisors were approaching our group, and everyone else scattered before him like river lotuses parting before a herd of fording elephants.

'Leelavati, you are my own daughter now,' the king said. 'Thank you for saving the honour of Ujjayani and Malwa.' He pulled a gold chain over his head, placed it around my neck, and then placed his hands on my head in blessing. I was overwhelmed at the respect he accorded me. And then he continued past us, and it was time for us to leave too.

'You were brilliant,' Mahendra marvelled, coming up to me and touching my arm. 'I never imagined you knew so much.'

He meant it as a compliment, but instead, it annoyed me. Was it necessary for him to be so surprised? 'I had no idea *you* knew so much either,' I responded. He *had* been the first one to support me though. 'You were brilliant too,' I added, a little grudgingly, and he smiled complacently.

I'd been scanning the crowd for Rahul and my heart jumped as my eyes found him at last. But the look on his face sent a chill through me. Why did he look so cold? It was then I realized that Mahendra's hand still rested on my arm in a faintly proprietary manner. I shrugged it off impatiently. Rahul was the only person who hadn't yet come up to congratulate me. Was he about to?

No, he averted his eyes and stayed by the royal entourage. He looked preoccupied but still, I had to thank him. But my courage seemed to have seeped into the ground. I tried to summon it back. The only reason we had won was because of his quick thinking. I *had* to thank him.

I walked up to him and tried to catch his eye again. 'You got here just in time,' I said to the back of his head. It came out rushed and breathless.

He turned. 'I didn't hear you, pardon me, Leela. It must be the noise.'

I raised my voice. 'I said, thank you for bringing Baba and the others. I could not have gone on much longer by myself.'

He dismissed it. 'It was nothing,' he said. 'You are the one to be thanked.'

'You are both to be thanked, and now you're going to spend the day thanking each other,' said Prince Subhrata, who had come up behind Rahul. 'That is what is wrong with young people nowadays; all this politeness and restraint. You should speak your heart instead. It's better for the soul.'

There was suddenly a very dangerous look on Rahul's face. 'What did you promise me, your highness?' he said, turning to the prince, his eyes flashing.

'That I shall hold my tongue,' the prince replied, looking not at all contrite. 'I am doing my best, my friend, really!' He turned to me. 'Goodbye, light of the world. You shine ever brighter. No, Rahul, there is no need to come with me. Stay here. It is a royal order.'

Rahul stood quietly beside me as the prince walked away; to leave would be to disobey a direct order. I didn't know what else to say to him, but I couldn't move from by his side. He let out a sigh. 'Here,' he said, without looking at me. 'This is the other thing I meant to give you.' I took the small silken pouch he held out. I knew from the weight of it that it held Ajji's armband.

I'd forgotten about the earrings. My throat tightened. 'Rahul,' I said. 'That is the most precious…'

'I know,' he said, cutting me short. I looked up, startled at the angry note in his voice. His eyes held the same anger and frustration I had seen a moment ago. I didn't know why, but I baulked at the face of it.

'I'd better go,' I said. 'Baba will be looking for me.'

I headed off with a purposeful air, but I could hardly see anything through a vision awash with tears.

I found Baba where I had left him, looking jubilant but weak.

The litter carriers stood beside him, ready to bear him home. They had been waiting for me.

'We should get you back home,' I told him. 'Amma will want to hear the news.'

Mahendra lifted him on to the litter and they raised him carefully off the ground. All the way home, he waved cheerily to the crowds that lined the streets. My throat now hurt from shouting my answers over the noise of the assembly, my head ached from hours of fierce concentration and my shoulders were knotted, as if the weight of the responsibility that I had carried today had been a physical burden. But I stayed beside Baba, even though I longed to run home as fast as my legs could carry me.

Our neighbourhood was in an uproar. Drums, cymbals, even pots and pans banged together greeting our arrival. Amma stood outside in the lane beside the front door, wearing the proudest smile I had ever seen on her face, and keeping all our well-wishers at bay.

'He's still sick,' she said, 'and Leela is tired. We can celebrate later, but right now they both need to rest.'

She was right. At that moment, I only wanted to sleep for a day and a night with my head in her lap.

'Leela, come here,' Amma said a few days later.

Things were almost back to normal at the observatory. Baba was on his feet and taking classes, as were the other teachers who had been ill. I was uncomfortable with all the attention I now attracted—no longer could I wander the streets lost in thought—people, known and unknown, stopped to smile and stare every time I ventured out. It was a relief to get home and shut the door against the world.

'What, Amma?' I asked absently. She smiled in a way that immediately caught my attention.

'Baba and I have something important to discuss with you,' she said. 'Do you know how many wedding proposals we have been flooded with since the assembly?' Amma couldn't stop smiling.

'No,' I said.

'So many proposals it is hardly possible to count. The best of families, the smartest and most handsome of young men. You made quite an impression that day.'

'Oh,' I said. 'But that doesn't change my chart, so what does it matter?'

'Oh, Leela, that is the best news of all,' Amma said. 'I cannot believe how auspicious the timing of this is. The stars are finally aligning for you!'

'That's hardly their usual way,' I said dryly, puzzled by her excitement.

'But they *are* aligning for you,' Amma insisted.

'What do you mean?' I asked, confused.

'Baba always knew of the likelihood of an auspicious conjunction in your seventeenth year,' Amma explained. 'But it was hard to calculate the exact time. Now he has finally managed to do so. There will be a rare conjunction of the three beneficial planets in two months time, and not just any conjunction—it is at the Bhrigu Bindu, the point Sage Bhrigu discovered, halfway between Rahu and the moon. When there is a conjunction of beneficial planets at the Bhrigu Bindu then all obstacles can be overcome, all negative effects vanquished.'

All negative effects vanquished?

'So...' I said, my head spinning with possibilities. 'There is no danger to anyone if a marriage is solemnized during the Bhrigu Bindu, whatever their chart?'

Amma nodded. 'No danger at all.'

'But Amma,' I said. 'It is two months away...'

'It's too soon, I know,' she said, wiping away a tear. 'And we haven't even selected a groom for you. Now with so many proposals flying in it's impossible to narrow down the best match...'

'So we have decided to hold a swayamvara,' Baba interrupted from the doorway.

A swayamvara? Would they really let me pick my own groom, from an assembly of bachelors, just as a royal princess was allowed to do?

Amma smiled at my incredulous expression. 'It is most unusual to have one for a Brahmin girl, but there is no real reason not to. Your Baba and I think you should pick your own match. What do you think?'

My face flushed. An impossible idea was forming in my head.

'I would like some time to think about it,' I said.

'She's being shy,' Amma told Baba, beaming. 'Oh, I have so much to do! The whole family has to travel here of course! I must plan invitations, accommodations, decorations. Two months is not a long time at all.'

I lost no time in finding Brinda. I didn't hold anything back—Baba's plan for a swayamvara at the time of the Bhrigu Bindu, the meeting with Rahul in the orchard, the ruby necklace, our conversations at the assembly.

Brinda's eyes grew wider and wider, but she waited till I finished to speak.

'You two are meant for each other,' she said at last. 'Who else would think fishing a sweeper out of a hole in the ground is romantic? I think there should be a separate caste for people like you—hopeless idealists.'

'Be serious, Brinda,' I said, pacing restlessly. 'What should I do? Amma and Baba are already picking out a list of boys to invite for the swayamvara. Is there a way Rahul can be among them?'

'All the boys your parents will invite will be overeducated Brahmins,' Brinda said matter-of-factly. 'So if *that* is the only time you can marry Rahul, these are your options; one, you could run away...'

'No,' I said. I could never do that to my family. 'What else?'

'I think it would be quite romantic,' Brinda said.

'No!' I repeated.

'Fine, then do nothing. Your families are so close that Rahul's family is sure to be invited. Even if he is only a guest at the swayamvara, you could just garland him.'

The bride at a swayamvara picked her groom by placing the wedding garland around his neck.

'But he will never come to the swayamvara if he thinks I'm marrying someone else!' I said.

'Then you must invite him yourself,' Brinda said. 'Tell him everything. He will come if he knows you plan to pick him. When you garland him your parents will be bound by your choice, according to the rules of the swayamvara. And nothing will happen to your precious groom because of the conjunction of the beneficial planets. It will be perfect.'

'You really think so?' I asked uncertainly.

'I do!' Brinda said. 'And you must go today!'

'Why?' I asked. I hadn't even had time to think it through yet.

'Rahul's leaving soon,' Brinda said. 'I found out through the Kanwar. They think that the Turkis may be getting ready to march on Anhilwara. It may not happen, but Malwa's sending a troop of cavalry there just in case. Rahul volunteered to go...'

No, he couldn't leave now, I thought, panic rising in my chest.
'When?' I asked. 'Do you know?'

'Tomorrow.'

'Then I have to go now.'

If I waited, I could miss him. Prepared or not, I had to go now.

'Now?' Brinda examined me critically from head to toe. 'First I have to do something about that ugly thing you're wearing.'

'Never mind that…' I started but stopped as she folded her arms stubbornly.

'You can't go in that crumpled, faded thing,' she said. 'Now change, or I refuse to help you.'

I sent word to Amma telling her that I was staying on at Brinda's. Amma was happy to let me. No one knew more about weddings than her, after all—she had even helped plan four of them for the Kanwar's sisters. I had not lied to Amma that I would be with Brinda until dinner. I *was*, only, we were not at her house, but in the back alley behind the Nagarseth's haveli.

'I'll wait here,' Brinda whispered, 'and warn you if anyone comes.'

I knew from the time I spent there with the Sethani that this was the best place to enter the haveli without being seen. Brinda's maid, a sturdy woman who had been the chief torturer during my beautification last week, had accompanied us. She dragged an earthen planter for me to step on so I could climb to the top of the high compound wall. It was a long drop down the other side, but I managed it. I ran for the stairs that led to the terrace on the second floor. I knew Rahul's room opened on to it. I crept up the stairs and peeped cautiously out the stairwell.

There was someone out there, alone, stripped to the waist,

lunging and striking at the empty air as if it was a shadow fighter. His movements were slow, deliberate and powerful. Only Rahul moved that gracefully. He turned around and I saw his face. He looked calm and focused, as if what he was doing was a form of meditation instead of a practice in how to pulverize an opponent. He dropped into a tight crouch then sprang into a wide stance, his arms whipping into a knife strike, muscles flexing. It was the form of fighting he had learnt in Java. Lethal, yet elegant, almost like a dance. I could have watched him all night.

But I didn't have all night. I took a deep breath and stepped out of the shadow of the stairwell.

'Rahul?'

My voice sounded small and weak. I cleared my throat anxiously.

He stopped abruptly at the sound of my voice.

'Leela? How did you get in here? Is everything all right?'

'Yes,' I said, stepping closer. 'Why do you assume there is something wrong every time you see me?'

'Because there usually is,' Rahul replied. 'Someone running you over on horseback, someone dangling down a well, rivals poisoning your father—somehow I just expect it. And why else would you be here so late at night?'

'Because I need to tell you something,' I said. 'Privately.'

'What?' he asked. I could see a pulse throb rapidly at the base of his neck. He suddenly looked very young in spite of his size.

I took a gulp of air and found I couldn't say what I had come here for.

'I wanted to thank you for finding my grandmother's jewellery,' I said instead. 'You have no idea how much it means to me.'

He inclined his head in acknowledgement of my thanks.

'It wasn't right that you had to sell them,' he said. 'I recognized them at the goldsmith's shop and purchased them with the intention of returning them to you.'

'And…I love you.' The words rushed out of my mouth before I could change my mind.

Said aloud, the words hovered in the air between us. I realized Rahul had been holding his breath only when he exhaled slowly.

'Oh,' he said.

He looked stunned. Did he not believe me? Oh, maybe he was in love with that Roopmati after all. I had made a huge mistake. Well, now it was done, so I would see it through. I remembered how straightforward he had been with me at the lamp tower. I used his words to frame my next question.

'Do you return my affection?' I asked plainly.

'Yes,' he said quietly. The frozen look on his face was starting to turn into something else. Something that made my pulse quicken.

'I hoped… I even wrote you a letter, but I do not know if you ever received it,' he said at last.

'I did,' I said.

'But you did not reply,' he said.

'I did not,' I admitted. 'It's hard to explain…'

'Is it because I'm of mixed race?' he said, with the air of someone seeking an answer to a long-pondered question.

'No!' I shook my head. 'How could you think that?'

'Then why, Leela?'

'I am a Manglik,' I could hardly believe I was saying the words, unburdening myself at last of the terrible secret I had kept from him. 'I was born under the influence of Mars—the worst possible kind. My horoscope says that anyone I marry will die within the year.'

There. I had said it. I watched him anxiously. How would he take it?

'Superstition,' he said. 'I do not believe in it.'

How easily he dismissed the thought that had tormented me for so many nights and days and years!

'But…your parents…don't they? The Sethani…'

'No,' he shook his head firmly. 'I honour her precisely because she does not believe in such things.' I was glad to hear they were close. It had not always been so, I knew. 'And even if I *did* believe it, did you really doubt that I would not take my chances with fate for the privilege of your hand?' A smile played on his lips.

He was serious. I had known he would disregard it. Still, I felt humbled.

'But Baba has found a solution. There is to be a conjunction in which the three beneficial planets—Budh, Brahaspat, Shukra—pass through the Bhrigu Bindu in two months. It is extremely rare and the only thing that can counter the position of Mars in my chart. The last one happened two hundred years ago.'

'Shh…' he said. 'This is no time for an astrology lesson.'

'Baba is inviting eligible young Brahmins to a swayamvara on that day, so I may choose a match for myself,' I continued. 'He will not think of you, but I…' I hesitated only for an instant, '…I invite you. I will be honoured if you attend my swayamvara.' It all came out in a rush. 'Will you?' I added softly.

'Yes,' Rahul said. 'Are you done?'

I nodded, letting the love shine from my face, unafraid. He held out his hand and I put mine in it, holding his gaze as he drew me slowly to him. I closed my eyes as he folded his arms around me. I could feel the taut length of his body against me, from my toes to my face. His body was damp with sweat yet he smelled clean. Someone was trembling, either him or I. He wound his fingers into my hair and I tilted my face to his.

A stone rattled on to the terrace, a warning from Brinda.

'Someone's coming!' I said, pushing him away. 'I must go.'

'Leela, wait!' he protested.

But I was already down the stairs, making for the wall where Brinda was waiting.

I could not be seen. It would ruin everything.

24

THERE WAS MUSIC EVERYWHERE EVEN THOUGH NO ONE WAS singing. Perhaps it had always been so and I had only now learnt to hear it. How strange it was to have no more secrets from Rahul. How strange to know that he knew how I felt. Now that things were sorted between us, the world felt right. Could it be possible that in two months we might be married?

I held up the new saris Amma had bought to the soft morning night. So far I had paid scant attention to my trousseau, but now I wanted to try on every last thing. What if I crossed paths with Rahul again? I chose a dark pink sari, the colour of ripe pomegranates, and braided my hair with fragrant harsingar flowers.

There was very little chance I would see him though, since Amma had arranged for the cook, the sweet-maker and the flower vendor to bring samples so they could plan the food and decorations for the wedding. I was supposed to help. As I expected, it was a tedious task.

'We'll need half a manna of fine grain as well as bearded corn,' the caterer said. 'And rice, milk and clarified butter. Seasonal vegetables too.'

'Fifty ser of besan laddoos, halwa and kheer...' the sweet-maker counted off.

Amma wrote the orders down meticulously. What did it matter? I thought dreamily. Who cared about mounds of grain

223

and bearded corn, or if the garlands were rose or marigold, or if the sweets were laddoo or kheer? If the groom was right, I was happy to have a garland of grass and weeds.

'We're home,' Baba called from the front door. 'Can we squeeze in a guest for lunch?'

'Always!' Amma said, dismissing the tradesmen. 'Leela, see to it that an extra place is set.'

I rose to go but caught my breath as I saw who Baba had brought home.

'I appreciate the invitation, but I can't stay,' Rahul was saying. 'I was just delivering some business documents for my father.'

Our eyes locked, and last night's words trembled between us.

Stay, my eyes said.

'Rahul, please thank the Sethani for returning Leela's jewellery to her,' Amma said. 'How the silly girl cried when that goldsmith sold it away! You would think a priceless ruby necklace would console her, but not our Leela.'

'It was nothing,' he said, his lips curving into a smile, and I blushed furiously. How I wished at that moment that I had tarried longer last night.

'You're sure you won't stay?' Amma asked.

He wouldn't, but his visit proved that last night wasn't a dream, that it had really happened. Was he afraid he had dreamed it as well?

'That boy needs to settle down as well,' said Amma after Rahul had left. 'But they are so picky about finding the right girl, especially after the last match was broken. It isn't right that he's wasting his time on fighting when his father needs him to take over the business and produce some heirs.'

'He's a bright boy, he'll find the right match,' Baba said. 'Just like Leela here.'

I loved Amma and Baba, but right then, I wanted to knock their heads together for their blindness.

I flew my kite that afternoon. It was three years old and yet it still worked perfectly. Somehow that didn't surprise me.

'Let me have a turn!' Loky begged.

'Not today!' I said firmly. He looked puzzled. I usually always indulged him. 'But you can make one of your own if you like. I still have extra paper.'

'Look, there's another one!' Loky cried, pointing over the rooftops.

And there it was—a bigger kite, shaped like a dragon, flying high over the town. It glided and danced playfully around my own.

'It's Rahul's,' Loky said, following the string with his eyes to the terrace of the Jagatseth's haveli. 'I'm going over there. *That's* the one I want to fly!'

I raised my face to the sun, keeping my eyes on the faraway figure of Rahul as our kites tugged together at the wind. In a while, the smaller figure of Loky joined him and a third kite soared out into the bright noon air.

✧

'Rahul sent a message for you,' Loky said. 'But what do I get for delivering it?'

'Just tell me,' I said.

His eyes rested lovingly on the sweet-maker's samples on my thali. 'Can I have a share of your sweets?' he asked.

'Yes, you can,' I said.

'Can I have it *all?*'

'Fine, you glutton. Now what's the message?' I asked.

'The old library at the observatory,' Loky said. 'During lunch tomorrow.'

'Thank you,' I said, and pushed the thali of laddoos and halwa towards him with a smile.

✧

The old library was tucked away high up in the tower of the observatory, and filled with faded, aging, tattered manuscripts. I had copied many a text within its musty walls. It was quieter here than the main library, and at lunchtime it would probably be empty. At least that was what I was hoping.

When the gong signalled the hour for lunch, I hurried upstairs. My heart was racing, and not just from the climb. I opened the heavy wooden door and walked in. It was cool and dim in the high-ceilinged room, for there were few windows, and the dry scent of old palm leaves filled the air. A pigeon cooed from somewhere high up.

There was a small knot of students in a corner at the far end of the library, bent over the low desks, scribing. And there was Rahul, waiting there by the window, just as I knew he would. My heart drummed an intricate rhythm of happiness and longing as I walked towards him.

'Leela,' he smiled into my eyes, and covered my hands with his, twining his fingers into mine.

'Rahul...' I said. If only the scribes weren't here...

'Why did you ask me to come?' I asked.

'Come sit by the window first,' he said. It was further away from the scribes, and a bookcase obstructed their view of us. I followed him and sat down on the low, wide window frame.

'I feel you should know more about my plans before you...' he hesitated, 'before you decide if you really wish to spend your life with me. Because it may not be what you had planned.'

'What plans?' I asked.

'I promised my grandfather that I would go back to see him,' he replied. 'We would have to leave in spring, take the coastal route as far as Ceylon, and then sail over the ocean to Srivijaya with the next monsoon. I cannot go back on my word to him, Leela. He is getting older and frailer each day. But perhaps you do not wish to travel so far away from your family? Will you, Leela? Will you come with me?'

I had always known that I would leave Amma and Baba someday. Every girl knew that. But so soon and so far? My youngest aunt's tearful face flashed in front of my eyes—*don't ever marry too far away from your parents, Leela*. The thought of leaving everything and everyone I know made my heart sink. And yet, that small word—'we'. How thrilling it was. *Us*. Together.

'We *will* return, won't we?' I asked.

'Yes, we will. I do not plan to live there forever. Maybe a year or two and then we will journey back. But I wanted to make sure you knew.'

'Two years?' I would miss Loky's graduation. 'That's a long time.'

'If you don't wish to come you could stay here until I return,' Rahul said, 'or I could,' he hesitated, conflicting emotions chasing each other across his face, 'I could perhaps explain to my grandfather why I can't come...'

'No!' I said. 'You have to go if you promised him.' I took a deep breath. 'I'll go with you.'

He smiled in relief. 'You may not know him, Leela, but he knows you. You'll see.'

His enthusiasm was contagious. Slowly, my panic subsided.

'And if you wish to continue to teach, there are many schools there where Ganit and Sanskrit are highly prized,' he continued.

'Scholars stop there to learn Sanskrit before making their way here to China. And you speak both now. When we come back, you can pick where you would like to live, or continue to teach here, if you so wish.'

He made it sound so easy and familiar. I smiled at the affection in his voice as he described the streets and homes and people where his grandfather lived. It was strange to me, but Rahul loved the place. With him beside me, I could grow accustomed to it too. I would follow him anywhere.

'Leela?' he asked. 'Are you listening?'

'Hmm, go on.'

'I also wanted to say that you would be under no compulsion to follow the Jain faith. My mother was raised a Buddhist and my father respected that. I will do the same.'

'Rahul?'

'Yes, Leela?'

'Why do you keep saying my name?' I said, distracted.

'Because I can,' he smiled. 'Why do you keep saying mine?'

'Did you mean what you said, about the superstition?' I asked.

'Yes,' he said. 'Not everyone believes that what the stars intend can be predicted, *if* they intend anything at all.'

'I...talked to this man once—an astrologer—who does not believe in the planets. It did seem, in a case he described to me, that the birth chart was wrong,' I said.

'And yet you want us to wait?' Rahul asked.

'It is only one case, I cannot be certain, and I can't risk your life,' I said. 'But let us not talk of that...it's nearly time for my class and I still haven't had my lunch.'

'I don't hear the gong. Do you?'

I frowned. It was true, the gong hadn't gone off, but it had been a long time, I was sure of it.

'Did *you* have something to do with that?' I asked suspiciously.

'I worked something out with your brother,' Rahul said. 'He's growing very smart, that Loky. He can make time stand still.'

'But how?' I asked, but Rahul wouldn't say.

I unknotted the cloth in which my lunch was tied and spread it out between us—buttered roti, spinach and cheese curry and plain lentils that Amma had packed for my lunch.

'You should know that I can't cook very well,' I said, in the spirit of honesty.

'You should know that neither can I,' Rahul said equally solemnly.

I offered him some of Amma's lentils.

'I'm not hungry.' He took my hand instead and kissed it, his chin prickly against my palm. My stomach plummeted to the river below.

'Rahul!'

'Leela!' he matched my tone, smiling. He lowered my hand, though he did not let go of it. 'What shall we talk of? The Turkis?'

I remembered Brinda's words. 'You're not leaving with the troop for Anhilwara, are you? I heard you volunteered to go.'

'That friend of yours knows everything,' he said. 'The Kanwar will never be the master of his house with her around, but a happier man will never be found,' his dimples showed again. 'Except for me, of course.'

He hadn't answered the question. 'Are you going?' I asked again.

'Not yet,' he said. 'I don't care to help Bhimdev Solanki with his pointless squabbling with neighbouring kings. But if they are attacked by Ghori, it is a different matter. King Vindhya Varman has promised Queen Naikidevi that Malwa will aid Anhilwara if the Turkis attack.'

'Why?' I asked. The thought of Rahul going to war was frightening.

'Because the Turkis are different,' Rahul said. 'With their tactics, training and speed, their mounted archers who are practically raised on horseback, their disregard of the rules of war *we're* used to following. No one kingdom can resist them on their own. The clans must unite unless we want to be vanquished, one after another.'

Perhaps he would be safer on a ship. After all, what are typhoons and pirates compared to ten thousand Turkis?

'You are not a kshatriya,' I said. 'It is not your duty to fight.'

'It is every free man's duty to fight for his freedom. I have given Prince Subhrata and the king my word,' Rahul said. 'If Malwa or its allies are attacked, I will fight against the Turkis.'

'I thought Jains do not believe in killing,' I said.

'Unless it is in self-defence,' he countered.

There would be no stopping him! I forgot about the scribes and cast myself against his chest. The beat of his heart was like a steady nagara drum sounding the summons to war.

And then, finally, the gong sounded.

It turned out that Loky had dropped a small pebble into the main water clock at the observatory. The pebble blocked a hole at the bottom of the hour bowl, the one that filled with water and sank every hour. So the timekeeper never rang the gong signalling the end of lunch and it went on and on, until someone finally realized the trick.

He was only punished lightly since everyone was in a genial mood after our recent victory. And since I had time to share a meal alone with Rahul, he had a very grateful sister.

25

'So, SHALL WE INCLUDE HIM?' AMMA ASKED.

I had forgotten which boy they were considering now. Every matchmaker in town, amateur or professional, had been to our house with at least one proposal. Baba wanted to sort them down to a dozen or so. The ones that were completely unsuited I didn't even hear about. Only the fifty-odd families that Baba thought were worth considering were discussed with me and the rest of the family, which had swelled considerably from just the four of us.

For the house was filling up fast; family was pouring in from all directions as it got closer and closer to the date of the swayamvara. From Bharuch, from Bijjadi Bida, from Dhar. Cousins, uncles, aunts. And Ajji, of course! And my youngest aunt, with her twin boys who were now toddlers, fascinated by things such as Moti.

But not everyone approved of Baba's decision to hold a swayamvara, and they let him know it. 'Why not just pick a boy,' grumbled my grandfather from Bijjadi Bida—Baba's father, the patriarch of the family, who had been a famous astronomer himself, as well as Baba's guru. 'Swayamvaras are only for diplomatic solutions to royal weddings, an easy way for the king to avoid offending anyone by rejecting their suit for his daughters.'

'Our girl is no less than a princess,' Ajji said fondly, and joined happily in the selection process. Finally, a list of fifteen boys was compiled and the invitations sent. There were three boys from Baba's hometown, including Mahendra. A boy from Mithala, one from Bengal, another from Tamil Nadu, even the monk who had been with the Nalandans at the assembly; he had renounced his vows to attend the swayamvara for a chance to win my hand.

Different as they were, all my suitors had a few things in common. They were all well educated, young and handsome, though the last, of course, could not be verified for those we had not seen in person. And, most importantly, they were all Brahmins. Even the monk, who had been a new convert to Buddhism, had gone back to the customs of his Brahmin family and donned the sacred thread again. I remembered him, the quiet one who had thanked me at the end of the assembly. Everyone in the family had a favourite, although Mahendra, in general, was the best regarded.

'And you, Leela?' Ajji asked. 'Is there anyone who catches your eye?'

I shook my head.

'Not telling, eh? Is it Mahendra?'

'I'm not talking about it,' I said.

What would she think of my real choice?

Considerations of caste aside, there was no real fault with Rahul. Yet these considerations were such that no one had ever thought of a match between us. And what about Rahul's parents? Would *they* accept me as their daughter-in-law?

Even brides who do not have to flout the norms of society had cold feet before a swayamvara. And here I was, about to pick an unsuitable match in full view of my family. My feet felt like the Gangotri glacier. But I was ready.

After the day at the observatory, I had not seen Rahul alone and only fleetingly even in company. I thought I glimpsed him one day in the audience when I sang with Nishikantji and some of his other students at the temple. And he was at the new Jain temple when we brought some of our out-of-town visitors to see it, for its fame had already spread far.

Rahul was a courteous guide, showing us around the magnificent structure with obvious pride. He had good reason too; the temple was adorned with some of the most refined form of shilpikari I had ever seen. Serene meditating Tirthankaras, ford crossers into salvation, were installed in the shrines instead of the colourful deities I was used to. But I was glad to see Saraswati, the goddess of learning, the patron of the arts and my favourite, prominently featured on the temple walls. Rahul paid me no special attention when the others were looking—my youngest aunt, perhaps remembering the episode on the ship, was especially watchful. But when we chanced to be alone for a moment, we held hands briefly, fingers entangled. Much too briefly, I thought.

My emotions were in turmoil. That morning, when the large wooden trunks Amma had commissioned to pack my trousseau arrived, Moti jumped into one. Everybody laughed, but I could not stop crying. I would miss him so much, I would miss all of them. In all my seventeen years, I had never been away from Amma for more than a few days. Now, as Amma packed my new saris, the copper vessels she had bought for my kitchen, the bedspread she had painstakingly embroidered herself—with a few clumsy stitches from me—I thought of how far away I had agreed to travel with Rahul. So very far away. What if I never came back? What if something happened to Amma when I was away? What if they disowned me? Amma, who was convinced that I was going to pick Mahendra and only move down the block, was mystified.

'There, there,' she said. 'I know it is a big step, but it is a happy day, Leela, a happy day.'

Suddenly I wanted to be alone, away from my happy, unsuspecting family. Otherwise, I would break down and confess our secret plan. It would be a simple matter for them to bar Rahul from attending the swayamvara if they chose. I couldn't risk it.

'Here's the barber's wife for you now,' Amma said looking up from the packing. 'Go quickly!'

I went more gladly than usual, the barber's wife not being my favourite person, always gossiping about other people and prying for juicy tidbits. But it would be a relief to get away from the crowded house. Perhaps a good rub-down with mustard oil under the warm sun and some solitude would soothe my restless mind.

I floated in the clear river water at the private bathing ghat for women. My hair felt weightless as it spread around me. Amma had insisted that I have a pre-bridal herbal scrub every day until the wedding, so I was subjected to the application of a thick, sweet-smelling paste by the barber's wife before rinsing it off in the cool river water. Tradition, Amma had said. It was part of the wedding preparations.

I waded out of the river, my bathing slip clinging to me. The barber's wife was waiting with a warm towel. My skin still smelled faintly of the sandalwood in the scrub as I lay in the warm sun, drying off, listening to her chatter. Today she seemed more animated than usual.

'It is war for sure now, miss,' said the barber's wife.

'Why? What has happened?' I asked.

'Ghori marches against Anhilwara with his army. Queen Naikidevi has ridden out for Arbuda, where she hopes to hold them off. She has asked Malwa for assistance. Ujjayani is closest to their position, so the troops here will be sent, I'm sure. The king intends to be keep his word, he cannot let Somnath fall again. It is a matter of honour.'

I sat up, horrified. This was not good! Rahul's cavalry would be called on. He had said that he would stand with Prince Subhrata Varman if they marched against the Turkis. He could not refuse to go now.

'Are you sure of the news?' I asked

She rolled her eyes at me. 'Barbers know everything—you should know that.'

'But there have been no summons on the army in the city,' I said, grasping at straws.

'They arrived early this morning from Dhar. They're camped outside the city. You should have heard the sounds—horses, chariots, elephants! Even now the troops in Ujjayani are being gathered to march,' she said.

'All the troops?' I asked, though I knew her answer.

'All of them,' she said. 'But don't worry, the battle will be far from here. Ujjayani and Malwa are in no danger. Your wedding will go as planned.'

I stared at the cool flowing water of the river, numb with shock. I had to find Rahul. Talk him out of going. His father was the most influential merchant in the land. He didn't have to fight.

A copper lota clanged noisily down the deserted granite steps of the ghat. I looked up startled. There was a flash of white at the top of the steps, between the trees that grew at the edge of the river.

'I think I'll go and sit in the shade for a while, it's hot,' I said.

'Stay close,' the barber's wife warned. 'There are soldiers in the streets today, and they don't respect the privacy of the women's grove.'

I climbed quickly up the steps to the trees.

As my eyes adjusted to the dark shadows of the grove, I

thought I heard a neigh. Turning in its direction I spotted a brown mare with white markings—Kalyanee!

Then Rahul stepped out from behind a tree. I cried out, my hand to my lips, for he was dressed in full armour, his helmet in his hand.

He looked grim, his face drawn into tight lines.

'I'm sorry to come here,' he said, lowering his gaze. 'It isn't appropriate, I know, but I had to see you and explain.'

I had not even remembered that I was still in my damp bathing shift, my hair tumbling loose down my back, my shoulders and knees bare.

'It's all right,' I said. 'There is no one at the ghat except the barber's wife.'

He could be going to his death. How did it matter that I looked ungroomed?

He turned towards me. I twisted my hair hastily to knot it up, but he raised a hand to stop me.

'Leave it,' he said. 'Please. I want to remember you like this.'

I dropped my hair, letting it fall all over my shoulders. For a moment, the shadow of war faded from his face as he smiled at me.

'Stay,' I said. 'This is not your fight.'

'I can't,' he said. 'If not for the prince and Malwa, I must go for the men I have trained for the last two years.'

So he honoured all his loyalties except the one to me.

'If you are not back in time, I will be forced to choose one of the suitors Baba has invited to my swayamvara,' I said. Would he miss the one chance to win me?

He laughed softly. 'You think I could let that happen? I will be back, Leela. You have my promise. You must know that if there is breath in my body, I will be back. Do you trust me?'

'Yes,' I said.

He turned to go. Was he already putting me out of his thoughts? I could not just let him walk away.

'Rahul!' I cried softly.

He looked back. I ran to him, wrapping my bare arms around him, and his arms closed tight around me, the cold chain mail digging into my back beneath the curtain of my hair.

That a kiss could be so wild and sweet, I did not know.

'Someone comes,' I said, when I could breathe.

'No one,' he said, gathering me back, ignoring the insistent beats of the nagara and the blast of the conch shells.

The summons! I closed my eyes, closed my ears, and stepped on to his metal clad boots to press even closer.

One last kiss. Another.

He slackened his hold. 'I must go.'

'Wait!' I tugged off Ajji's earrings and knotted them into a corner of his scarf. I did not tell him to be careful, to be safe, to please, please, come back in time, though the words hovered on my lips. He had read them already in my eyes and my embrace.

He closed his fingers around my simple token and pressed his face to my hair one last time. Then he drew away and was gone.

Hooves clattered, fading into the distance. Alone under the silent trees, I shivered in the sunshine that could not stop the chill from seeping into my bones.

26

$\mathscr{F}$AR AWAY IN THE DISTANCE, ATOP THE HIGHEST OF THE surrounding hills, a bright red flag went up. If I narrowed my eyes to slits against the dazzling glare of the midday sun, I could just make out a horseman riding hard towards Ujjayani.

I checked the shadow on the sun clock I'd set up. The flag signal was half a yojana away from Ujjayani. If my calculations were correct, it would take the horseman between three quarters to one-and-a-half ghatika to reach Ujjayani. Could it be Rahul? Would there at least be some news of him?

'Leela?'

Amma's voice startled me—I hadn't heard her coming up the stairs to the terrace. 'You'll ruin your complexion in the hot sun, and the swayamvara not two days away!'

I had stolen away so carefully that I had thought it would take her at least a little while to find me.

'There's a rider coming in, Amma,' I said. 'He will have news of the war.'

'Let's tell your Baba,' said Amma. 'He'll go down to the marketplace and hear what the messenger has to say. You should come downstairs and eat some lunch.'

I followed her downstairs even though I was certain I could not swallow a morsel.

The preparations for the swayamvara were in full swing. Today they were building the mandap where the ceremony was to take place. It had been Loky's task, as brother of the bride, to hold steady each of the four bamboo poles in turn as my cousins stamped down the earth at the base.

After it has been secured and blessed by a priest, the structure was ready to be decorated. The flower vendor had brought a cartload of fresh flowers some already strung into long garlands, some loose. Along with him, came a familiar face, Bittan, for the flower vendor was none other than her husband. She looked glowing, heavy with child.

'We are so proud that you picked us to provide the flowers for your wedding,' she said. 'Believe me, we'll spare no effort. I'll make your wedding garlands myself.'

'I didn't know you were expecting,' I said, smiling and drawing her close. 'You shouldn't be working at a time like this.'

'I'm fine,' she said. 'And it's *your* wedding. I wouldn't miss it for the world.'

'Still,' I said. 'Don't tire yourself out!'

'I'll sit right here by you,' she said. 'Only let me help!'

'I'd like to help too,' my youngest aunt said, joining in. 'I'll string the second garland, if you show me the pattern.'

She settled in next to Bittan, among the baskets of roses, marigolds, jasmine and frangipani. They talked about Bittan's baby, the suitors and the war. But my youngest aunt continued to watch me with concern as she pierced the flower stems deftly with her needle and pulled them along the length of the string. When Bittan turned away, she laid a hand on mine.

'Leela, I have been meaning to ask—are you truly happy with this arrangement?'

She was thinking about that day on Rahul's ship.

'I am fine,' I said. 'Really.'

'I have been watching how you hang on to every word of any news of the war,' she said. 'Isn't Rahul fighting? Is there any news of him?'

I gripped my hands together so hard it hurt.

'No,' I could tell my voice sounded strained.

'Leela,' she said gently. 'If you need to talk, I am here. Better talk now, when there is still time.'

I said nothing. When I looked up, I saw that Bittan's eyes were wide with concern.

'Listen,' she said softly when my youngest aunt had left to tend her children. 'Do you remember my cousin Viru?'

'Of course,' I said. 'Did he marry his sweetheart after all?'

'Yes,' she said. 'And he is fine, I swear, nothing happened to him. It was all worth it, the tampering of the birth chart.'

Why was she telling me this?

'I always wondered why you helped me,' she said. 'And now I know, everyone knows, that you're a Manglik. It's good that you've found this mahurat to marry, but if there is someone who can't be here because of the war... What I'm saying is—don't marry the wrong man at the right time. Wait. The stars will take care of themselves.'

She held up the finished wedding garland. It was beautiful.

'Think very carefully before you place this around your suitor's neck,' she said as she handed the garland to me.

If anyone knew how I felt, it was Brinda, for the Kanwar had marched with Prince Subhrata Varman as well. I was amazed at her strength, but she was the daughter, sister, and now fiancée of a long line of kshatriya warriors. She had seen them being sent to war before, and some, for the last time.

'It isn't the first time for him, Leela,' she said. 'Twice before they have ridden to battle and returned safe and victorious each time.'

'He is barely twenty,' I said, shocked.

She shrugged matter-of-factly. 'My cousin Vijay died in battle before he was fifteen. This is what they do, Leela. It can't be helped.' But I could see the sorrow in her eyes.

'You know what I wish?' she said suddenly. 'I wish we had run away, the Kanwar and I. It is permissible for warriors to have a runaway gandharva wedding. I have waited so many years and now even you are to be married before me!'

Her rueful smile took away the sting from those words.

'Let's have a double swayamvara, then,' I teased. 'You can garland the Kanwar.'

She laughed at that.

Baba returned from the marketplace with news of the war. 'There have been heavy casualties in the cavalry,' he said. 'They rode in time to relieve the forces of Anhilwara, which were in dire need of reinforcement. They would have fallen without Malwa's help. They've stopped the Turkis at the foot of Arbuda—for now.'

My heart beat frantically, wild with fear. Rahul commanded five hundred horsemen in the cavalry.

'Do we know if,' I swallowed hard, '...if anyone we know has been hurt?'

'Prince Subhrata Varman is unharmed,' Baba said. 'But they don't have news of anyone else.'

'We'll know soon enough,' Amma sighed.

'Queen Naikidevi is leading the troops herself,' Baba said. 'Her bravery has improved morale no end. Mulraj is far too young for the task, though he is king, so it is up to her and Bhimdev Solanki.'

'When will it be over?' I asked.

'For now, the fighting continues,' Baba said. 'The Turkis have regrouped. They will not retreat so easily.'

'Will Malwa's army stay on?' I asked.

'I'm afraid so,' Baba said. 'They will stay till the end.'

'Don't move!' the barber's wife's sister said gently. I sat, still as a stone, while she bent over my upturned palm. She squeezed a thin string of dark green henna paste from a small cone, her hand moving rapidly to form intricate patterns over my skin. 'If you smudge it, the pattern will be ruined,' she reminded me. 'You must let it dry completely.'

The courtyard was full of music and loud voices, laughing and singing. In the courtyard, the men had been banished. The womenfolk had taken over, getting their palms decorated with henna, dancing to bawdy wedding songs, laughing, singing and letting their hair down.

'Do you like this style?' the woman asked.

My palms, the backs of my hands, my wrist and my arms were covered in lotus blossoms, peacocks and paisley motifs. They were beautiful.

I nodded.

'You have such elegant hands; it is a pleasure to decorate them.'

Ajji and my youngest aunt tucked my sari up around my knees so that she could decorate my feet and ankles the same way.

The cool henna tickled my feet but I didn't feel like laughing. All news from the battlefield had been bad recently.

The dholaki beat a happy rhythm and a pair of young girls, cousins from Bijjadi Bida, unrecognizably grown from the toddlers I remembered them as, danced while everyone else clapped along.

We have raised our girl with tender care
Do not make her work hard, mother-in-law
Do not make her grind the grain
With the heavy milling stone…

I had been sitting still for ages and the delicate swirls of dark green henna paste had dried to a deep brown on my skin. Ajji brushed a mixture of lime juice and oil on my hands to stop it from flaking off and to deepen the colour. Where the paste cracked, the colour—a rich, bridal red—shone through.

'I'm hot, Amma, I want to go up to the terrace,' I complained.

'No, you'll ruin your henna,' Amma said.

I got up and left anyway.

'Stop that girl! Oh never mind, someone go with her and see she doesn't smudge it. That would be such a bad omen!' Amma cried after me as I swept out of the courtyard.

'I'll go,' Brinda said and followed me out.

It was dark on the terrace. Small night lamps flickered all over Ujjayani. Below, I could see the glow from the fires where the sweet-makers had set up their kitchens outside the walls of the house. They were already preparing the wedding feast. But the light I was looking for was the one on the hilltop far away in the distance—the one that would signal an incoming messenger.

But the hills were dark.

I closed my eyes and Rahul's face floated before me. I remembered his promise—*if there is breath in my body, I will be back.*

What if he didn't come? What if he was dead? A shuddering sob shook my chest and panic coursed through my veins.

Brinda was at my elbow, with an arm around me.

'He'll come,' she said. But my doubt was reflected in her voice.

What if he did, but was too late? What if the swayamvara had already been staged and Rahul was not there?

'If he doesn't come, there will be no wedding,' I said.

Brinda said nothing, but her arm tightened around me.

And what of the disgrace to the family? To spend such lavish amounts of money, invite not one, but fifteen eligible young men, stage such an elaborate ceremony—only to be flouted openly by a disobedient daughter. Baba would be publicly humiliated. But the alternative, too, was unbearable.

'He'll come,' Brinda repeated, her voice stronger this time. Was she thinking of the Kanwar?

I wished I could share her certainty.

27

$\mathcal{F}$OUR MORE HOURS.

The guests had arrived. The suitors and their families had been welcomed. Someone pulled me to the window so I could see, through the stonework screen, all the men who had been invited. Brinda had been tasked with making sure I could identify each of them correctly. I tried to pay attention, but it was as if everyone was speaking to me through a long tunnel. Apart from Mahendra and the two boys from Bijjadi Bida that my grandfather had picked out, I couldn't tell which one was which.

'You must get dressed now, Leela,' Amma held up my wedding sari, a deep green paithani silk, spangled with gold zari along its nine yard length. I was used to light cotton saris that were half the length of a nauwari, and needed help to put it on. Amma tucked and draped until it hung in rich heavy folds down to my feet. Brinda fastened a pearl mundavalya headband around my forehead. Its red tasseled ends brushed my shoulders. At my neck, the ruby necklace glowed like fire against my skin.

Amma placed the veil over my hair. It was the same colour as my sari but the fabric was lighter, almost translucent. She squeezed my hands, like when I was little, and pushed matching rows of glass bangles over my wrist, green and gold. Brinda clasped silver anklets at my feet.

Amma kissed my forehead, her eyes misty with tears. 'I must

now go greet the guests. Stay here until the gong sounds, then Brinda and the other girls will bring you out.'

✧

'Loky, did you see a flag?' I asked.

Loky shook his head, looking at me with Baba's serious gaze. How grown-up he seemed suddenly, as if he understood. Perhaps he did.

I could not check for the flags myself so I had asked him to do it for me. Three hours left for the start of the swayamvara. Three hours twenty-three minutes till the start of the mahurat signalling the auspicious conjunction of the planets. Three hours and forty-eight minutes till the end of the conjunction. It took at least one hour for even the fastest of horsemen to ride into Ujjayani from the time the flag went up. Rahul had less than two and a half hours to get here.

I had not explained to Loky why I needed to check for the flags, but I knew he sensed something.

'You should see the clock,' Loky said. 'It is so much more complicated than the one at the observatory.'

'What clock?' I asked absent-mindedly.

'The clock Baba has set up so that the timekeeper may sound the gong for the start of the swayamvara,' Loky said. 'He can't keep checking the time every minute with all that he has to do, Amma says. So he has designed the most accurate clock in the world. We tested it at the observatory. But how would you know, you've barely been to the observatory lately.'

'What is it like?' I asked. It was a better distraction than anything else at the wedding.

'It has three water bowls floating inside each other. Their holes have been calibrated to tell the start of the swayamvara, the start of the auspicious conjunction and the end. Baba set it up himself this morning. The timekeeper is watching it without blinking,' Loky added.

I nodded, but fear was rising up in my throat again. Where *was* Rahul?

'Go check for the flag, Loky,' I begged, and he hurried away.

I tried to remain calm as I waited for him to return. Surely he was taking hours?

'There's no flag,' Loky said when he came back.

He looked uncharacteristically solemn. There was less than an hour left to the swayamvar. If there was no flag, there was no possible way Rahul would be here in time.

'Are you sure?' I said.

Brinda walked in and put a hand on Loky's shoulder.

'There is no flag,' she confirmed. 'I checked too.'

My heart stopped.

Downstairs, people laughed and talked, ate the excellent delicacies prepared by the wedding cooks, complimented each other on their fine dresses and jewellery and spared no thought for the men fighting and dying far away on the battlefield.

I heard them, but louder than that I heard the clang of sword on sword, the trumpeting of war elephants, the thunder of hooves and the cries of men dying far away at the foot of Arbuda. I saw Rahul, lifeless and still, the cold marble of the temples he died to defend rising above him.

I wanted to scream. But now was not the time. Tomorrow, I promised myself. I would cry tomorrow. Today there was a wedding to stall and my parents' honour to be saved. It was the least I could do.

But there was something I had to do first. I pulled the kite out from behind a pile of old clothes and opened the window screen. The wind caught at the paper kite and I let go of the string little by little until it soared high above the garden. Then I let go. The kite climbed into the clear blue sky, free. I watched as it climbed higher and higher till it became a speck. A part of me flew away with it. The rest still had work to do.

I turned to my brother.

'I need your help, Loky,' I said. 'We need to make time stand still.'

A gleaming copper pot stood in a place of honour on the terrace. An older man sat by it, watching it intently, almost without blinking.

'Not you again!' he said scowling at Loky. 'Your Baba has told me to not let you or that mongrel dog of yours anywhere near the clock.'

Loky had been hovering around him all morning.

'Pardon me,' I said quietly, 'Could *I* have a look?'

The old man's jaw dropped at the sight of me in all my bridal finery.

'Why certainly, lady,' he said.

I walked closer and leant over the side. It was ingenious. The large pot contained three shiny sinking bowls floating in clear water, one nested within the other. They had been perfectly calibrated and tested. Baba would even have taken into account the evaporation rate according to the heat of the day.

I lifted a hand to my neck as if to pull my hair away from the water. The pearls I had loosened from my necklace, none of them larger than a peppercorn, fell and sank into the water.

Loky had used a tiny piece of gravel to block the water clock at the observatory. He had looked at the pearls—small enough to escape notice—and said confidently that it would work. I hoped he was right.

The old man was looking at my face, not the clock. 'Thank you,' I said, smiling at him sweetly. 'I must go.'

As I walked away, a breeze picked up and a mass of unseasonable clouds floated our way, partially blocking the sun. My shoulders slumped in relief; the sun clock would not work without a shadow. They had only the water clock to go by.

'Exquisite!'

'So lovely!' my cousins exclaimed as they led me down the steps to the garden. Brinda held my arm but stayed silent.

The garden was crowded with people, all staring at me. The mandap had been set up on one side of the garden. The suitors were assembled at the other end. There was Mahendra, glowing with hope and anticipation. I felt a pang of guilt as I glanced at him. The other men were lined up next to him. When the gong went off, I would have to walk along the line and place the heavy wedding garland I held in my hands around the neck of my chosen groom.

A crack of lightning streaked across the sky, but no raindrops fell from the heavy clouds yet. People looked up and smiled, because rain at a wedding is the most auspicious sign of all. A group of men hurried into the garden and hastily started to erect the rain tents that Baba had ordered in case it did. It was just as well. In the confusion, people would not realize how much time had actually passed.

The girls next to me giggled and looked over the suitors.

I could only pick one—perhaps some of the others would be interested in one of them. Only Brinda didn't glance their way, her face as tight as my nerves.

Amma had a frown on her face. Although Baba was the famous astronomer, calculator of the motion of the planets, maker of ingenious clocks, Amma had a better sense of real time than he. She was starting to walk over towards Baba.

'Brinda…' I said under my breath but she was already gone.

I could see Amma head away from Baba and towards me.

How much time had passed?

Baba was done giving instructions to the men with the tents. He was looking worried now and was starting to look up at the rooftop from where the timekeeper was supposed to be sounding the gong. He started walking towards the stairs. I could just look at him helplessly as he strode past me and climbed up the stairs two at a time.

'NO!' Baba's anguished cry was heard by everyone.

As if on cue, a crack of thunder from the gathering clouds followed his cry.

The flower garland nearly fell from my trembling hands.

'What is it?' Amma said. 'What happened?'

Baba emerged from the door to the stairs.

'The auspicious moment has passed!' he said. 'The clock was blocked. Sabotage.'

'How?' Amma said.

'I don't know, but I *will* find out. It must be the timekeeper. He must have been bribed by my enemies. He claims that the only one who went near it was Loky.'

'Loky would never do that,' Amma cried. Then a shadow of

doubt crept up her face. 'I think...'

'Where is that boy anyway?' Baba thundered.

'Amma, no,' I said. I couldn't let Loky take the blame in my stead. 'It *may* have been me.'

'What?' Amma said turning to me in astonishment.

'I was...I was looking at the clock,' I said. 'And I think something fell into the water from my necklace. Perhaps one of the gems had come loose...'

Despair was written all over Baba's face. How badly I had let him down! I could feel my eyes tear up.

'What have you done, my child?' Baba said helplessly. 'There is no other moment when you can marry.'

'Than I shall remain unwed,' I said softly.

'She did it deliberately!' someone whispered.

'Amma, can I speak to you alone?' I begged.

'Leave us,' Amma said to the cousins and aunts who surrounded us. They left, but I could hear the murmurs that were spreading among the guests. People were whispering, shaking their heads and gesturing to one another agitatedly.

'You talk to your daughter,' Baba said grimly to Amma, 'and I will go talk to our guests.'

I always became Amma's daughter whenever I got into trouble.

'Leela, what really happened?' Amma asked.

'I was looking over the water...' I began.

'I heard what you *said*,' Amma said. There was grief and anger in her voice. 'We wanted you to have the freedom to choose for yourself. We never wanted you to feel you had to settle for someone because of your horoscope. And *this* is what you do? Did none of these fine men appeal to you? Who do you want then, Leela?'

'It doesn't matter now. The time has passed...' I said, a sob escaping me despite my best efforts to suppress it, 'and who knows if he still lives...'

'Who?' Amma said. 'Who is it?'

But I was not listening any more. I could hear something far off in the distance, over the noise of the people at the wedding, over the thunder rolling down from the clouds. This was a different sound. It was the sound of galloping hooves.

'I see a flag, I see a flag, I see a FLAG!' Loky sang from the rooftop.

The sound got louder and closer every moment. Then a neigh sounded and the gates were flung open. Outside, I could see that a brown mare with white markings waited, hot and exhausted— Kalyanee. And there was Rahul at the doorway.

He was dressed in armour and covered in dust, his face flushed from his long ride, and yet he looked pale and drawn. His left shoulder was wrapped in a clumsily-tied bandage, soaked with blood.

He was alive!

His eyes searched the gathering, which had fallen silent at his appearance, until he found me. He knew at a glance that no wedding had taken place, for the parting in my hair was bare of red sindoor powder. I could see the question in his eyes.

Too late, I said silently, I know you tried, but it's too late.

No, his eyes said, I'm here now, it'll be all right.

But I knew it wouldn't be. It would never be right again. It was much too late for that.

Everything lurched around me. A strange halo was streaking the corners of my vision. I blinked, but it would not go away. The sky was cracking into tiny fragments before my eyes and the voices around me seemed to be coming from a great distance.

I reeled, and then the world went black.

Where was I?

Someone was holding a cup to my lips. Amma.

'Drink this,' she said. 'No, don't speak. First drink. What do you expect when you don't eat anything for two days?'

Had it been a dream? I had seen Rahul… No, it had been real. I pushed the cup away. 'Is he hurt?' I asked.

Amma did not ask me who I meant. She looked at me with patient resignation. 'Even that hard fall didn't bring you to your senses then?'

I shook my head.

'In that case, ask him yourself,' she said.

'What do you mean?' I asked in confusion. Now that I had my bearings, I knew we were in Amma's treatment room. The smell of dry herbs and spices filled the air.

'You have five minutes,' Amma said in the direction of the window and closed the door quietly behind her as she left.

Rahul crossed the distance between us in two strides and knelt at my side.

He wrapped his arms around me, burying his face in the fold of my stomach as I sat up on the cot. He was bare-chested, his wound dressed in a clean bandage—Amma's work. I clung to him, overwhelmed with gratitude that he was safe.

How long had I been unconscious?

I tried to speak. 'You're safe!' I whispered. 'I thought, I was afraid that…'

He looked up at me. How tired he looked, and so changed, like he had seen the most terrible things. The war had made him different. I traced a cut on his cheek tenderly with my henna-covered fingers.

'I'm fine,' he said, 'and thankful that you are not married off. I was afraid too.'

I spread my hands helplessly. 'It is too late for us now.'

'No,' he shook his head. 'I am not leaving here without you after all this.'

'Don't you understand? The time when I could have married without fear is past.'

'I was never afraid to marry you,' he said.

'But *I* am,' I said. My stomach still knotted with fear when I thought of putting Rahul in danger again.

'It is not true what they say about the stars,' he said. 'You know it. You said it yourself. Remember the astronomer you had told me about?'

'Yes, but...'

It is one thing to know a thing in your head, and another to believe it in your heart. I was afraid. How could I wilfully endanger Rahul especially when I had nearly lost him once?

'Leela, don't let fear stand in our way,' he said. 'Please, I beg of you. What did the stars predict for all the men lost in the war? Do you know how many men I have watched die? How many I have killed?'

His voice broke and dropped to a whisper. 'And to see a friend...the bravest of friends, with the best stars in the world and everything to live for... When such a friend falls, Leela, how can anyone believe what the stars say any more?'

His tone filled me with dread.

'Subhrata?' I whispered.

He shook his head. 'Brinda must be told...' he said slowly.

'*No*,' I said, filled with horror. 'Not the Kanwar!' Brinda's face flashed before me, blushing happily as she talked about the Kanwar's youngest sister's marriage and what it meant for their future.

Rahul looked at me helplessly, powerless to deny the truth. Kanwar Randheer Singh had joined his ancestors.

'It's not fair,' I said bitterly. I had been dry-eyed these past many days, but now I could not stop the great gasping sobs from racking my ribs. 'She waited for him for so long...'

And suddenly, as I my grieved for my friend's sudden loss, a realization, clear as a temple bell, sounded in my mind.

The stars did not control us.

I took a steadying breath. 'I love you,' I said to Rahul. 'I always have. And I know there is truth in what you say. Life is too short to spend railing against our fates.'

He lifted me off my feet, his hands around my waist, and I clung to him. The solid, reassuring warmth of his body belied the desperation of our circumstances, but I still took comfort from it, if only for a moment. But there were problems still, I knew. For there were others I loved too.

'But I will not leave this house without my parents' blessing. I would rather be unwed all my life. How will you convince them to give me away? I come from fifteen generations of astronomers. You cannot make Baba think that the stars do not matter.'

'And if somehow I do?' he said. 'Will you marry me then?'

He kissed my forehead, my hair, my lips—every touch a promise.

'Yes,' I said, returning every kiss, each one a farewell. There was a sound at the door. We moved apart.

Amma walked in.

'Rahul,' she said. 'Leela's father and grandfather have asked you to come before them.'

28

J WAS NOT ALONE FOR LONG.

Brinda slipped into the room soon after Amma left with Rahul. I stared at her, choked with despair.

'Come! Don't you want to hear what they say to him?' Brinda asked, pulling on my hand.

I clasped both her hands in mine, tears streaming down from my eyes. She stared at me, her face changing as she read mine.

'Brinda…' I managed to sob.

A strange, still look had settled on her face, a look more anguished than a roomful of keening mourners.

'Rahul's waiting,' she said finally, her voice so faint I could barely hear it, 'and I *will* see you married. There will be time for…other news later.'

Did she not understand? Of course she did. And yet she thought of *me*. To speak of death now would be to curse my wedding, if there was one at all, with ill omens. How could she be so brave? I couldn't tear my eyes away from her face. But she clutched my hand in an iron grip and pulled me along through the verandah to a room next to Baba's study.

'Listen,' she ordered, opening the door connecting to the study just a crack. I could see Baba, my grandfather, two of my uncles, Ajji and Amma. I was sure there were other people listening at the other door.

'Rahul Jagatseth,' Baba said. 'What do you have to say for yourself?'

'Acharya, I intended to be here for the swayamvara...' Rahul began.

'Yet we did not invite you,' Baba said sternly. 'And the swayamvara is over. The auspicious time when my daughter could have wed has passed.'

'Any time is auspicious for a marriage to a lady such as your daughter,' Rahul said.

'How can you speak of marriage?' Baba thundered. 'How can you ask for the hand of a Brahmin girl?'

The other men nodded in agreement, humming like a swarm of bees around a jasmine shrub.

'I have been your student, Acharya, as has my father. You know us well. In what way are we inferior to any Brahmin?' Rahul asked.

'You speak of your father!' Baba said. 'And yet your parents never came to us with a proposal. Do they even know what you planned? Did you even consider asking for their blessings before presuming to press your suit? What would they think of the danger to your life if you married a Manglik?'

Rahul held his gaze steadily. 'The risk is only to myself and it is a risk I choose to take.'

'Not merely to you,' Baba said icily. 'My daughter will be at risk of becoming a widow. That is not what I would wish for her.'

'Acharya, there is evidence that all predictions based on the birth chart do not come to pass,' Rahul said quietly. 'An excellent astrologer of my acquaintance knows of a case when a marriage was entered into despite the girl's Mangal yog. The prediction did not materialize.'

Instantly there were loud protests from all the astrologers in the room.

'And who is this astrologer?' Baba asked.

'I am not at liberty to say,' Rahul said.

'Then can you name the couple?' Baba asked.

'No, Acharya,' Rahul said.

'It is that charlatan from across the river, isn't it?' said one of my uncles. 'He's just a drunken mess.'

'My source is wise, accomplished and sober,' Rahul said.

'But since you cannot name him, I cannot credit anything you say,' Baba said.

I bit my lip. Even if Viru's story convinced Baba, the others would dismiss it outright.

Rahul was looking at the door. 'As for my parents—my father is away, otherwise I would certainly ask for his blessings. And my mother...' he hesitated, 'my mother...'

'...is here,' said the Sethani, appearing at the door of Baba's study.

Who had sent for her? Amma? The Sethani went to Rahul, and he bent to touch her feet. She laid her hand on his head, blessing him, and raised him up.

'Is the injury serious?' she asked, turning towards Amma.

'No,' Amma said. 'And I have dressed it. It will heal.'

'I am thankful you have returned safely, my son,' she said.

'Where is Baba?' Rahul asked.

'Away,' she said. 'He will not return until tomorrow. What has happened here?'

'Your son,' Amma said heavily, 'asks for the hand of my daughter.'

The Sethani showed no surprise. 'And what do you say?' she asked.

'What do I say? What is there to say!' Baba cried. 'There is the matter of caste. My daughter is a Brahmin; your son is not.

There is the problem of faith—we have raised our daughter in the Vedic traditions and your son is a Jain, a naastik. And then there is her horoscope—she is Manglik. It is not a match any right-thinking person would bless.'

'The problems of caste and faith remain,' the Sethani said, 'but you may put the matter of the horoscope out of your mind.'

What?

'But Leela is a Manglik. Do you not know what that is?' Baba said slowly, as if speaking to a dull-witted person. But I knew that the Sethani had sharper wits than anyone else I knew. So what *did* she mean?

'Yes, I do,' the Sethani said patiently. 'A Manglik is one with Mars unhappily situated at the time of their birth; doomed to discord and childlessness in their marriage, and in some cases, the death of their spouse. I know this very well.'

'Then you know that anyone she marries might be faced with death,' Baba said perplexed. 'And yet you say there is no problem.'

'Anyone but Rahul,' the Sethani corrected. 'But Rahul would be safe. You see, Rahul is a Manglik too.'

29

$\mathcal{R}$AHUL STARED AT HIS STEPMOTHER AS A MAN SENTENCED to die might look at someone offering him a sudden offer of clemency.

There was stunned silence in the room for a few moments. Then Baba finally spoke, 'If a man born with the Mangal yog, joins in wedlock with a woman with the Mangal yog, the yog ceases to have any effect. So it says in the Brihat Samhita.'

'It is as you say,' the Sethani said. 'We have been trying to find a Manglik match for Rahul in our community for many years, without success. Perhaps it is because the wealthy rarely have bad horoscopes?' Her scornful gaze swept across all the astrologers in the room.

'What about his earlier engagement?' Baba asked.

'You understand that everything I say here must be kept completely confidential, on your honour as a Brahmin. The horoscopes of unwed girls are a highly sensitive matter. But yes, the match was arranged in such a hurry for precisely that reason. We discovered that the daughter of Oswal Seth, a respected merchant, was a Manglik, so we immediately arranged a match. But the two were not compatible, so our families agreed to break it off. We still haven't found another Manglik match for him in our community.'

'You never told me!' Rahul said. 'I only knew that astrological compatibility suddenly became important to Baba after my mother passed away. It was hard to understand why. Why didn't you tell me the truth?'

'He didn't want you to know,' the Sethani said. 'Your father never considered horoscopes until he lost your mother. After that, he changed. He wanted to spare you the pain of losing a spouse, a pain he well understood.'

A flash of understanding passed between mother and son.

'But you suspected Leela was a Manglik,' Rahul said. 'Did you not think of her?'

'She is a Brahmin,' the Sethani said. 'I love her like a daughter, but the match would not have been acceptable to her family.'

I was struggling to keep up with this as I strained to hear the conversation from the other room. I knew from my studies of the Phalit texts that what the Sethani said was true. But it seemed so...convenient.

But if I convince them, somehow? Will you marry me then?

And I had said yes.

No, I would not question it. What mattered now was if it would convince Baba and the others.

My grandfather was speaking now, his face red with anger. 'You are right. The match *is* unacceptable. He is no Brahmin. He doesn't wear the sacred thread. He does not worship the gods and perform the fire sacrifices of the twice-born.'

'Wait,' Baba stopped him. 'Do you have his horoscope with you?' he asked the Sethani. 'I would like to verify what you say.'

The Sethani handed him a scroll. Baba unrolled it carefully.

'Very interesting,' Baba said at last. 'It is a beautifully drawn chart. I think I recognize the style. Who was the astrologer who made it?'

'I don't know. My husband had it made before we were married,' the Sethani replied.

'I see,' Baba said. 'Yes, it would work. It would be a good match. Great, even. Who would have thought?'

'Impossible! If you allow this match it will set a bad precedent,' my grandfather cried. 'Is this what we want the other young people to learn? That intermarrying between the castes is permissible? You will destroy our name and our lineage. This is what the scriptures warn against.'

Some of my uncles started to quote verses to support my grandfather's assertion. It was not difficult. The Dharmashastra was full of them.

'But it seems it is fate that their stars are as well matched as their sentiments,' Baba said slowly. He was looking at Amma, not at my grandfather. 'I have always thought well of this boy. Perhaps it is better she marries him than remain unwed.'

There was a collective gasp from the room. My heart started to beat wildly.

'If she does, it will be at a terrible price,' my grandfather warned.

'What price?' Rahul demanded.

'I do not speak of money,' my grandfather said scornfully. 'I know well enough that your family has more money than the treasury of Malwa. But if my granddaughter dares to defy convention and take your hand, then after she crosses the threshold of this house, she can never return. No house in this family will ever open their doors to her again.'

Amma gasped and turned to Baba.

But Baba was quiet. He was not used to speaking against his father. Still, he tried. 'It is a heavy price,' he said finally.

'I have said it,' my grandfather said. 'I am still the head of this family, Bhaskara, not you.'

'Then let her choose,' Baba said slowly.

Amma was openly weeping now.

I could feel the house around me shudder. It had sheltered me these past seventeen years, I had played in its courtyard, watered the sacred tulsi at its heart, painted its threshold with rice paste, burnt my fingers in its cooking fire, said my prayers at its shrine. And Amma, Baba, Loky—how could I walk away from them?

Then I looked at Rahul standing, head bowed, at the centre of my family, and the Sethani standing quietly beside him, one hand on his arm.

I had made him a promise.

Where was the garland? It must still be in the courtyard. No, a red-eyed Brinda was holding it up for me. When did she get it? It did not matter. I took it from her hands, opened the door we had been listening at and walked into the room. They were unprepared. No one had expected me to arrive so soon.

I did not look towards Baba or Amma. I walked straight past everyone to Rahul, lifting the garland as high as I could. His eyes widened and instinctively, he stooped. I dropped the garland around his neck. How strange the flowers looked, all drooped and wilting now, against his bandaged shoulder.

Then my youngest aunt, who was standing beside Rahul, pressed the matching garland into his hands. He took it from her and placed it carefully around my neck, his eyes soft as they took at my tear-streaked face. We turned to face my family together.

'Preposterous!' my grandfather exclaimed. 'We cannot allow this mockery of tradition. Did you not hear, girl? If you choose him, you are dead to us!'

There was commotion. People shouted, lamented, cursed. I stared at my feet. I could see Rahul's hands balled into fists by my side. There was more commotion outside. I thought I heard the sound of hooves. Then the door burst open.

'Well, did you make it?' Prince Subhrata Varman cried, entering the room without ceremony, in the manner of an old family friend. 'Oho! Look at our young bridegroom here. It is about time, lad, about time!'

The room fell silent.

'How is your father?' Rahul asked quietly.

The prince's face crumpled.

'He…was martyred in battle,' he replied. 'Just an hour after you left, my friend. A warrior's death.'

'Then you are king now, my liege,' Rahul said, bowing before him.

'To you, I am always a friend,' the prince smiled. 'That is why I came here first. In case there was any,' he looked around belligerently, his hand at his sword, '…trouble.'

My grandfather and uncles glared at their new king but were cowed into silence.

'There is no trouble,' Rahul said, 'but the thought is much appreciated.'

'Your majesty,' Baba said. Subhrata, King Subhrata Varman, touched his feet. Baba put a hand on his helmeted head in blessing. 'Blessings on your victory, my king. You have saved us from Ghori!'

'I am in need of your prayers, venerable Acharya,' the king said.

'You always have them,' said Baba.

Then Baba looked around the room. 'My daughter has made her choice. I will see to it that she is wed to the groom she has picked. My father's commands will be obeyed, but let me give my only daughter away with dignity. We owe her that much.'

My grandfather stomped out of the room. My uncles also left with him.

'Your royal highness,' Baba said. 'I will understand if you do not wish to stay for the wedding.'

'I have waited too long to see my friend wed,' the king said. 'So I will stay. Tomorrow I will shave my head and begin the period of mourning before the coronation. And it seems you are in need of wedding guests, and we have a victory to celebrate! Perhaps my lieutenants can also stay for the feast?'

✧

And so we were wed.

Although most of our earlier guests had left, I was surprised to see who remained. Mahendra for one, looking rueful but resigned. Bittan and her husband, who had somehow appeared, uninvited, in the garden. And, of course, the victorious soldiers of Malwa.

Amma and Brinda brought me to the wedding altar beneath the flower-bedecked mandap, where Rahul waited. Before I stepped into it, I wrapped my arms around my friend, tears flowing silently down my face. Amma caught the look in my eyes and hers, and gasped. She quietly put an arm around Brinda and led her away.

'Where is the priest?' Baba asked. No one knew.

'I'll perform the ceremony,' said a familiar voice, and there was Kumarilla Mishra, ready to officiate in place of the vanished priest.

I watched Brinda carefully from my place at the altar. A tall soldier was talking to her. It was the Kanwar's younger brother, Randheer Singh. *Kanwar* Randheer Singh, since he had now taken his brother's place. Brinda's small shoulders shook as she cried, her head bowed. Then she raised her arms. I turned my face away as she brought them down hard to smash her glass bangles on the stone wall behind her—the universal symbol of widowhood. When I looked again, I saw that Randheer Singh had clasped both her hands in his and stopped her from doing so. As she collapsed, sobbing against him, I noticed how much like his brother he suddenly seemed, the sorrow on his face wiping away his usual carefree expression. Perhaps, I thought, perhaps, with time...

Rahul squeezed my hand quietly. He had been watching too.

I turned my attention to our wedding.

'The Jain ceremony is a little different,' the Sethani was saying.

'I know it is,' Kumarilla Mishra said. 'But it really is not *very* different. Perhaps you can help me through it so that the wedding may be performed according to both traditions?'

The fire altar at the centre of the mandap was lit with agni, the sacred fire, to bear witness to our vows. The glow from the flame flickered over Rahul, gilding him gold as he sat by my side, casting offerings into the fire. Loky did the kanyadaan, giving me away, standing as tall as he could as he poured rice through my hands into the fire. Rahul's scarf and mine were tied together as I put my hand into his. We walked four times around the fire, taking turns to lead each other, once each for the four goals of life—duty, prosperity, love and salvation. Then I placed my foot upon a stone, promising to be as steadfast as it was.

Then we took the seven steps and the seven vows. Kumarilla Mishra spoke the vows first, and we repeated them in Sanskrit. There was no need to translate them for us, as it was for others. Both Rahul and I knew the meaning of our vows as we repeated them:

We have taken the Seven Steps. You have become mine forever. I have become yours. I am the sky, you are the earth. I am the life source, you are its carrier. I am speech, you are thought. I am music, you are verse. May the night be honey-sweet for us. May the morning be honey-sweet for us. May the earth be honey-sweet for us. May the heavens be honey-sweet for us. May the plants be honey-sweet for us. May the sun be all honey for us. May the cows yield us honey-sweet milk. As the heavens are stable, as the earth is stable, as the mountains are stable, as the whole universe is stable, so may our union be permanently settled.

'You have made these promises before your parents, before agni, the sacred fire, and before that eternal witness, the sun,' Kumarilla Mishra said. 'Now look upon the Dhruva Tara, my children. Yes, it is daylight and you cannot see it, yet we know it is there. Promise to be as constant to each other as the polestar.'

Rahul looked dutifully at the sky, but I didn't. Instead, I looked at Rahul. He was my Dhruva Tara, my constant guiding star, the only star I would chart my course to.

They showered us with rice and rose petals. Someone blew a conch shell. Then we rose and touched the feet of our parents and our elders together.

Rahul waited at the door as I said my goodbyes.

I laid my hands in the basin of turmeric paste Amma held and pressed them to the wall of the kitchen. The imprint of my hands stared back at me. Every daughter left this mark behind for her parents to remember her by when she left her childhood home for that of her husband's. This would be the last sign of me in this house.

Amma wiped away her tears and washed the paste off my hands with clean water.

'I am so sorry for everything,' I whispered to her between tears. 'I have brought disgrace on you and Baba.'

'Shh...' she said, hugging me close. 'It is no disgrace to have a daughter like you, Leela. I have worried so long about what will become of you. But you have found your place at last, and my mind is at rest. You be happy now. That's all that we want.'

'You may not visit us, but perhaps we can visit you,' Baba said practically. 'That wasn't part of the condition, was it, my girl?'

I stared at him, relief coursing through my veins. I had wondered why he had agreed to such a harsh demand from my grandfather. How thankful I was for Baba's quick thinking!

I looked for Brinda, but she had left. Amma and my youngest aunt walked me to the door, but not before someone had stopped us. Aajoba, my other grandfather, Amma's father, had walked downstairs on his aching feet to bless me before I left.

'I hear that fellow Maheshwara has disowned you,' he said, calling my paternal grandfather by his name. 'But I am the patriarch of my own house, thank the gods. You were born in my house, the daughter of my daughter. The doors of my house will always be open to you, Leela, and to your children and grandchildren. You may visit us in Bharuch whenever you wish.'

I touched his feet, washing them with my tears as he placed his old hands on my head.

I may be an outcast, I thought, but the people I cared most about were by my side.

Amma filled the edge of my scarf with rice. I threw it backwards over my shoulder as I walked through the door—a gesture that brought good fortune to the household I was leaving forever. Loky clung to my waist and Moti licked my feet. Baba stood outside the door, looking uncomfortable, but his eyes were red too.

'Where is the doli? I'm sure I ordered one, didn't I?' he said.

'Yes, but they left thinking that the swayamvara was cancelled, Baba,' Loky said.

'Then how is she supposed to go to the Jagatseths' haveli? Walk? That isn't appropriate!'

'Don't worry, Acharya,' Rahul said. 'I have my horse.'

Someone brought Kalyanee forward. She look rubbed down, rested and very, very tall.

I had never ridden a horse in my life. How could I start now in all these fine clothes and jewellery?

My youngest aunt giggled suddenly. 'Perfect,' she sighed. 'Much better than a palanquin.'

Then Rahul's hands were at my waist, lifting me up to the horse's saddle.

'Oh, be careful!' Amma cried. Thank heaven the mare stood quiet and calm. I perched, side saddle, trying to look as dignified as I could with my veil askew. Then Rahul swung up behind me. His muscled arm came around me firmly. 'Are you okay?' he asked.

I steadied myself against him. 'Yes,' I replied.

'Then let's go home,' he said.

With a click of his heels, Kalyanee moved forward. I looked back at the group of familiar faces standing before the house, my eyes smarting once again. I blinked the tears away, swallowed the lump in my throat. That's when I noticed it—my tattered paper kite hanging from the saddle. How had he found it?

'It fell on me out of the sky as I was riding to you,' Rahul said. 'I didn't even slow down to catch the string. It was meant to be, Leela.' I locked my arms firmly around his waist, leaning my cheek against his chest as the horse broke into a canter.

The clouds were moving away now. In spite of the thunder and lightning, the rain had never really begun. Scattered raindrops fell on us from the dark clouds like a benediction. As I looked ahead, a shaft of sunlight broke through the clouds and silvered the wet ground.

Epilogue

THE ASTROLOGER ACROSS THE RIVER HAD SHUT HIS SHOP. It wasn't that business had dried up—quite the opposite, in fact— but he simply did not need to work anymore. The handsome sum his last job brought meant he could retire. He had made more money on it than he had made for the past ten years of work.

It had been a strange transaction for many reasons. First, for the amount of money offered and the quality of manuscript demanded. He had to give up drinking and stay sober for a week before he could even attempt to make the quality of chart needed by his customer. Second, the secrecy the customer had insisted on. She had only visited his shop after dark, under a thick veil. The only thing he knew about her was that she was middle-aged, sure of herself, and rich enough to have men who guarded her when she came. And that she had pox scars on her hand.

But most puzzling of all, this was the first and only time in his career that he was paid to change a perfectly auspicious chart to an inauspicious one.

Perhaps it was because he was sober, but he had qualms about his customer's motives. Why would anyone change a non-Manglik horoscope to a Manglik one?

'Does the person whose chart this is know that you are changing it?' he had asked his customer before handing it over.

'I'm doing it at his request,' she had replied, sounding amused at his uncharacteristic concern. 'Although, I suppose I

270

can take credit for teaching him to take recourse to alternatives, as insurance, in case plans go awry. But it is no business of yours. You will do well to forget this transaction ever took place.'

He was no fool and he had had his suspicions. Yet, even his cynical heart could not but respect such a motive. He would keep his suspicions to himself for the rest of his life.

'So when did she know?' I asked Rahul. Peacocks preened in the courtyard at the Jagatseths' haveli in Bharuch. I could see them through the latticed sandstone screen of the room. Our room.

Rahul smiled and pulled me close. 'Right after I rode away with the cavalry. I left a letter explaining everything. I asked my mother to have my birth chart altered, just in case I was late. She was the one who taught me to always have an alternate plan ready for everything in life—business, war and love.'

'Do you think she will like Srivijaya?' I asked him. We were to leave within the week, and not return for at least two years.

'Both of you will,' he said. 'Baba and I will do our best to make you comfortable there. So will everyone else. I can't wait to show you our large library, and for you to meet my grandfather.'

He rose up on his elbow and pulled something off the table next to the bed. 'Speaking of books, two have arrived for you. The first is from Rashid.'

'The book by his poet mathematician?' I asked.

'Yes, indeed,' Rahul said. 'The second is one your Baba sent for you. He was anxious that you receive it before we sail.'

'A book from Baba,' I cried. 'Why didn't you show it to me before?'

'You may recall that we were otherwise occupied,' he pointed out, the ready dimples showing through the stubble on his cheeks.

I blushed and took the book from him.

There was a letter with it.

My dear daughter,

I have finalized the text of the Siddhanta Shiromani and have decided to name the first part of it, the book on arithmetic—Leelavati. I enjoyed composing the verses when you were little, and you have taught enough classes on arithmetic to deserve the honour. I am sending you the first copy so you may read it on your voyage. Scribes here are now diligently making copies to be sent out to every corner of India where education is respected. Wherever the world values knowledge, your name shall remain.

Amma wanted me to mention that your friend Brinda sends her love. The family of Kanwar Ranveer Singh has requested her hand for their younger son, Kanwar Randheer Singh. Amma thinks it may be for the best. Do not forget to bring back any books from Srivijaya that you think would interest me. Your Amma and I will pray for your safe return. Our blessings, as always,

Baba

I opened the book at the first page and started to read.

Acknowledgements

This book would not exist without the support of my family and friends. I'd like to warmly acknowledge and thank the following people:

My mum, for her complete faith in every project I have ever attempted, however strange and unlikely.

Papa, for being our gateway to all things literary, and for proudly preserving my first book—*Rony, the Pony*—handwritten and illustrated when I was six.

My sister Minni, for demanding the next installment of 'Leela' by 9 a.m. every Saturday, Brisbane time.

My sister Ruhi, for loving this story to tears.

My sister Anuja—an amazing writer—for her help with the plot, her publishing advice and everything else.

My first teen readers—Niharika Alva in India, Nalini Singh in Australia and Ayesha Chauhan in the US—for their unanimous approval. Ayesha read this while undergoing treatment for cancer, and tragically, passed away soon after. This book is dedicated to her sparkling and courageous spirit.

My writing group—Kate Narita, Natalie Reid, Sue Lovejoy, Amy Benoit, JoAnn DiVerdi Miller, Allison Vinkels and most of all, April Prince. Also Sarah Albee, Don Hinkle and Christy Lenzi for their feedback. My Natick writing buddies, Martha Calderaro and Heather Kelly, for their critique and support. My friends from Uma's Alumni, and our teacher, Uma Krishnaswami, for being a wonderful mentor and friend.

The team at Red Turtle/Rupa—Sudeshna Shome Ghosh for believing in this story and taking it on, Sohini Pal for her thoughtful and thorough edits, Maithili Doshi Aphale and Smruthi Gargi Eswar for the stunning cover art, and everyone else who worked on this project.

My dog and cat for being the best companions a writer could have. And the three people that matter the most—my husband Chandra, and my children, Ravi and Anika. Thanks for putting up with me through the long road of getting this book researched, written, repped, rejected and (finally) published. You are the best.